THE SILENT BLUEBIRD

ELLE M. HOLMES

ISBN: 978-1-7358412-0-5

Cover Design by Connor King

For my friends that helped me get here,
the best parents a girl could have hoped for,
and to my C.K that keeps this L.L. in line and in love.

THE SILENT BLUEBIRD

Prologue

His footsteps echoed across the marble as Dr. John Scott navigated the intricate maze of hallways within Georgetown University. He was no stranger to these hallowed halls, but this evening held an air of mystery that electrified the atmosphere around him. Yesterday he'd received a voicemail from his old friend and colleague Charles Carter:

"John, we've done it. We're testing it for some General tomorrow at 5 p.m. Please come. I know it's been a while, but I'd really like you to be there." His voice sounded weak, yet there was a certain excitement buried in its timbre. The kind only heard from someone on the edge of greatness.

John could scarcely guess at what Charles had uncovered. After six years of silence, hearing the voice of his old friend conjured memories from the dark expanse of his own past. Last-minute cram sessions, hacky sack challenges in the quad, late nights when Charles would come crashing into the apartment. Each step closer to his destination pulled John further down the rabbit hole of their friendship until its abrupt end six years earlier.

The last time the two friends spoke it was 1981 and to say they had a falling out back then was putting it lightly. While they'd both been hired on at Georgetown as Adjunct Professors, Charles wasn't satisfied with lecturing. He was a researcher, a dog with a bone, so to speak. And it had been the same bone for years: unlocking the secrets of the human mind.

One seemingly insignificant Thursday night in '81, Charles was on his latest bender, spewing all sorts of ideas to anyone that would listen at the bar just off campus. Ideas that if one could tap into the thoughts of men, the free-flow of information would undermine the need for infrastructure as it was known. No need for police when everyone would know what the other was thinking. No need for politicians to put a limit on sharing knowledge. It would be a world solely based on the pursuit of knowledge—a lofty albeit naïve goal. As Charles continued his sermon on the barstool, John noticed the other patrons beginning to stare at his friend with more than a little contempt.

That's when John tried to step in and corral him back to the university for the night—Charles had been living out of his office for months instead of their shared apartment in Lyon Park.

"Charles, you can't say those things around everyone. What you're working on, I don't think the world is ready for it yet," John said as he tried to maneuver the inebriated man down the street, crossing into campus grounds.

"Oh shut up, John! You've always been too much of a fuddy-duddy, even in grad school. You never went out with us, you just worked and studied and ran off to that girl's house all the time," Charles said as he fell off the curb, almost crashing into a group of undergrads on their way across campus. "And who are you to tell *me* about telling people things? You never tell anyone *anything*.

You play it so close to the vest, thinking that somehow, ya know, it's better or whatever. It's not, John. It's not. That's a load of malarkey, if everyone knew about everything, just think how much we could accomplish as a society! No more stupid secrets, no more fighting over what we think the other person is thinking or doing or all the boobish stuff people fight about."

"That's not true. Come on, buddy, let's get you home. You don't mean that." John struggled to get Charles through the double doors of his building, his inebriated ramblings echoing down the empty hall. It proved especially difficult to get the man into at least a semi-upright position as John tried to lean him against the wall while unlocking the door to the office.

"I do mean it. You're a crackpot, John. You try to hide what you're working on, not because you don't want anyone to see it, but because you don't want anyone to see that you've got nothing. *N-o-t-t-thing*." Charles's wild gesture sent him stumbling, but he managed to get a foot under himself at the last moment. "You just like to go around and criticize everyone else's work because you will never be as smart as any of us and will never do anything worthwhile with your life. You've always been nothing and will always be *nothing*!" he screamed out as he stumbled his way to the couch facing his desk. Clearly Charles had forsaken cleaning up after himself; the stench of old Chinese takeout and curdled coffee creamer was enough to make anyone sick, and John didn't want to be there when the already drunk Charles got a good enough whiff.

John stared down at the mess of a grown man who

he thought had been his friend. His jaw tightened. *Is that what you really believe?* John thought to himself as anger threatened to overtake reason. *If you only knew the alternative.* He let out a breath and shook his hands, realizing he'd balled them into fists. "You're drunk and have no idea what you're talking about, Charles. And I don't need to explain myself to you." He turned to leave.

"That's right, get back on your high horse and run off. Go off into John-land where you matter and no one else exists. You'll see, one day I'm going to be someone, and the world will know my name and my work. No one will ever know the name John Scott."

Shortly thereafter, John left the university. He resigned from his teaching position and started a new life away from the world of academia, choosing to pursue a different goal. John did up marrying "that girl" he always ran off to see and they were happy. Charles was right about one thing, though: the scientific community forgot the name Dr. John Scott, an anonymity he came to value. But not Charles. Charles Carter never forgot him.

Fast forward six years and Charles—now the head of neuroscience research at Georgetown University—had reentered John's life with a simple voicemail.

What did you get yourself into now, old friend? John wondered as he turned the last corner into the research lab on level five. He had always thought these hallways had a haunted air about them. As if the long-dormant diseases studied within their walls could resurrect themselves at any moment to claim their next victim. John tried to shake the uneasy feeling he had walking into Charles's lab. If he had finally achieved his goal, it would have a profound influence not only on John's life but on humanity as a whole.

The labs at Georgetown had remained the same structurally, but the interiors had grown and advanced as quickly as the computer age progressed. The old DN100s that John had been familiar with before were now replaced with Lambdas that filled every inch of free space in the room. Computer terminals lined the walls with one workstation in the center. At least John imagined it was a workstation; the entire thing was concealed underneath a large, white cloth, overhead lights pointing at it from every direction. What little workspace remained in the room was occupied by a menagerie of research assistants, lab techs, and military men all presumably here for Charles's great unveiling.

The moment John entered the room, Charles caught sight of him. "John! You made it!" He ran over with the gusto of a child reuniting with his long-lost dog.

The years hadn't been kind to Charles. His auburn, curly hair was already receding from the corners of his forehead. Gray teased at his sideburns. His gaunt face and the dark circles under his eyes indicated that he hadn't had a good night's sleep in some time. Not to mention a neglect of regular meals, typical for a man who had focused too much on one pursuit.

"It's great to see you," Charles continued, "I'm so glad you made it. We need to talk, after the test. You and I need to go grab a beer or something. So much has happened…" Charles's anxious gaze bounced across John's face, as if trying to unearth some meaning behind his guarded expression.

"Yeah, of course." The two men exchanged a look of remorse and more than a bit of gratitude. Gratitude at their reunion and remorse for having lost touch—they were once thick as thieves but had allowed petty disputes and time to separate them.

"But first, science!" Charles turned to the rest of the room, surveying the horde of research assistants and military men. John recognized General Eli Kalani in the center of the group and they exchanged a quick glance. He was surrounded by a number of lesser military men, including a young lieutenant who looked especially eager to please.

As John continued to review the room, he remembered a few of the assistants from his teaching days, but there were two he didn't recognize. A young man with dark black hair, cut unfashionably short for the eighties, and a middle-aged woman whose face looked to be pulled back as tight as her bun. She seemed too old to be a research assistant, but John hoped that maybe Charles had finally found a research partner that could put up with him for more than a week.

"Ladies and gentlemen," Charles began, "I called you all here to be witness to the future of human knowledge. For years we've been in the dark about our deepest intentions. Restricted by the fear of others' opinions, our work constrained within the limits of our technology. Too many people hiding their agendas behind a curtain of uncertainty. But tonight we aim to pull down the curtain and turn on the lights. Sasha, if you would please begin."

Sasha, the middle-aged woman, pulled off the cloth covering the central workstation to reveal a single monitor encased in a plexiglass box. A green line blinked at the top left-hand side of the screen.

"Now keep in mind this device is tuned to me and no one else right now. Young man," Charles said, pointing to one of the lieutenants standing near General Kalani, "we've never met before tonight, correct?"

"No, sir. I don't believe we have," he responded hesitantly, looking to General Kalani for approval on his response.

"Great. So I wouldn't have known what your name is before tonight. Can I ask then, what is your name and rank?"

"Lieutenant Tyler Ashmore, sir," the man said with a pride that could only come from a member of the US Army.

"Thank you very much," Charles responded as he closed his eyes. Buzzing began to sound from every corner of the room and the green line began to move. *Lieutenant Tyler Ashmore* flashed across the screen.

"That's it?" one of the other young lieutenants asked. "What exactly are we looking at, sir?"

He's actually done it, John thought to himself.

"Ah! Now that's the question, isn't it, young man? I call it the CarterScott Device." Charles looked at his old friend, acknowledging him with a genuine smile as if to seek redemption. John caught the glance and nodded his head in acceptance. "You see—"

The lights went dark.

A loud bang echoed throughout the small room. *Was that a gunshot?* John thought, frantically searching for somewhere to take cover. He barricaded himself behind one of the terminals at the side of the room as more shots rang out into the air. Only three seconds passed before the red emergency lights flickered on. John peeked from behind the terminal to see a wasteland of bodies and the young, dark-haired research assistant pointing a gun at Charles, who was blocking the monitor.

"What are you doing, Bruno?" screamed Charles.

"Move, *signore*." The young assistant stood firm and defiant against his mentor.

"No! I don't know what you think you're doing, Bruno, but I can't let you take my machine." Charles rose to the challenge with more courage than John thought the man possessed.

"Domino." John let the word slip from his mouth without realizing it.

Bruno whipped his head around in the direction of the noise, narrowing his eyes as they landed on John. "You're one of them, aren't you?"

Charles took this opportunity to lunge forward, attempting to grab the gun in the confusion. Unfortunately, he never had been exceptionally fast. The young man barely flinched as he pulled the trigger, dropping Charles to the floor. In one motion, Bruno grabbed the small monitor and turned the gun toward John. "Stay back, old man."

At that moment General Kalani managed to pull himself up on the desk and began firing. The emergency lights continued to flicker as the young man darted out of the way. Bullets ricocheted around the room, and one seemed to hit its target as Bruno shouted in pain. Then he was out the door, machine in tow.

John scrambled over to his friend. "Charles, hold on, we're going to get you help."

"You were right, old friend, guess I finally told the wrong person about my work." Charles coughed up blood as he reached for his pocket, pulling out a small, rectangular device and handing it to John. "At least I didn't tell them everything…"

He closed his eyes and John felt the light of a brilliant scientist go out. Even though it had started as an assignment—to get close to this young scientist with radical ideas and notions of grandeur—over the years, he had truly become a close friend. He was there through so many good times, and though Charles never knew the full extent, he was there for John's bad times too. Whenever things seemed to be getting to John, Charles was always there with a beer and a good laugh. For all that he was and all they'd been through, the world would be a bit darker without Charles Carter in it.

"We have to go," said General Kalani, putting a hand on John's shoulder. "We can't stay here."

"I know," replied John. His chest tightened and a tear fell from his face as he rose, having to say goodbye to his friend for the last time.

"We have to get to the Library," General Kalani started, his eyes darting around the room, surveying the carnage. "We need to tell them what's happened. Did Charles really crack the code on zetas?"

"It looks like it." John exhaled as he rose to leave. The air felt thicker somehow, as if the souls of the recently departed lingered ever so slightly in the gloom of the red emergency lighting.

General Kalani looked down at Lieutenant Tyler Ashmore—he was only twenty-four. He'd been assigned to Kalani's detail just last month and now he was dead. Kalani couldn't help but imagine his own son lying there. His heart began to pound as he fought to suppress the thought. "We're going to need more help."

"*You're* going to need more help. I'm out," John said, turning to face General Kalani. Fear and rage battled inside him as the repercussions of the evening played out in a hundred different scenarios in John's mind. "They know who I am now. I have a family to think about, General."

"You can't be serious? The Library needs you now more than ever." Kalani felt an anger rising within him, tempered only by the sorrow of loss. "There are so few of us left."

"I know, but I can't help them anymore. I'm getting my wife and son and getting out of here." John looked around the room. He knew it wouldn't be easy to leave, but he couldn't risk this happening to his family. "But you're right, you will need help. Form a team, hell, form a whole agency if you need to. You're a general, you have the power. But keep the information tight. Tell them nothing beyond what they absolutely need to know to do their job. Keep the rest of the Library secret. The fewer people that know the history, the better. Domino got too close this time. We can't risk another leak."

"But what will their jobs be?" Kalani asked, his eyes still pleading with John not to leave.

"Protect and serve the people. And above all, keep the Library hidden."

Chapter 1

Sarah Mercedes Smith, or Sadie as she liked to go by, stood surrounded by the fifth-grade class of Watkins Elementary, hoping to mold young minds and shape the future of society. Or at least settle for making it through another tour without losing a child. One girl wearing a pink sweater raised her hand. "Ms. Smith, why don't animals wear clothes?"

Sadie had heard this question more often than any normal adult should in her tenure at the Smithsonian. She'd supported herself through school by working as a tour guide at the Natural History Museum and every tour had a child just like this one, full of questions, all thinking they were the first to ask them. She had hoped that finally getting her degree and being promoted through the ranks to Curatorial Assistant in the antiquities department meant that she wouldn't be on tour duty anymore. But occasionally the museum educator would be overwhelmed with school field trips and when too many docents called out, Sadie was somehow the first call to fill in. Not that she disliked the job, she loved the museum and sharing her historical knowledge with eager young minds, it was the less than eager ones she found troublesome.

"Well, sweetie, that's because their clothes are built-in with their fur. They have the most luxurious coats, don't you think?" Sadie said in response.

"Yeah, they look super soft. Can I touch the leopard?"

"Not these, but—"

"Actually, it's not a leopard, it's a jaguar," said one of the other students as he crossed his arms. He wore a blazer over his school uniform, which looked out of place compared to his classmates. "*Panthera Onca* of the family *Felidae*, and it's the third largest cat in the world."

And that was the other type of child in every group, the one that knows it all and wants everyone to be aware of that fact. Sadie was never one to discourage sharing knowledge, but there was a right and a wrong way to do it. This was certainly the latter. "Well, did you know that this one has a name?"

The boy paused, looking confused. "That doesn't really matter."

"Of course it matters! You and I have names, why not this jaguar? So, who does know his name?"

"Smitty!" the girl in the pink sweater, clearly the most outspoken of the group, yelled as she jumped up and down, pointing at the sign, having found another excuse to call out.

"That's right! And it's the reason why he's one of my favorite exhibits here at the Natural History Museum. We share almost the same name. Smith and Smitty." The sound of children's laughter filled the exhibit. *There are still good times to be had at this job*, thought Sadie. "Now, let's continue with the tour. Up next—"

"Look!" Pink Sweater screamed as she pointed behind Sadie toward the Rotunda. As Sadie turned around she could hear screams and shouts joining in throughout the Hall of Mammals. A young boy had climbed onto the back of the thirteen-foot African elephant that stood in the center of the Rotunda and was making his way up the trunk.

Sadie's jaw dropped, along with her stomach, and she darted through the crowd, trying to get to the boy, never taking her eyes off of him. She watched in horror as he reached the top and teetered. Sadie ran with all her might, praying that she would make it there in time.

She didn't.

He landed with a scream.

She plunged through the throng of people to find the boy cradled safely in the arms of a stranger wearing a distressed leather jacket.

"You okay, buddy?" said the stranger.

"Yeah! That was awesome! You ran so fast, can we do it again?" asked the apparently unharmed young boy. Sadie stood there panting, having seen her whole career pass before her eyes as she ran through the crowd. She decided that she needed to punch up her cardio workouts at the gym. Her hair had fallen from its ponytail, her jacket was slightly askew, her hand trembled. She pulled herself together, trying to maintain some sense of decorum in front of the museum patrons now observing her with stunned silence.

"Thank you so much, sir, you saved the day," she said, merely glancing at the stranger before turning to the boy. "Where are your parents, young man?"

Then a mom with two more children in tow burst through the crowd.

"Billy! How could you? Are you okay? You know better than to horse around like that. Thank you, sir, for saving my son," Billy's mom said to the man while simultaneously giving Sadie a disapproving look, as if it was her fault.

The woman grabbed Billy's hand and started toward the door, "Just wait until your father hears about this."

"That kid is so going to get it when he gets home," said the stranger, walking up next to Sadie, "at least based on the fathers I know."

"Yeah, wouldn't want to be him tonight. That was incredible, the way you caught him. Well done, sir. I'm Sadie, by the way." Sadie really looked at the man for the first time, noticing the kind blue eyes of this mysterious stranger. Maybe it was the adrenaline pumping through her veins, but Sadie couldn't help but feel an attraction toward him. His smile was debonair yet genuine. He gave off a sort of strength that she couldn't quite place or understand, given his seemingly slim frame. There was something about him that seemed mildly familiar to her, it scratched at the back her mind like a cat wishing to be let in, only to run off once the door was opened. Or maybe she just liked the way the front lock of his curly, dark hair fell over his forehead, reminding her of Clark Kent and giving an overall superhero-ish look to his entire persona. "Do I know you? You look so familiar..."

"Uh, I don't think so, unless you've been dreaming about me." He smiled with not-so-subtle confidence.

"Oh, ha, one of those guys then," Sadie said, rolling her eyes. The man's face immediately flushed red.

"No, no, please don't judge me on that. I couldn't help it. My name's James," he said, reaching out to shake Sadie's hand. "And as for the boy, it was nothing. Right place at the right time kind of thing."

"Guess so. I'm glad you were, would've drastically ruined my day. And I imagine his." Sadie realized she was still shaking hands with this stranger. "So, can I get my hand back?"

"Oh, yes, sorry about that!" James relinquished Sadie's hand and ran his own through his dark hair. "I just—I mean, you ran pretty fast yourself, didn't you?"

"As fast as you can in heels." Sadie found herself smiling at the man. She felt a sharp tug at her arm.

"Ms. Smith, come on we have to see more animals." Pink Sweater was back and apparently eager to continue with the tour.

"Well, I should probably get back to work, shaping young minds and all that."

"Of course, I won't keep you," James said, almost hesitantly, turning to leave. Then he paused and looked back. "Would you—"

"Yes," said Sadie.

"What?" James cocked his head, narrowing his eyes at her.

"I'd love to get a coffee later. I get off at six. If that's what you were going to ask, that is." Even Sadie was taken aback by her quick, and rather forward, suggestion.

"Yeah, actually… how did you…" A look of confusion stretched across James's face.

"Girl's intuition. I'll see you later?" she said as Pink Sweater dragged her back to the rest of her tour.

"Um yes, I'll wait for you out front then."

Sadie turned and left James standing in bewilderment, hiding her hot, flushed cheeks and a coy smile that would surely give away her excitement. *What harm is a coffee?* she thought to herself.

The rest of the day went by in a blur. Before she knew it, 5:30 came and Sadie was heading back to her office with a mixture of anxiety and excitement about her coffee date. *It's coffee, that's not really a date, right?* A stack of paperwork was waiting on the desk for her; a challenge to her evening plans. *The wheel that is the Smithsonian never stops rolling, not even for tour duty*, she thought.

"Oh yeah, Stead wants you to look into a new exhibit proposition." Allyn Green stood at the doorway of Sadie's office. If one were to picture a historian, it would be Allyn. He was a bespectacled, vest-wearing man—never without pocket protectors—with a tall, thin build and a pale complexion. But he was also one of the most genuine people here at the Smithsonian. While others worried about being the next rising star in the field, he was happy to be working in the nation's home *"for the increase and diffusion of knowledge."* Or at least that's how the Smithsonian had started, according to Allyn.

"What's the proposition?" Sadie frowned as she searched the papers for a due date.

"Um, not sure, something about the evolution of human communication," he said, taking a seat in front of Sadie's desk. "I don't know, it's not mineral so immaterial in my book." He broke into a laugh. "Get it, book because of human communication?" Allyn looked at Sadie for confirmation but found only silence. "Ah, my humor is wasted on you people."

As Sadie stared blankly at the first file, she felt the ends of her lips curl into a soft smile of their own volition, her mind drifting to her own 'human communication' with James earlier that afternoon.

"Allyn, don't you have work to finish?" a voice questioned from the hall.

Dr. Jonas Andrews appeared in the doorway, wearing his usual disapproving dad look. Jonas was Sadie's direct boss, the Curator to Sadie's Curatorial Assistant. A handsome man, who didn't look a day over forty, despite being in his early fifties, his salt and pepper hair the only tell of his age. He prided himself on maintaining a strict regimen of clean eating, 5 a.m. kayak workouts on the Potomac, and the occasional cheat day involving a box of banana Twinkies, but no one except Sadie knew about that last part.

"Oh hey Dr. Andrews, umm yes, yes I do." Allyn spun out of the chair and through the door with all the grace and poise of a newborn giraffe.

"Bye, Allyn!" Sadie laughed and looked over to Jonas. "Hey Jonas, how was your day?"

"Not as eventful as yours apparently. The boy wasn't in your tour group, was he?"

"Oh, no, thankfully. But since I was the closest one at the time and the main witness, I get the joy of all the paperwork." Sadie shook her head. "Honestly, I don't even know how he managed to climb up there in the first place, I mean he's six years old and maybe four foot tall. But that guy was there to catch him, so it all worked out."

"Mmhmm, and the smile on your face?" Jonas asked with a coy smile of his own.

Sadie hadn't even realized she was still smiling. "Hmm? Oh nothing, just Allyn, you know. Same old Allyn." She hoped the heat she felt rising in her cheeks wasn't obvious on her face.

"Sadie, I've known you both for going on four years now and not once have I heard Allyn tell a joke that is actually funny." Jonas sighed. "But I'll let you keep this one. Just don't forget to review that proposition tonight." He turned to leave, wincing slightly as he pivoted on his left leg. "You should be plenty caffeinated anyway," he added with a wink.

"Will do, sir. See you tomorrow." *How does that man always know what's going on in this museum?* thought Sadie. She placed the file in her bag and headed out for the night.

As Sadie walked down the steps of the Smithsonian, her eyes scanned the horizon until they finally settled on the savior-of-falling-children. She took a deep breath; the chilly November air felt clean and fresh, filling her with a sense of "anything can happen."

"Hi there," Sadie said as she walked over to James, trying to hide the nervousness she felt inside. She didn't really know what she was doing with this guy, she wasn't used to being the one to suggest any sort of social activity, content to stay home or at work, or any familiar place with familiar people for that matter.

"Hi," James responded cheerfully. A little too cheerfully. Was he more nervous than Sadie?

"So I see you waited, sorry for running a little late. I got held up with my boss." Butterflies erupted inside of her. Maybe it was the thrill from earlier that day that still subtly lingered, maybe it was the fear of what could've happened had this man not been there, or maybe it was just the attention from a random, good-looking stranger.

"Not a problem at all, it's given me plenty of time to not decide on a coffee shop," he responded with that debonair smile. "But I figure there's this little place just around the corner. Sometimes the simplest answer is the best one."

"Sure. Lead on." She smiled as the pair traversed the short distance to a rather familiar coffee shop for Sadie. "Café Cuppa?"

"Yeah, is that okay? Have you been here before?" James looked as if he'd made a horrendous mistake.

"Of course! I love this place. Actually, I'm probably here three or four times a week between forgetting my coffee in the morning or needing a break from cataloging in the afternoon."

"Perfect." James's shoulders dropped, visibly relaxing as he smiled and held open the door.

Inside that small coffee shop, time ceased to exist. The universe consisted purely for the enjoyment of their two souls, so perfectly matched. Every moment pulled Sadie further and further into James. His eyes, with a mysterious sapphire sparkle, seemed to whisper reassuringly to her unspoken anxieties, "I'm here now, it's okay." The only interruption was the bouncing curl of hair that would dance across his forehead with any sudden laugh his body could no longer contain. A laugh that filled the coffee shop, resonating in every corner long after he had stopped. They flitted from subject to subject, as if eager to finally lose themselves in a conversation started eons ago. Sadie could feel the sum of these parts disassembling the wall she had spent so long building around herself. A hard defense built out of necessity, and yet, with every breath, she could feel James tearing it down brick by brick.

The table began to buzz. James glanced down at his phone. "I'm so sorry, I have to take this. Do you mind?"

"Not at all," Sadie responded.

James walked out of the noisy coffee shop, turning in the doorway to look at Sadie with a smile and a wave. Sadie smiled back at him. As he began pacing in front of the windows, speaking rapidly into his cell, she glanced around the coffee shop. She hadn't noticed before, but at some point the place had emptied out, save for a few couples tucked away happily in their booths.

James was still pacing outside. Sadie fiddled with the silver ring she always wore on her right pinky finger. She'd had it since she was a child. She couldn't remember where she'd gotten it, only that she'd always had it. It was inscribed with a Latin phrase: *Praesidio in Statera*—meaning "Protect the Balance." She'd tried researching it before but never found anything. Sadie hadn't been able to bring herself to get rid of it though, as if it held some secret key to where she came from, and it had become a bit of a nervous habit to fiddle with it whenever she was anxious.

Sadie looked back outside to see only the general bustle of Washington DC at night. *Where did he go?* She waited ten minutes, twenty minutes, thirty minutes for him to come back in. The waitress finally came up to inform her that they were closing, so she finished her cold coffee, paid the tab, and went outside, hoping for any sign of James, to no avail. She was alone again.

Sadie stared up at the night sky. One of the other advantages of the latest cold front: clear skies. As a child, Sadie found herself staring up at the sky more often than not. No matter what the "home" of the month was, she used to sneak out of her room at night and lie on the roof, gazing at the stars. Granted, growing up in the city limited the number of stars, but not the feeling they gave her. It seemed that no matter the problems she had by day, at night they could disappear into the sky and she could remember how big the universe really was. That she was just a speck on a floating dot in the middle of a murky galaxy, one of probably billions in the universe. When seen from that perspective, what did it matter if adults were fighting downstairs over money, or foster siblings were squabbling over chores? Her favorite nights were the meteor showers, when she would stay up on the roof until dew formed on her jacket. Perseids being the best in the Northern Hemisphere, she waited all year to see if she could count more than the last.

Sadie turned as the coffee shop manager locked the door and hurried on his way home. The tourist crowd had already given way to the locals wining and dining their way from Capitol Hill. A handsome couple rushed by her, huddled together for warmth against the cool, crisp air that blew through the breezeway in front of Café Cuppa. Sadie felt the familiar tug of loneliness creep into the back of her mind. She was a woman of duality, she wanted a sense of belonging, but she was very much afraid to trust that it could ever happen to her.

The chatter of passersby quieted as each found their destination, and Sadie accepted that James was not coming back. *It was just coffee, after all*, she thought to herself, it shouldn't have been that upsetting. She had experienced enough disappointment in her life that being left at a coffee shop was merely a drop in the ocean. Still, she found herself let down after what could've been an interesting night. Sadie turned toward the subway station to head home alone, telling herself she was content in the safe yet solitary life to which she'd become accustomed.

Chapter 1.5

Elsewhere

"They found her body at the bottom of an old subway terminal." Those words hung in the air, thickened it, choking the life out of the room. Killian refused to breathe them in as he sat devastated in his brother's living room. Killian Quinn, the esteemed Agent of the Zeta Defense Agency, the self-proclaimed powerhouse of ability, couldn't even remember the simple act of breathing. His partner, Nebraska Hill, hadn't been heard from all day, though that wasn't out of the ordinary. She had a habit of doing her own thing. She was the senior member of their duo, after all, and felt no need to explain her every move to Killian, or anyone for that matter. And no one questioned it, she'd always turn up to work on time the next day. But this time was different. This time she wasn't coming back.

"Killian, did you hear me?" his brother asked. "I said they found her body at the bottom of an old subway station." Desmond Kalani, Killian's big brother in more ways than one, stood over him and placed a hand on his shoulder. The hulking man was not only ten years Killian's senior but had sixty pounds on him as well. While they shared the same mother, Desmond clearly took after his Samoan father, whereas Killian tended toward their mother's Irish heritage and build. Desmond had always been there for him, taking on the fatherly role at home and continuing that trend when he got Killian the Agent job at the Zeta Defense Agency—or ZDA—which Desmond headed.

"But… how? I mean, she was small, but she could—" The questions raced through Killian's mind faster than his mouth could keep up. "And what was she doing down there at that time of—"

"They don't know," Desmond interrupted, handing him a glass of scotch. "Perhaps it was just a matter of her being in the wrong place at the wrong time. She didn't have anything on her—authorities only found me because her fingerprints registered in the system and alerted my office. The police suspect it was a mugging gone bad and she must've fallen off the platform in the scuffle. I'm sorry, Killian. She was a good Agent, and she'll always be remembered as such."

That was of little comfort to Killian. Nebraska Hill had been his partner for six years. He thought of the countless assignments they'd received, the late-night stakeouts that grew their partnership from her merely tolerating him to the jovial camaraderie of friends, the scrapes they'd made it through. All of them had to have been more dangerous than a simple mugger. That wasn't how Nebraska's story was supposed to end. Dead on a subway track, alone in the dark, at the hands of some lowlife that had no idea who she was or what she'd accomplished with her life. No idea of what he had stolen from the world.

"I'm so sorry, Killian." Desmond's voice pulled Killian back from his thoughts. "Know that we will do everything we can to find whoever did this."

"And make them pay," finished Killian as he downed

the rest of his glass and headed for the door.

"Killian, don't go do something stupid like getting yourself killed," warned Desmond, "it's not what she would've wanted."

Like you'd know what she would've wanted, Killian thought. *I knew her better than most.* "I'll be careful, big brother. Goodnight." He closed the door behind him, heading out for the nearest bar. Tonight would be about celebrating his partner, tomorrow he would begin the hunt.

∞

The bartender was cleaning up for the night when Killian found himself at the bottom of the bottle.

"Sorry, buddy, we've gotta close up," he said, looking at Killian. "As they say, 'you don't have to go home, but you can't stay here.' Though you probably should just head home, I'll call you a cab."

"I can walk, thank you very much," Killian slurred back as he practically fell off the stool. "I'm completely in control of myself."

He trudged his way to the door and down the dimly lit street. It was late enough that dew was beginning to form along the cobblestones. He allowed his thoughts to drift to Nebraska, to the Agency, to Her. Her, The Girl, the one that always found her way to the forefront of Killian's thoughts. Nebraska had been there the first time he saw Her. It was four years ago, but he could remember it like it was yesterday.

"So, what's on the docket today?" Killian asked as Nebraska walked up to him.

"We're getting assigned to a new Penumbrial, she's right here in DC," Nebraska replied, handing him the file.

"Seems like a pretty thin file," said Killian, feeling the weight, or lack thereof. "What's her history, background?"

"That's our job to find out. She's new to the system, so while we wait for the analysts to get us more information, I want you to find out everything you can on this girl. Where she goes, you go. What she does, you do. And as always, don't let her see you. You're still not great at the inconspicuous part of tailing someone." Nebraska gave him a look of parental disappointment then smiled wryly at him. In the two years they'd been partnered, Killian had actually begun to win the ol' bird over.

"That was one time, and the guy was hyper observant or something! Besides he was in on it all along, I think it was an unfair test," Killian retorted.

"Regardless, try better this time. I know you can do it, just be careful and less reckless, Rookie."

"Fine. Alright, Case Number 602, let's get acquainted." He opened the small file again, regarding the face of a young woman with dark brown hair, caramel skin, and glasses that covered her enigmatic green eyes. He checked his watch. *Probably enough time to catch her as she leaves work*, he thought to himself.

Killian sat at the corner of Constitution Avenue and 10th Street, waiting for her while reading up on what little was known of this woman. Parents both out of the picture, bounced around from foster home to foster home since she was two, graduated *summa cum laude* from Georgetown. *So she's smart*, Killian thought, *probably a nerd*.

Then he saw her. It was like the world stopped. For

a brief instant, nothing else existed for Killian Quinn. The sounds around him muted, the cars froze in time, he had never experienced anything like this before. He was powerless to move. He heard only the thumping sound of his heart. The world slowly began to turn again as the woman walked down the museum's steps. She was wearing black leggings with brown boots, a blue blazer, and a white t-shirt with a little bluebird on it. 602 was the kind of pretty that, Killian assumed, wouldn't give normal people the time of day, a kind of natural beauty that looked absolutely effortless. *So she's smart* and *beautiful,* he observed—the world was at her fingertips.

A crowd let off the bus and shuffled past Killian. One of them bumped him in the shoulder, bringing him back to reality.

"Hey, watch it!" He couldn't see anyone paying him any particular attention so turned back toward 602. "Agh! Where'd she go?"

He crossed the busy street filled with five o'clock traffic and managed to catch up to 602 again just outside the subway station entrance.

He followed her and sat down the car from her for the few stops back to her apartment. The entire time she stayed engrossed in a novel that looked too heavy to hold, let alone read. That was until a group of teenagers got on at Navy Yard-Ballpark. They came in and sat on either side of a younger redheaded kid sitting across from 602.

"Hey fart-face, where's our money?" one of the more brutish teenagers said to the kid as he slapped the backpack out of his lap. *Fart-face? Really? That's been used for years, buddy, get a new line,* Killian scoffed.

"I-I don't have any. My mom gave me a card," the frightened redhead responded. He tried to pick up his pack, but one of the other obnoxious teens kicked it further. He sat back, defeated. That's when 602 looked up from her book. She walked down the train, picked up the bag, and brought it back to her seat.

"Come sit next to me, sweetie," she said to the boy, "this is the smart side of the train." The teens watched, stunned, as their victim got up and sat next to 602. A nervous smile began to spread across his chubby cheeks. "What's your name?" she asked.

"Willy," he responded while he clutched his backpack to his chest. He was clearly overjoyed at having defeated his bullies, but Killian could also see the smirk that only comes from an awestruck young boy.

"Nice to meet you, Willy." Then she shot an icy look at the teens, one that sent chills down Killian's back fifteen feet down the car, and returned to reading her book.

"Whatever," the ringleader said to his crew. "Let's go." He rose to leave and promptly fell flat on his face, having tripped over 602's outstretched leg. Meanwhile, she hadn't even bothered to look up from her book but gave Willy a subtle fist bump behind it. Killian actually laughed out loud at the interaction. So she was smart, beautiful, *and* kind. Not to mention she had a penchant for vengeance. *I like this one,* he thought.

Once 602 was safely in her apartment, Killian called Nebraska to relay the day. "The Bluebird has landed, Brask."

"Don't call me that," she retorted, "and what do you mean by Bluebird?"

"Yeah, 602. She had this little bluebird on her shirt today, figured we could give her a codename. Ya know, like the secret service does to the President? So her codename is Bluebird."

As Killian walked away, he turned and looked back at 602, now Bluebird, through her window. Little did he know then that this woman would change the course of his life in the not so distant future.

"I am *not* calling a grown woman 'Bluebird,'" replied Nebraska on the other end of the line.

"Just you wait, I'll win you over yet, Brask." Then he hung up before she had a chance to correct him again and headed back to the ZDA.

Nebraska… When I find the scum that… Killian's thoughts trailed off as he arrived back to his apartment, barely able to see the single keyhole in the lock through his alcohol-induced double vision. He managed to get inside after only three attempts. It wasn't until he plopped himself down on the couch that he noticed a thick Manila envelope on the floor by the door. He could only make out one word on the front.

"Rookie!" he exclaimed as he shuffled across the floor to the envelope, knocking over a table. The items on top crashed to the ground, including a framed picture of Killian, Nebraska, and Desmond at the Agency. Killian was in the middle, smiling ear to ear, with his arms around Desmond and Nebraska's necks.

The frame lay cracked on the floor, but Killian ignored it as he scurried to the envelope. There was no return address, just Killian's and the two stamps needed to send such a heavy package, but he ripped it open regardless. Only one person called him Rookie, and that was Nebraska. Through gritted teeth, he opened the envelope. Inside he found a strange, rectangular device and a large file with a single sheet of paper clipped to the front.

"How in the world…" The shock sobered him up enough to read the letter:

Hey Rookie, if you're reading this then I'm sorry to say that for the first time in our partnership, I made a mistake. I'm hoping you will never need to read this, that I'll have removed this letter from the mailbox before it's picked up tomorrow morning. But in the off chance I don't, here's what you need to know. First of all, keep this strictly confidential, as I don't know who is involved. In the meantime, trust no one.

For the last few months, I've suspected a mole within the Agency. It started when Oliver and Agent Bell lost their Penumbrial and were reassigned to administrative duty. Personal biases aside, Oliver was one of the best Agents I'd ever known, there was no way he would've done anything to harm the Agency or his assignment. He changed in the following weeks, more withdrawn than ever. Then when he died in the car accident—second worst day of my life—I knew there was more to it than a random disappearance.

So I began to look into it, to clear his name, and in the process I began to notice other things going wrong. Nothing as big as missing persons, but operations that were fouled up at the last minute. Money being siphoned off or lost through various channels. Unexpected "delays" in research developments.

Which brings me to tonight. I've been going through phone records in and out of the Agency, trying to find anything out of the ordinary and stumbled across an anomaly—a call going out to a number not associated with any current cases. Didn't think anything of it at first, plenty of people can misdial, but then I noticed it lasted twenty-nine seconds—just under the trace time. Small, yes, but I followed it anyway. The number was registered to an office downtown, but when I went to check it out, it was empty, up for lease, and had been for years. There was only one other number recorded for outgoing or incoming calls to that address, a seemingly innocuous public phone. Every Monday night, like clockwork, that phone calls the empty office for exactly twenty-nine seconds. Tonight, I'm going to find out who's making those calls and finally get some answers.

Call me paranoid, but I feel like someone is catching on. I've "requisitioned" a CarterScott device to lock and block, to make sure no one can listen—for lack of a better term—in on what I'm doing. But if you're reading this, then it wasn't enough, or maybe it was too little too late. Hopefully the device will serve you better than it did me. Use it wisely, Rookie. Find the mole, fix the Agency. You can do this. You're a good Agent, don't let anyone tell you differently. Why do you think I stuck with you all these years? You went from rook to senior Agent faster than anyone before, and it had nothing to do with your brother, or even me, for that matter. Alright, partially because of my brilliance rubbing off on you, but still, you've got something special. There's no one else I'd trust to have my back. But don't overinflate that ego just yet, you're still reckless. Use that head of yours for more than ramming into things. You'll figure this out. Alright, enough sentiment.

Hopefully you'll never read this anyway.

I've included all of my notes, persons of interest, and records of anomalies in the Agency. It's in your hands now.

Take care, my friend.

Killian sat on the floor, motionless. *I knew she wouldn't have let some random guy catch her off guard,* he thought. He grabbed the CarterScott device. It was smaller than he'd imagined. It looked more like an old school e-reader than a top-secret government device. He'd heard stories of the thing from the Agency, rumors from Agent to Agent about the ZDA back in the eighties. But he'd never imagined that the original would still work.

He turned it on.

The device pinged as the screen came to life, revealing Nebraska's latest entry. Killian was afraid to read it. He knew it wouldn't end well but felt as though he had to get the story, the full story.

    Great. A storm. And me without my good socks. Why do I never bring extra socks...

    Corner of 12th and Independence, public phone inside. Phone's ringing... come on eyes, focus! Can't see anything in this rain.

    Is that... there's someone, a figure, but can't make out the face, even with binoculars. Tall man, cloak, and a wide-brimmed hat.

    Twenty-nine seconds, on the dot. He's already on the move. Why the rush? Following him across the grounds to 17th.

    Oh, that's clever. Down into the Dupont

Underground. Abandoned tunnels, lots of cover, perfect for someone who doesn't want to be found.

He's not losing me, though. God, it's creepy in here. Dark, granted, but the air is thick and heavy, almost haunted. Suffocating. Nope, nope, not going there. Calm down. It's a tunnel, light at both ends. Entry and exit. No time for claustrophobic thoughts.

Why is the ground shaking? What the... never mind. Just the train. Of course it's the train. Get it together. Stay focused. There's debris and broken glass everywhere, one careless step and he'll know I'm here.

He's still moving ahead, further into the network of tunnels. It's a wreck down here—where is this guy going?

I don't think he's noticed me so why all the cloak and dagger? Hat down, collar up, can't even catch his reflection on any metal surfaces. Why is everything down here metal? Must be well-trained. A professional. He's favoring his left leg slightly... the only distinguishing identifier.

He stopped. Why? Are we... did we loop back toward the entrance? Or is this the other end of the tunnel? He's turning the corner.

A dead-end? The tunnel's caved in, a mess of concrete and rebar and he's nowhere in sight. What did I miss? It's so dark...

There! A staircase. Lightning above made

it visible for just a second. He's there, at the steps, looking right at me.

"Freeze!"

Dark again. Are those footsteps running toward the exit?

Lightning. He's right there.

So close. I can almost reach him. I can feel his coat right at my fingertips. Got you!

Weightlessness. Falling. How? He pushed, I stepped back. The edge... I must've been closer to the edge of the platform than I thought. Still falling. Reach, Nebraska! Reach for something, anything. Brace yourself. Was there anything on the tracks? Thank God no trains have run through here in years. The third rail should be off. Was there anything else there?

Pain. Oh God...

Something is wrong. I landed, right? Why is my side on fire? Oh God...

Lightning. He's there, the figure. Standing over me on the platform. There's something next to me, something shiny? A blood-covered piece of rebar is sticking out of my side. Oh God...

Please, not here. He's moving. What is he doing? He's coming for me. I need help. Brave face, Nebraska, you can get out of this. It smells like metal and... and rain. The soft, gentle rain, like that time Oliver and I... No, not Oliver, not now. Focus, Nebraska. The wound. It's bleeding bad. I'm bleeding bad.

He's coming closer, so close. Reach for my gun, reach for him, reach for anything. He bats my hand away. Why won't he help me? "Please, help me."

He doesn't help. Why would he help? His hands are in my pockets. Why is it so cold? All I want is to feel you holding me again, Oliver, so warm. So safe. What is he looking for? "Please, help me." Not here. Anywhere but here.

He's back on the platform. Lightning again.

"No!" It can't. He can't. "Please don't leave me."

He's gone. I'm alone in the darkness. No, please, not here. It's so cold. No one knows I'm down here... no help is coming. That's the last Greenbelt train rumbling. It's okay, Nebraska, take a minute. You can get through.... Just rest a minute, rest your eyes, push away the tears. Mom and Dad will never know what I've done with my life. Oliver-your eyes, your sweet face. I'm sorry, my love, I tried.

No, I'm not done yet. I have to keep trying. I can make it out of here. I have to. I can't stay. I can't die in this awful place. Die? Please no, I can't go, not yet, not before... Killian. Oh God, Killian, you can't, don't... I'm so... Oliver...

The poets say we all die alone, but Killian was never one for poetry or fancy words. He preferred action and results. He sat there on his apartment floor, reliving the last moments of his partner's life, helpless to do anything to change it. His hands fell into his lap and he cried. He cried for his friend, for her life, for his loss. He would finish what she started. He had no choice.

Chapter 2

Mornings had never been, nor would ever be, Sadie Smith's strong suit. The five-foot walk from bed to bath in her modest 1-1 apartment was, although short, still no match for morning sleepiness. No matter how many times she had made the groggy trek, she seemed incapable of not hitting the corner foot of her dresser. It could've been that the dresser was just an inch too long for the wall, but she had fallen in love with the antique piece at a vintage shop years ago and wasn't going to let a silly thing like wall-length stop her from enjoying the ambiance she believed it added to her cozy existence. The throbbing pain from a stubbed toe had become as consistent as her morning alarm, so was thusly ignored. Sadie reached for the faucet, hoping that splashing cold water on her face would be enough to wash at least some of the sleep out of her eyes before making her way to the kitchen.

"Good morning, Redy," she said to the Betta fish swimming peacefully amid the roots of the Lucky Bamboo plant he called home. He came up to the glass, anxious for breakfast. "Happy Friday to you too, sir."

Sadie had found him one night after a few too many glasses of wine with her college roommate and self-appointed best friend, Piper. On a whim, she ended up in a pet store that was open way too late and spotted Redy—a solitary fish that needed little care to survive and had a penchant for anti-socialism, a kindred spirit. Now he was her constant welcome-home companion.

As she walked toward her coffee machine, Sadie looked at her phone.

"8 a.m.?" she exclaimed. "I'm late!" She rushed to throw on whatever presentable piece of clothing she could find and ran out the door with little more than a "later" shouted to Redy as the door closed. Coffee would have to wait.

Her commute to work went by in about the same manner as her week had, a blur. Ever since the fiasco that was the tour on Tuesday, she had been longing for Friday. While the boy that decided to climb the elephant wasn't in her tour group, she had filled out the paperwork, making her the easiest scapegoat for the museum. "*A complete lack of supervision*," wrote the mother in a letter addressed to the director. To avoid any further action, Sadie had been taken off the tour guide roster for the time being. Definitely not the worst repercussion in her mind.

Though she often found her thoughts drifting back to the event, not for the boy, but to James and their missed connection. Instead of the usual snacking at her desk, Sadie had been taking her lunch down in the museum cafeteria all week in the off chance James would show himself again. She told herself it was to give him a piece of her mind for ditching her.

It wasn't.

Sadie was the type of individual that liked to keep people at arms-length for exactly this reason. "If you never expect anything, you'll never be disappointed," she would say. "Expectation is the blight of happiness." But somehow, without conscious effort, she'd allowed a meager seed of that expectation to climb into her heart when it came to James.

"Ground control to Major Sadie." Allyn stood at the door with the Friday donuts he always brought and a cup of coffee in her favorite mug. "You still with us?"

Sadie had been drifting, again. "Yeah, sorry. Just thinking. What do you have today?"

"Looks like all that's left is the only-slightly-more-eccentric-than-standard-glazed donut: boring old chocolate-glazed. So you know, your favorite." He smiled at her.

"You're the best, Allyn. I'm so ready for the week to be over but Fried-Dough Friday makes it all worth it."

Allyn was nothing if not a creature of habit. It didn't stop at donuts every Friday, even his clothing choices were routine. He wore the same color vest on each day of the week.

He had told Sadie about his color schedule on the first day they met. Sadie was still a tour guide part-time but had secured an internship working with the Exhibitions & Collections Management Department. Allyn had only recently been hired on in the Division of Science himself, so they were sitting through the same orientation program. Sadie still remembered the first time she saw him. He was wearing a blue vest, of course, and his Smithsonian lab coat with a, *Hello, My Name Is Allyn*" sticker over it. But in the sea of intellectuals that worked at the Smithsonian Science Division, Allyn was still rejected as the nerd to end all nerds.

He tried to go to each table that morning and introduce himself, only to be ignored by every one of them.

Sadie had seen it before, the new kid in school trying to find their niche at lunch. Hell, Sadie had been that kid before, eight times in fact. Eight new schools, eight new rejections. Every time she felt just as alone as Allyn looked. After the sixth introduction, he admitted defeat and found a seat by himself at a desk toward the back of the room, something Sadie could never stand to see.

"Hi, I'm Sadie," she said, initiating contact. Allyn's eyes lit up, a goofy grin spread wide across his face.

"Hello! My name is Allyn Montoya," he said, pointing to his sticker. "You killed my father, prepare to die." He laughed at his own movie reference.

"I love the *Princess Bride!*" Sadie smiled and chuckled along. "Is your name really Montoya?"

"No… it's Green, but Green doesn't work as well." He gave her a nervous, embarrassed smile. "It's stupid, I know."

"No, not at all. It's nice to meet you, Allyn Green. Is this seat taken?" she asked, motioning toward the chair next to Allyn.

"Of course! I mean, no, it's not taken, but of course you can sit there." He moved his backpack away from the desk, spilling pencils, a notebook, and a small hand lens all over the floor. "Oh, sorry, I'll get that."

"Let me help you." Sadie bent down to help pick up the poor man's belongings, most of which seemed brand new for the occasion. The hand lens, though, was different, it was well-worn and the metal casing was engraved with the words: *Look up from the shadows, share the bright side.* "Here you go," she said after examining the piece. "I like that quote, is it from something?"

"No," he said, taking it back and placing it gingerly

in his bag. "It was just something my mom always said when I was a kid. She bought it for me when I decided I wanted to spend my life with rocks—a reminder to look up every once in a while and share happiness. So now that's what I do, look up and smile to all I meet."

"Sounds like you have a smart mom," Sadie said and a tinge of sadness gnawed at the back of her mind. *Push it down, Sadie.*

"She was," he said as he pushed his glasses back up his nose. "She passed away from cancer last year." His voice shook at the end of the sentence. Sadie almost felt the anguish in those words.

"I'm so sorry," she replied, not quite knowing what else to say. She wanted to tell him he wasn't alone, that she had lost her mom and dad, but decided it wasn't the same. How can you compare losing a couple of people you don't even remember to losing the person who raised you, supported you, loved you?

"It's okay. She was always proud of me, and she made it to my graduation, so I've got that." He almost started to tear up but smiled through it regardless. "Now that we've got the depressing stuff out of the way, what department are you working in?"

"Oh, umm… actually, I'm an intern, with Exhibitions and Collections Management," Sadie said sheepishly. "But I love history and the Smithsonian, so honestly I'm just happy to be here at all at this point."

"Me too! Not the intern part, but the happy to be here part. Did you know that the Smithsonian was founded with a singular purpose: the increase and diffusion of knowledge among men? And women too, of course." The dark traces of sadness faded from Allyn's face and instead he lit up like a ball of incandescent happiness.

"I did not." Sadie smiled. "But I do now. That's a pretty lofty goal."

"It is! And I plan to help in that effort."

"While looking on the bright side?" she asked, her smile widening.

"Yep! That's why I wore my blue vest today. It's actually forty-three percent of the population's favorite color, and since most people hate Mondays, I figure it's a way to brighten their day, seeing their favorite color." He looked at Sadie, eyebrows raised, as if eager for her reaction.

"Very nice, I like it."

Allyn's eyebrows settled and his smile grew. "Yeah, and on Fridays I wear red because it's an exciting color and most people are excited that it's Friday. It's also an 'attractive' color in the eyes of many," he said with an awkward wink.

He may have started that first week with only two color-coded days, but since he had come up with options for the rest. Tuesday was green because it was his favorite color and he'd always had a strange affinity for Tuesdays. Wednesdays had become tan, like a camel, after he spent an entire month going, "What day is it? Hump day!" Thursday was black, though he never explained why. After a few cagey answers, Sadie decided it was best to leave it be, clearly Allyn was not going to divulge that part of his psyche. But regardless, his consistency was comforting. Having had very little of it growing up, she longed for any semblance of stability, and something as small as Allyn's sweater calendar was appreciated.

"I do what I can. Good thing you're not diabetic or donuts would probably be a dangerous pick-me-up," Allyn stated plainly, bringing Sadie back to the present. He took a big bite of his jelly donut, most of which slipped out the back and onto his shoe. "Oh, and Stead sent out a memo, our weekly status got moved up to 10 a.m."

Valerie Stead, the woman who, for all intents and purposes, ran the Smithsonian. Even though she was only the Museum Manager of the Natural History Museum, every other manager in existence came to her with questions or requests. She had her fingers on the pulse of the place better than anyone else in the building—and she made sure everyone knew it.

"Oh okay, glad I got here on time then." Sadie rolled her eyes as she looked at her watch. The woman was cold and demanding in every way, but tardiness was an especially significant act of provocation.

"How'd it go with that request, by the way, for the new exhibit?"

Oh no, Sadie thought. In the haze of the week, she had completely forgotten to look over the file; it lay untouched in her bag. She immediately opened it to look for any sort of timeline that Stead had in mind.

"Potential opening in ninety days..." Sadie met Allyn's eyes. They looked as if they were about to pop out of his head. "Think she'll ask about it today?" she asked, although she already knew the answer.

"Ninety days? That crazy," responded Allyn. "There's no way she'd want it done in three months. Most exhibits take at least a year to go from inception to display. I mean, how big can a communication display be? ...But

I digress, she's definitely going to ask for an update if this is truly being fast-tracked. Better read up on it now. You've got twenty minutes, my friend. I'll be right back with another cup of brain juice for you." He gestured toward his coffee mug.

"Thanks, Allyn." Sadie began reading with the vim and vigor of a student cramming before an exam. She had always prided herself on her ability to prepare well in advance of any test or project. Of course, loving to study didn't hurt.

"I know that look," Jonas said from the doorway. "Passed Allyn in the hallway, he said this was for you. Though I'm not sure coffee will help you read any faster. You're already the fastest speed reader on my team." He placed her favorite mug on her desk.

It was a mug from "Central Perk" that Piper had bought her, since it was one of the few shows they could agree on watching. "You know you've always got a friend and soul-sister in me, and now you can bring this to work for a caffeine kick in the pants to remind you of that fact," she had said when she gave it to Sadie at graduation. "And don't let all those boring scientists you're going to work with at the Smithsonian bring you down to their level. I've worked hard to bring some pop-culture to your life and I'm not about to let those nerds ruin all my work." She meant well, but Sadie found some amusement in the knowledge that if Piper had ever seen Jonas Andrews, she probably would've switched majors.

"Hey Jonas, yeah, somehow managed to forget about this thing all week between the paperwork and everything."

"Well, thankfully I did do my homework, between

the two of us we should be fine. Let's go, you're not going to get anything extra in the last five minutes. Better to be on time."

Sadie got up and rounded her desk, but cut the corner too sharply. She rammed her hip into the corner, an action that happened so often she mostly ignored the pain and focused more on not spilling her coffee.

"Did the two seconds you would've saved cutting that corner really have made a difference?" Jonas questioned as he watched Sadie take a few awkward steps to recenter herself and let the pain fade.

"You never know," she said with a laugh.

∞

The meeting progressed as normal, with each department giving updates on their latest projects and such. They talked about the annual Food History Gala, which always made everyone in attendance hungry as they discussed the dishes that the winner of the Julia Child Award was best known for. So far, neither Sadie nor her project had been brought up. Leaving her thankful and looking to Jonas with hopeful eyes.

"Thank you to everyone for your input and updates," Director Valerie Stead announced as she stood up from the back of the room. This was a woman who commanded attention and respect by her mere presence. Not a hair dared be out of place and her glasses seemed to stand at attention on her face for fear of disappointing her. Stead's accent proved she was born in England, but Sadie was never able to have a conversation with her long enough to ask where exactly in England she was from. It was a very posh accent though, so probably London. She still wore stockings under her skirt, a remnant from the past when women thought it disdainful to show skin in public. But her shoes, her shoes were always fantastic. Never overstated, yet never outdated either. Classic black pumps that somehow didn't make a sound when she walked, perfect for sneaking up on an unsuspecting employee not fully engrossed in their work. "Ms. Smith. What about our new communication display? Any updates?"

"Communication has been updated quite a lot actually, since our beginnings with cave drawings," Sadie responded as more of a knee-jerk reaction than a real answer. She looked up to meet Stead's unamused eyes. Realizing she had said that out loud, Sadie immediately wanted to melt into the floor. "I'm sorry, what I meant was—"

"What she meant was, we think we're going to have a great display for this one." Dr. Jonas Andrews to the rescue. "The material lends itself to an interactive exhibit. We're working with the technology department to see what we can do about creating a projected canvas on stone that guests can 'draw' on, leaving their own mark on history before progressing through each step of the evolution of communication."

Sadie seethed with anger at herself for forgetting about the project then needing Jonas to swoop in and save her like that.

"Very good, Dr. Andrews," said Stead, seemingly appeased by his answer, for the moment, at least. "We look forward to seeing this one come to life. Thank you, everyone. Have a good day."

And with that, the meeting adjourned. Sadie could

only look to Jonas with grateful eyes as Stead approached him. Watching their conversation from afar, she wasn't able to shake the thought that it centered around her lack of preparation, and she felt her position at the Smithsonian slipping into jeopardy. Sadie knew she shouldn't be worried, in the four years she'd been working with the curatorial staff, not once had she given any of them doubt as to her abilities. Still, that small part of her that felt she always needed to prove herself, to work hard enough to be valued, screamed self-doubt in the back of her mind. Stead glanced at her, then quickly returned to the conversation with Jonas.

Sadie found herself subconsciously holding her breath as Stead nodded and walked away, leaving Jonas free to join her.

"Thanks, Jonas," she said through almost gritted teeth, still kicking herself for allowing her mind to be too distracted to work on the project. "Your idea sounds awesome. Does the tech department really think that's something we can do?"

"I have no idea, I haven't talked to them. That's your job." Jonas looked at Sadie seriously, as if this were a teaching moment between a father and his delinquent daughter. "I came up with the idea, now you can run with it, Assistant Curator."

"Right, I'll get on that. I promise this time. No more distractions." Though James still lingered in the back of Sadie's mind, begging for more attention. The thought of his infectious laughter and that beguiling smile made her blush. Sadie forced the idea from her head. *Focus,* she thought.

"See that there aren't. I'm heading out for a lunch meeting and then will be working remotely for the rest of the day. I'll see you Monday, Sadie, have a good weekend," Jonas said as he turned to walk away, again favoring his left leg.

"Thanks, Jonas… Hey, what happened to your leg? Are you okay?"

"Ah, so it is noticeable. I hit a rock on my ride Sunday and must've tweaked my ankle. It's getting better, but I guess I'm not as good at hiding it as I thought. No need to worry, my dear, time heals all wounds," he said with a wink as he left the room.

∞

At 5:30 on the dot, Sadie closed the office door behind her. She could hardly wait for a low-key weekend spent with Redy, a bottle of 19 Crimes, and the historical fiction novel she had bought featuring a woman sent back in time to eighteenth-century Scotland. Yes, they already had a TV show about it, but she'd always been one to read the book first, and this series would be no exception. She could almost hear the 1,100 pages calling her name.

The elevator doors began to close and she ran to catch them. "Hold the elevator!"

Sadie got there just as they shut, but to her surprise, the doors dinged and re-opened for her.

Valerie Stead stood behind them.

"Oh, um, thanks," Sadie said, now embarrassed to be in the confined space of an elevator with a woman whom, Sadie believed, had been severely underwhelmed by their meeting this morning.

"You're welcome," she replied coolly. The pair stood quietly, listening to the instrumental piano stylings of a Billy Joel hit that was playing over the scratchy elevator speakers. "I meant to tell you last week, I appreciated your work on the Byzantine project, and I look forward to what you and Dr. Andrews will come up with for this new project."

What? Sadie thought. She looked at Stead for confirmation that she hadn't imagined the words. *Something I did was good enough for her?* She thought she saw a glint of approval in Stead's eye, the ends of her lips moving to a slight upturn, but no. Not from Stead. Expressionless was an understatement. She would've made an excellent poker player in another life. "Thank you, ma'am. Means a lot."

The elevator doors opened and Sadie waited to let Stead go first. She didn't move.

"That's okay, I forgot something upstairs. Have a good night, Ms. Smith."

With that, Sadie left the elevator and watched the doors close over her shoulder, before continuing on her way home.

The day hadn't been a total loss after all, and she vowed to make sure this project didn't wreck the little bit of approval she seemed to have finally gained from Valerie Stead.

Chapter 3

Sadie had just walked into her apartment when her phone began to buzz. It was a text from Piper.

Hey, girl! We're hitting O'Malley's tonight, you should join! I'll be by in ten to pick you up.

Due to a registrar's mistake, Sadie and Piper had ended up being roommates their freshman year at Georgetown. Typically, the university tried to place students together that had the same major, but Piper's communication major was in stark contrast to Sadie's double majors in history and psychology. Despite their differences, they had stayed friends through it all. And Piper Montgomery was not one to be ignored.

"Ugh…" Sadie sighed audibly.

I don't know, Piper, it's been a long week.

She hoped that would satisfy her friend. Really, Sadie didn't want to get stuck in another one of Piper's schemes. Piper saw it as her life's ambition to get Sadie a date. Not that she hadn't been on dates before, but studying the acoustic resonance of the Arctic beluga whale at Point Barrow in Alaska and sharing a cup of hot cocoa with a man named Sven apparently didn't count for Piper.

"I thought you said he barely spoke English, how do you expect to get to know someone if you can't even talk to each other? I mean, there are ways, but…" she had said with a salacious laugh. "But how cute could a guy named Sven be? Don't you worry, girl, I'll get you a Jax or Jason or Jamal. Someone with a bit of oomph!" Sadie didn't necessarily know what kind of "oomph" Piper had in mind, but she liked Sven. And the three months they'd spent on that exhibition had definitely gone by faster with him there. Of course, after the three months, he left without a word and went back to Iceland. Another page in the book left on a cliffhanger. Six months ago, Sadie saw his wedding photos on Facebook.

Piper's response buzzed in.

Too bad. I'll be there in five. And try those new shoes I got you last week. They'll be perfect.

That's how things always went with Piper. There was never really a choice, it was her way or, well, that's it. Sadie decided it wasn't worth the fight, she'd have lost anyway, and a drink out would probably help get her mind off Tuesday night. She still didn't understand why it mattered to her, maybe it was the missed opportunity, or maybe the fact it was yet another relationship that was "just not going to work out." Either way, Sadie was ready to get the notion of James out of her head.

She quickly tried to make herself at least somewhat presentable, more to avoid another lecture from Piper, but why not make an effort? And she did love the shoes Piper had bought her. They were black, round-toed wedges, open heel with a single buckle strap. The perfect balance of comfort and chic.

A loud, rapid-fire knocking on the door signaled Piper's arrival. "Sadie, open up! We're already running late," she yelled.

"I'm coming! And how can we be late when you just

told me about this ten minutes ago?" Sadie asked as she opened the door.

"Because I know if I give you too long to mull it over you'll undoubtedly bail on me," Piper responded as she gave Sadie her customary once-over.

It wasn't untrue, the more time Sadie had to think about something, the more time she had to come up with a better excuse as to why she couldn't do it.

"Cute outfit," Piper said. "It's almost like you have a fashionista best friend that picked out each piece of it. Except for the sweater, that's all you, but whatever. Let's go!"

With that, Sadie was pulled down the stairs and into the cab waiting below.

∞

When people think of an Irish pub, what they're probably picturing is O'Malley's—dim lighting, low ceilings, wooden everything. From the lavish crown molding to the heavy tables to the ornate bench ends, all of them dark wood. The walls were covered with old photos and posters of classic Guinness advertisements. The photos were particularly interesting, a scattered mix of black and white family portraits from "the old country" and pictures of doors, hundreds of doors. It looked like every door in Ireland had been photographed and sent to O'Malley's to add ambiance to the space. Speaking of which, space was not something there was a lot of. It looked more like someone had bought an old house and turned it into a bar. There were essentially three sections of tables, one for private parties, one near the dartboards, and one featuring a small stage, complete with a piano for cranking out classic Irish drinking songs. A wrap-around bar extended through all three, so that draughts of everyone's favorite pints and a wide selection of Irish whiskey were easily accessible, no matter where you sat.

O'Malley's was full, as per usual for a Friday night, but Piper and her friends always managed to grab the corner booth, perfectly situated midway between the bar and dartboards. The ideal spot to spy on people at the bar, with the live band close enough to hear but not so loud they couldn't talk over it.

As Sadie walked past the jolly patrons, she could've sworn she saw the mysterious James heading toward the door. *No, couldn't be*, she thought. She turned for a closer look, but of course, it wasn't him. This man was too short. Just another dark-haired charmer taking his date on to their next stop. Sadie again tried to push the thought of James out of her mind as she walked toward their usual table. The other four members of the group were already downing their first round of Irish slammers when Sadie and Piper arrived.

"I can't believe you guys started without us!" Piper yelled in a playful manner.

"We weren't sure when you were getting here, but I did already order you a drink, baby," said Ethan, Piper's latest toy. He was tall, handsome, and knew it. Everything about him screamed that he was the star quarterback of his high school football team, content to relive the "glory days" of his past instead of pursuing anything worthwhile in the present. Sadie thought him nice enough but knew he wouldn't last long. Piper was notorious for being fickle when it came to men.

"Aw thanks," she replied as she sat on his knee and kissed him. "A cosmo, right?"

"Here's your Guinness, sir," the waitress said as she delivered a pint of the black stuff to the table.

"Oh. Ummm, sorry. I thought you'd want a beer since we're at a pub, and bonus, they're two-for-one right now." Ethan smiled, not realizing the mistake he'd just made. Not only did he get Piper Montgomery a beer, a beverage she vowed never to cross her lips again after one too many keggers on campus, but he'd also tried to budget his spending for the night.

Poor sap, Sadie thought.

"It's okay, Piper, I'll take the beer and we can go get you another drink," Sadie said in an attempt to deflect the anger she could almost feel coming from Piper's direction. "You know, they say God invented whiskey to keep the Irish from ruling the world. But Arthur Guinness found another way and now the Irish have a place in most bars across the globe." The other five people seated at the table stared at Sadie for a moment, then continued on with their conversations. Random factoids were a personal passion of Sadie's, even if they weren't anyone else's. Either way, she'd downgraded Piper's anger from a ten to at least a five at this point. Mission accomplished. Sadie grabbed Piper's arm and headed toward the bar.

"I can't believe him? It's like he doesn't know me at all," Piper lamented.

"Well, he doesn't. You've been dating for what, two weeks now?" Sadie shrugged. "What did you expect?"

"A little respect, at least. I mean, do I even look like a beer drinker?"

No, definitely not, thought Sadie, as they joined the crowd of patrons trying to get their orders in before happy hour ended. Her friend was more the Diane Chambers type than a Marion Ravenwood.

"Hey, that guy keeps staring at us," Piper said as she pointed out a man in his late twenties who was sitting alone at the bar enjoying a Guinness. "Do you know him?"

"Not that I recognize," Sadie replied, following her gaze. The man glanced in their direction, poorly pretending to survey the room, then looked away as he pushed up his rimless glasses. They helped to soften his general demeanor. At first sight, the man seemed rather intimidating, being a head taller than the people around him. He had a strong, handsome face and wore a neatly trimmed goatee. He definitely stood out in a crowd, and it definitely looked like he was watching the two women. As soon as he noticed them staring in his direction, he sheepishly tried to divert his eyes to the TV, attempting to look interested in the game that was on. Unfortunately for him, it was a commercial break.

"He's kinda cute actually." Piper bit her lip. "Let's go over and meet him, shall we? Don't want to be rude or anything." She began walking toward the man, pulling along Sadie with her.

"I don't know if that's a good idea, Piper, he looks kind of nervous or I don't know, kind of off. We can't just—" Sadie was cut off before she could finish her objection.

"Hi. My friend and I saw you staring at us, so we thought we'd come to say hi and give you the chance to buy us a drink," said Piper, with all the confidence and gusto in the world, knowing no one ever turned her down.

"Oh, umm, hi." The man's eyes flitted back and forth between them. "Yeah, I'm sorry, I uh… sure, why not. Hey Sam," he said to the bartender, "get these ladies whatever they want. On my tab."

"Why thank you, sir," said Piper. "We'll have two blue Long Islands."

Sadie shook her head. "Piper, no, actually, can I have a water, please?"

"What's wrong with you? Get a drink! This nice man is buying us a drink. I'm sorry, what's your name?"

"Petey," the man replied.

"Petey? Really? Well okay then, Petey is buying us a drink, don't be rude and reject his kindness," she said as she grabbed Petey's broad shoulder, ever-so-slightly caressing his dark umber skin. A grin shot across Petey's face. Clearly, he wasn't opposed to showing his "kindness."

"Really, it's okay," said Petey. "Get whatever you want. Sam's a buddy, he'll make it however you like."

Sadie hesitated; she hadn't planned on being out late tonight. Instead, she'd wanted to make some headway on her latest novel before having to spend the weekend working. "Alright, fine. Can I get a Kentucky Mule then? With Old Forrester, if you have it, Maker's if you don't." *If I'm going to get a free drink, might as well enjoy it,* she thought.

"Girl after my own heart." Petey smiled. "Skip straight to the bourbon. And Old Forrester, good choice. I like an Eagle Rare personally, but Old Forrester is good too." He had an infectious smile and Sadie couldn't help but grin back.

"Eagle Rare is fantastic straight, but if I'm mixing it, it's going to be Old Forrester," she replied. In her early twenties, Sadie's love of history had led her down a rabbit hole about the introduction of bourbon way back in the 1820s. There was so much legend and lore surrounding how and where exactly it originated, she couldn't help but be intrigued. "Did you know that the Scotts originally brought the distilling process to America in the eighteenth century, but whether it was introduced by Jacob Spears or Elijah Craig remains a legend to this day? Also still in question is whether it was named for Bourbon County in Kentucky or Bourbon Street in New Orleans." Historical questions were another addiction for Sadie, once a question was asked, she would doggedly pursue the answer until she was satisfied. And often those answers found their way into her everyday conversations.

"Really?" replied Petey. "I never knew that. So is Elijah Craig the oldest bourbon?"

"Actually, that would be Buffalo Trace, th—"

"And that's Sadie and her history. Where do you store all this info, girl? Oh well, to each their own," said Piper, trying to reinsert herself in the conversation. "So where are your friends, Petey, or are you flying solo tonight?"

"Ah, yes, friends, I've heard of those. Problem with them is you have to meet people and, well, you actually have to like people for that to happen," Petey responded wryly.

"You sound too much like our Sadie, here, doesn't he?" Piper grabbed Sadie's shoulders and shook her in a way that Sadie always hated. "I happen to be an excellent judge of people and I have a few of them back at our table. Why don't you come over with us and I'll even sweeten the deal and let you win the first round of darts?"

Piper always did have a way with people, particularly men, and getting them to do exactly what she wanted.

"As tempting as that sounds, I think I'll just stay here and enjoy my single beer before heading out," he said, turning back to face the bartender and ask for his bill.

"Nonsense!" Piper exclaimed as she grabbed his arm and began pulling him behind her. "It'll be fun. As I'm always telling Sadie here, what's the point of life if you don't go out and live a little."

Petey looked at Sadie with an almost "*Is she serious? Please help me!*" look on his face. All Sadie could do was mouth "sorry" and shrug her shoulders.

"Welcome to Piper's world," she whispered to him as he was dragged along beside her, attempting to grab his belongings from the bar before they were out of reach.

The hours passed and the drinks flowed while Petey ingratiated himself into their little group. Well, with everyone except Ethan that is. Piper had made it abundantly clear that they were in a fight and had broken up for tonight. So he sat in the corner nursing a beer with a sullen look on his face as if he were in time out.

Petey, on the other hand, had turned out to be quite the dart player and comedian. For someone who didn't like people, his dry wit, amplified by the multitudinous rounds of beer, was certainly a hit, especially for Piper, who was all but throwing herself at him at every opportunity.

"I used to be six foot three," Petey bellowed out the punch line of his latest joke, followed by his rather unique laugh. It was somewhere between a squeal and a scream, not so high-pitched as to be harsh, but definitely not a sound one would expect from a man of his size. He, and those around the table, laughed so hard at his joke that they were all out of breath. The half-drunk pints in front of them shook as Petey slammed on the wood and stomped his feet as if to assist his lungs in keeping him alive. Even Sadie found herself laughing along.

"Hey Sadie," Piper yelled across the table. "Remember that one time when my mom came up for parents' weekend in college? Oh it was SO embarrassing though, for you, of course. I laughed for days!"

"Yes Piper, I was there too." Sadie smiled with mild annoyance.

"Yeah, so Sadie and I had just started becoming friends, it was a rocky start, but…" and Piper continued with the story, but Sadie had already stopped listening. She did remember that weekend, better than she honestly wanted to. Piper's mom had come up with a car full of gifts for Piper, everything from purses to scarves for winter, afraid her little girl would freeze in the city. It wasn't the gifts that got to Sadie, it was their closeness. She vividly remembered sitting there watching Piper's mom gush over how proud she was of Piper, her little girl that was all grown up and ready to face the world. She even brought a box of homemade cookies for them. It was unapologetically the perfect representation of a mother's love and concern for her daughter, and Sadie wanted every ounce of it.

But Sadie had pushed against that side of her. It was a fantasy, a charade. One that would never be hers. That was why, when Piper invited Sadie to join them on a shopping spree, she opted to stay in, using the excuse of a paper deadline. In truth, though, as soon as they left she gathered every unread book in their apartment, a gallon of ice cream, and sought the comfort of their trusty gray beanbag chair. Stereotypical, yes, but she never doubted the healing power of historical fiction and overly sugary dairy products.

Even as Sadie sat in O'Malley's thinking about that weekend, listening to Piper's story continue on, she could feel the relentless lump growing in her throat and heat swelling behind her eyes. *Whatever*, she thought. Wherever Sadie's mom was now, it was her loss. Sadie had learned the hard way to shove that stuff down and lock it away, don't let it muck up the present.

"As exciting as Piper's stories of our past are, I'm going to go grab another Guinness and throw more sharp objects at the wall," Sadie said as she got up from the table, trying to busy her mind.

"Oooo can you get me an Irish slammer, sweetie?" Piper cried.

"Oh me too!"

"Me three," the table erupted in requests.

"I'll just send a whole round over, how's that?" And Sadie turned, leaving the table cheering behind her, to gain the safety of solitude, if only for a moment.

While the others did their shots, Petey sauntered over to Sadie, who was practicing for the next darts challenge. "So," he said as Sadie threw another dart and completely missed the board. "Not the next world dart champion then are we?"

"Ha, I'm already the reigning champ, I just don't want to make them feel bad. Don't tell anyone though," Sadie said with a wink.

Petey let out a roar of laughter. "Right, and I'm a secret agent, but don't tell nobody either." He picked up a handful of darts and started throwing them between Sadie's shots. "So Sadie, what's your story? Besides being a dart champion and superhero."

"Superhero?" she questioned, almost coughing up the sip of beer she'd just taken. "What makes you think I'm a superhero?"

"The name. Your last name's Smith, right? Heard Sam call you Ms. Smith after he ID'd you." Sadie looked at Petey as if to say, "So what?" and he grinned. "Sadie Smith, it's a superhero name. Like all the other greats, Bruce Banner, Peter Parker, Scott Summers."

"Ah, well technically Sadie is short for Mercedes, but my first name is Sarah, so still works, I guess." She threw her next dart and missed again.

"Sarah Mercedes Smith… why Sadie then?"

"Umm," she paused, calculating how much of her past she wanted to reveal to this stranger, "it's been a nickname since I was a kid. One of the families I lived with, when I was probably seven or eight, had a daughter named Becca, who was about three at the time, and to learn how to speak she would practice people's full names when she met them. Mercedes was a tad hard for her so she would go around the house yelling 'Sa Sadie Smit,' and I guess Sadie sorta stuck."

Petey took another swig of his beer and shrugged. "Better than being Sa forever. Imagine people having to say, "sup Sa' all the time. That would be annoying. Sadie was a good choice."

As Sadie continued throwing darts, a short Hispanic man walked right up to her and, with a flirtatious wink, said, "*Disculpe, mamacita, pero que hace una flor como tu, en un decierto como esta? Tienes sed? Ven para acá y te doy lo que necesitas.*"

"Yeah, sorry, I don't actually speak Spanish," replied Sadie, taken aback by the man's forwardness.

"Oh, forgive me, I was merely asking if I could buy you another drink, a beautiful desert rose such as yourself should never be without refreshment when Julio is around," the man said as he leaned on the high top table nearest Petey and Sadie.

"Umm." Sadie let a small chuckle escape from her mouth. "I'm good. Thanks, though."

"Suit yourself, señorita, but I will be just over there if you should get thirsty," Julio replied with a quick smack of his lips.

"Alright, buddy, that's a hard no, but have fun with your boys over there. Buh-bye." Petey stepped in and waved the young man away. He turned back to Sadie and the pair shared a chuckle of disbelief. "Does that happen often?"

"What, the horrible pick-up lines part or the people assuming I speak Spanish part?" asked Sadie.

"Either?" Petey raised an eyebrow as if he hadn't realized there were two options.

"That was the first time I've been called a desert rose, but as for the Spanish bit, yeah, all the time. People always assume I speak their language based on my looks, but I don't." She took another swig from her beer and returned to the dartboard.

Petey seemed to study her. "To be fair, you do look

Hispanic, even with the green eyes. Never thought to pick it up in school?"

"Nope, took Latin," Sadie said, throwing another dart.

"Because that's useful, being a dead language and all."

"I'm a historian; dead languages are an occupational hazard." Sadie threw her last dart and hit a bullseye.

"Ahh, I did it!" she celebrated, jumping up and down.

"What, well done! That deserves a shot. Let's go!"

Sadie followed Petey to the bar for a shot of Eagle Rare, his choice, and then they rejoined the rest of the group. Soon, the live band began playing and the drinks continued to flow. The night flew by and Sadie hadn't once thought about what's-his-name, the guy that bailed with no explanation. As the band finished their last song, she checked her watch. It was almost midnight. She was glad to have had a night out, but she really did have a lot she wanted to accomplish this weekend—and being out until the early hours was not on the list.

"Alright, how about we go hit up that new speakeasy place across town?" Piper blurted out, wanting to continue the evening's antics. "I hear they have an awesome whiskey selection, Petey. You'd love it!"

"I do love whiskey, let's do it." Petey stood up far too quickly, almost knocking over the table and losing his balance in the process. "To the cabbie!"

"Coming, Sadie?" Piper asked, turning toward her friend.

"As much fun as that sounds, I better be getting home. I have a lot of work to do this weekend." She should get started on that new exhibit, after all. "Thanks for making me come out with you tonight, though. It was a lot of fun and I needed it."

"Ah okay, fine! Well, I'll let you know how the night goes," Piper said with a wink and a nod toward Petey, who was trying to traverse the ocean of pub patrons below him. He really was tall, easily six foot five.

Sadie bent down to grab her bag and found a backpack sitting on the bench. "Oh, someone—" She looked up, but the group was already gone. She decided she would just text Piper and let her know that she had the bag in case anyone wanted to come and get it from her.

By the time Sadie's Uber dropped her off, she could barely keep her eyes open. She haphazardly threw her stuff, and the backpack, on her coffee table, watching it slide all the way across and fall off the other side. *I'll deal with that in the morning,* Sadie thought to herself. She heard a small thud but couldn't be bothered to look back as she quickly got ready for bed and settled into her jersey sheets for the night.

"Goodnight, Redy," she said and fell asleep to the white noise of downtown DC that echoed from outside her bedroom window.

Chapter 4

A thunderous pounding shook Sadie's front door.

"Sadie, open up!" It was Piper.

What time is it? Sadie thought to herself as she checked her phone. Not only it was 8 a.m., but she also had five missed calls from Piper. *What on earth is she doing here this early?* Sadie quickly threw on the trusty hoodie hanging on her bedpost before running to the door.

"What is so urgent?" she asked, a little annoyed at having been awoken so early on a Saturday morning. Piper was wearing the same clothes as the night before. "Have you even been home yet?"

"Hey girl, um no." Piper chortled, clearly still buzzed. "Oh, here's your paper, who still gets a paper, by the way? Whatever, ummm, so do you still have that backpack? No one mentioned it last night, but I also didn't check my texts until this morning when we were all getting breakfast. It could be Jason's, but I'm hoping it's Petey's." She giggled. "Then I'll have an 'in' to see him again later." Piper gave a very poor wink, really more of an exaggerated blink.

"Piper, you don't even know who this guy is," Sadie cautioned while grabbing the backpack from the floor. "What if he's a creeper?" *Or worse.*

"Whatever, you worry too much! All I know is that he was a lot of fun last night and stayed partying with us everywhere we went. Can't be that bad of a guy. K, gotta go, love you," Piper retorted as she spun and ran down the stairs, almost falling. "I'm good!"

"Be careful! And get some sleep!"

Sadie closed the door, hoping that Piper was right, and headed to the kitchen for coffee, her morning survival tool. As she waited for the pot to percolate, she leaned over the counter to feed Redy.

"Good morning, sorry if she woke you up too. Crazy Piper, always up to something, I guess."

She glanced past Redy's bowl and noticed a glint on the living room floor beneath the couch. She strolled over to discover a small, Kindle-like device, but upon closer inspection it seemed less advanced than that. *What in the world?* Sadie thought. Yellowed with age, it had a simple dark screen with three buttons below and was roughly the same size and weight as a paperback novel. She pushed one of the buttons and a loading symbol flashed across the screen as her kettle began to whistle. The display reminded her of VCRs back in the day.

The loading symbol was moving at a snail's pace so she decided to pour her coffee and catch up on current events while she waited. Sadie took pleasure in being one of the few people that still supported a physical newspaper. There was something to be said for the smell of fresh ink on newsprint, and the tactile feel of the paper reminded her of its history. The newsies that used to call out the reports every morning. When people actually had to wait to "read all about it" the day after it happened, instead of being inundated by Tweets and phone alerts at every new celebrity relationship. When the news was still newsworthy.

She skimmed over the headlines: "Millionaire CEO of Escavez Industries Found Dead from Apparent Overdose," "Woman Identified in Subway Murder," and "New Baby Hippo Born at the National Zoo." She'd heard about the hippo at work all week; it seemed the entire Smithsonian was on "Hippo Watch." They had even set up a live webcam and covered it in the company newsletter. They named the little guy Oulike, and he was the cutest baby hippo ever.

The device chimed from the counter, and Sadie picked it up to find the screen filled with text. *So it is an e-reader*, she said to herself. She placed it back on the counter, deciding to message Piper to ask if the backpack owner had lost this as well.

As she distractedly scrolled through social media on her phone, completely forgetting why she had grabbed it in the first place, the device kept catching her eye. She knew it wasn't hers, but thought, *What's the harm in reading a book?*

Finally giving in to her desire, Sadie picked up the device again. The screen lit up and she began to read:

SUBJECT: KILLIAN QUINN

"Okay, I've just reset it, so in three days, make sure you reset it again."

"Three days? Why three days... wait, please tell me you didn't take the original CarterScott prototype, Killian?"

"I did nothing of the sort!" He's always such a worrier. "Brask did. And then left it for me."

"And you neglected to turn it in?"

"Why would I do that? She trusted me to finish this and that's what I'm going to do. She left me this envelope for a reason. I have to believe that she was onto something. We can't trust anyone else at the ZDA, and I can't trust that they're not going to be checking in on me with Nebraska gone, especially if they find out she took this."

"Fine. What do you want me to do with it?"

"For now, keep it safe and don't forget to reset it. I left my phone at home so you're the only person that'll know where I am. I think it's better if I stay off the grid for a few days, just in case. Meaning, check the device and I'll let you know if I need help, the range should be long enough to cover the city. Oh, and I need your hacker skills."

"Of course you do. What do you need?"

"Well, she tracked a number to an empty office space, but even though it's empty, there was only one other business in there—Banyan Acquisitions and Development. Fairly certain it's nothing, they look legit enough, but next time you find yourself in a devious mood, can you check 'em out?"

"Acquisitions and Development? That's the trademark name of shell corporations. But sure, I'll look into it."

"Thanks. And one last thing..."

"Why are you hesitating? I don't like when you hesitate, Killian. It normally means you're about to ask for something above and beyond."

"Yeah, so I know you're not going to like it, but can you please look after 602 for me?"

"No."

"No? What do you mean 'No'?"

"I mean no. I'm terrible at all that spy stuff, you know this. That's why I'm the 'desk guy' and not the 'go out and protect people and do stuff guy.' That's your life, *Agent Quinn*, not mine."

"I know, but I need you to do this for me. I can't be worrying about her while I'm trying to figure out the rest of this mess." Play up the puppy dog eyes and maybe he'll go for it...

"Fine. But if something goes wrong, it's not my fault."

Ha! Knew that would work. "Thanks, buddy, you're the best. Hey, do you have a gun?"

"I'm sorry, what now?

"A gun? Do you have one?"

"No, why would I have a gun?" You've got to be kidding me.

"Umm, because you work for a covert agency tasked with protecting people? Why wouldn't you have a gun?"

"I don't like guns."

"But don't you need—whatever, here, take mine."

"I don't want it."

"Well you need something if you're going to protect 602. I'm not leaving her unprotected. Go ahead and sigh all you want, you're taking it."

"Don't you need it more than me?"

"I'm tailing people, that's all right now. And if I happen to get into a scrape–"

"Which normally happens with you."

"–then I'll take one off of the first guy I take out. Easy-peasy." Please just believe me and take the gun.

"Right, easy." Thank goodness. "So where are you off to now?"

"One of the photos Nebraska had in her file is an 'enforcer' for hire. Some guy named Derek Haynes. Used to be based in New York but has since relocated to DC. Guess he has a penchant for the docks. I plan on sniffing him out, see if I can figure out who he's working for."

"You have fun with that. I'll be here, enjoying my beer."

"And then watching out for 602...?"

"Yeah, yeah, yeah, I said I would. Don't you have a world to save or something?"

"Or something. Later."

I need you to come through for me on this one, buddy. I have to believe he will.

That usually familiar door ring now sounds like a bell tolling for my own demise. He was right though, what is next? What are you supposed to do when you're "off the grid?" There are enough shady individuals down at the docks that value privacy. If I head there now, I could probably get a room for the night without calling attention to myself.

It's almost pretty along here, with the streetlights reflecting on the cobblestones and light rain coming down. What was that? Oh, just a tabby chasing a rather plump rat. "Stupid alley cats."

I really hope that old thing works the same way as the new ones and jams all other devices. Nebraska had to have known it did, why risk keeping it if it wasn't necessary? No, I have to trust her.

Can't stop thinking about Desmond's words, "*she was a good Agent, she'll be remembered as such.*" She was so much more than that. She was the best. She was my mentor. My friend. Definitely not how it started six years ago. Nebraksa Hill, the twenty-year veteran of the Agency, the no-nonsense ball of fire, the living legend herself assigned to a rook like me. The amount of disdain such a tiny woman could convey with a look... incredible. She never even let her hair down, literally, in case it potentially interfered with the task at hand.

That's who Nebraska was. An Agent through and through. She gave her life to the ZOA and this is how it ended. Left for dead in a subway tunnel and a few empty platitudes like, "she was a good Agent." I have to finish what she started. I won't let her death be in vain.

I see a bar boasting "PRIVATE" rooms for rent. I don't think I want to know what normally goes on in this place.

"I need a room For the night." This "inn-keeper," For lack of a better word, is a piece of work. Mid-seventies, or maybe he's just had that hard of a life. Straggly gray hair Flying every which way as iF it's trying to escape From under the threadbare beanie he's wearing. Why does everything around here smell like rotting Fish? Including this guy.

"That'll be Fifty dollars. Do you have a name For the room?"

Oh, look, no teeth. A serious winner here, Folks. "Here's seventy that says the name is John Doe."

"Room 21."

Wow, this place is great. To the left, we have our—likely illegal—poker games going on, and to the right, you'll Find more than a Few women looking For a good time.

Room 21, okay, up the stairs and down the hall, last door on the left. Good, as Far away as possible. Oh, seriously, the stench of rotten Fish is even in the rooms? I'm never eating Fish again.

Well, it's not much, but it's warm, private, and definitely "off-the-grid."

Dammit, Nebraska, dying alone in the gutter like that. Why didn't she just tell me! I could've been there... I could've helped... No use Fretting about the past, Killian. You can't change it, but you *can* avenge it. I promise, Nebraska, I'll Figure out who did this to you.

Damn, those foghorns are loud. Tomorrow is a new day. Just get some sleep—hey, the bed isn't too terrible—and figure out where to go from here.

Interesting opening chapter, Sadie thought to herself. She looked up to see her briefcase sitting untouched near the door. *I should probably focus on the exhibit for a while.* She sighed as she set down the device and walked over to her briefcase, settling in for a morning of actual work.

Chapter 5

Three hours passed before Sadie hit a mental wall in her project. She looked up from her laptop at the device still sitting on her coffee table, begging to be read.

"How 'bout some lunch, Redy, maybe that'll clear my head," she said to the fish who sat on her kitchen counter. He responded with bubbles and the same figure-eight swimming pattern.

Sadie flipped on the TV for background noise as she made a chicken salad sandwich. Mad Money was on with Jim Cramer spewing his normal nonsense at a decibel too high for weekend TV. "Sell, sell, sell, Dynamo! You heard me, jump ship and run over to Lockwood, folks. That's where—" Sadie flipped the channel. "Curse your sudden and inevitable betray—" She flipped again. "Could I *be* wearing any more clothes?" She could always count on Friends for a good laugh, even though she'd seen every episode at least four times, so she left it on and returned to her sandwich.

"So this Killian guy," Sadie looked at Redy, "I'm thinking obviously Irish looks with a name like Killian Quinn, red, wavy hair, freckles, the whole nine yards. He gets this 'device' from his dead partner, then immediately gives it away, then storms off to some dockside hellhole? First of all, I didn't think those types of places even existed, but to find it so quickly? What kind of guy is this?"

Redy continued his swimming. The bubbles rose to the surface as if counting the seconds that Sadie looked on in silence, awaiting a response. "You're right, I guess I just have to learn more about him, don't I?"

She grabbed her plate, walked over to her gray beanbag chair, and settled in to read the next chapter of Killian's story.

Note to self, shady "hotels" come with horrible beds, if you can even call that a bed or this a hotel for that matter. Whoa, it's 11 a.m. already? I need some food.

So, Middy—by the way, that's what I've decided to call you from now on. Short for, ya know, Midnight. Ha! That's what you get for telling me your hacker name. Of course you'd pick Midnight, but hey, who am I to judge. And Middy sounds fun, plus it gives you plausible deniability.

Anyway, Middy, know what I could go for right about now? Remember back in '14 when we followed that one guy up to New York and we had to stay hunkered outside his place for a week? And there was that little bagel shop around the corner? The one with the homeless dude that always sat out front with his dog, Rusty? ...Was the dog named Rusty or the guy? Whatever, the bagels though, I could go for one of those bagels right now. They always say it's the water that makes stuff better up there, like the pizza and bagels and stuff. We

should look into getting a water main "requisitioned" down our way, we'd make a killing opening up shop down here touting New
York water bagels. Feel free to add that to
your to-do list, while I continue to walk these
foul-smelling, fish-ified streets.

There's a pub already open for lunch across
the way, Finch's. Seems like a disreputable
enough place, if our guy Derek is a regular
around here, they'd probably know about it.

Oh man—empty room save a few patrons
that genuinely look leftover from last night
and a single bartender removing the stools off
the bar. Guess they just opened. Surprisingly
enough, the fish smell hasn't followed me in.
Or maybe it did and it's being completely overwhelmed by the smell of stale beer. This place
can't have passed a health inspection in years,
not that they probably care.

"Hey, do you have anything to eat?" I'm
telling you Middy, the bartender is exactly what
you would expect from a place like this. Short,
brutish, scars across his arms—no stranger to a
fight. And his full sleeve tattoos tell quite a tale.
He's got the Navy's crossed cannons but looks
like he's tried to bury them beneath a fleet of
other nautical imagery: an anchor, a daggered
rose, and a golden dragon. Clearly this guy has
been around the world a time or two. Instead
of a response, I get a groan followed by some
muttering of unintelligible words.

"Guess that's a no then." This place is sad even for a dump. But there are a lot of cameras, especially around that door at the back. Leading to something nefarious, I imagine. Should probably keep an eye on that one. The patrons though, all three of them, look strung out to dry, hanging over chairs, tables, and even one on the piano bench.

"Here."

The embittered ol' salt of a bartender just plopped a sandwich down in front of me. No idea what's in it, hopefully some kind of meat and cheese.

Huh, actually not terrible. I should learn to be less suspicious of gruff people and their food offerings.

"You'll want a pint with that too, I imagine?"

"Umm, yeah, sure. Why not, right? Gotta start sometime."

Another groan and mumble. Not the most talkative of fellows. Now how do I go about seeing if anyone in this place knows our pal Derek?

Well, what do ya know—a group of sailors just turned up, not the military kind, by any means, cargo sailors based on their haggard appearance and the stench that entered with them. Middy, next time I get the bright idea to head to the docks, please give me something for the smell. There's gotta be something I can do, because right now I'm ready to cut my own nose off. If it wouldn't harm this perfectly formed face, that is. Go ahead, roll your eyes, I know you're doing it anyway.

The door is swinging open again—a waitress. Guess they know their clientele and their hours. She's cute, blonde hair, blue eyes. You'd like her, Middy.

"Sorry I'm late, Joe, car wouldn't start again and I had to take the bus."

Yet another groan from Joe, as we now know the bartender. The verbosity of this man is truly astounding.

"Hey pretty lady, sorry 'bout your car, you can start my engine any time you want." It's one of the cargo sailors, the ringleader based on the laughter coming from his buddies.

"I'm pretty sure a goat could start your engine, Richie." She's got some spunk. Ha, you'd really like her, Middy.

Richie's buddies are all laughing, but he does not look amused. Clearly self-confidence isn't his strong suit. Is this guy actually making a grab for her?

"Now that wasn't very nice, Sami."

"Let go of me, Rich."

"Someone better teach you some manners, girl." And now he's twisting her arm. Alright, I've had enough.

"And you'd be the one to teach her then? I think in order to teach, you should probably have at least a somewhat decent grasp of a subject, and seeing as you seem like the type of guy to have only grasped one thing in life—yourself—I'm gonna go out on a limb here and say you shouldn't be teaching anyone anything. So why don't you and your buddies go back to your table and let her get to work?"

"What did you say, boy?" Oh, "boy?" Okay, so we're gonna go there then.

"You heard me. Or is English beyond your scope of intelligence as well?"

"Why I oughta…"

"Oughta what? Shower, yeah, you probably should do that. I could smell you from way over there when you walked in. It would be best for all of us, honestly."

"You lookin' for a fight?" And now he's rolling up his sleeves and walking over to me. This should be fun.

"Ya know, I never go looking for a fight, but gosh darn-it, they seem to find me so often."

Four assailants. Number four seems to favor his right leg, a quick kick to the knee would take him out for the day. Number three has a pack of smokes in his shirt pocket and yellowed smoker's teeth. An open hand jab to the throat would send him into a coughing fit and out of the fight. That leaves Richie and guy number two. Number two is a little smaller, a strong left hook after I take out number three would buy me some time with Richie.

Number four makes the first move. Kick to the knee. Throat strike to number three. Left hook to number two. Three down before Richie makes a move. Let's see what you got, buddy. Every move from this guy is slow and lumbering. Dodge. Jab. He's stepping back to launch his full weight behind him, but I'm already out of the way and he falls face first into the floor. Someone's behind me—number two. Open palm hit to the chest and he's flying back, tripping over the chair behind him.

Now Richie's running full speed toward me, leading with his fist. Oh, this is going to be good. One slight step to the right, leave my foot out, and BOOM. Richie's down, head into the bar. Numbers two through four are now scrambling to pick their disoriented leader up and out the door.

"Thanks for the lesson, guys. Same time tomorrow?" Damn, that guy's head was hard.

"Really, a knock-down-drag-out brawl in a seedy dive bar?" Sadie rolled her eyes. "Talk about over the top." She looked over at Redy, as if he would concur with her thoughts. He continued his normal swimming pattern among the roots of his bamboo plant. Sadie shook her head at her own lunacy and turned back to the story.

"Hey. You." It's the girl. Sami, I think? "Thanks for that."

"It was no problem, really. Some people didn't have mothers that taught them respect and it clearly shows."

"Well I wish more guys around here had a mom like yours. Here, let me get you some ice. My name's Sami, by the way." Ha, I remembered it.

"Killian. Nice to meet you, Sami. Hey, you wouldn't by chance know a guy named Derek, hangs around these parts sometimes?" Never know unless you ask, right?

"Derek Haynes? Yeah, I know him." Obvious disdain. Must be talking about the right guy. "He comes in most afternoons, should be here anytime." She continues to rub ice on my knuckles. "If you want, you can hang out until he gets here. It's a slow day, I should have some free time since you scared away my normal customers." Uh oh, she's doing that coquettish eyebrow thing.

"Oh, ha, thanks, but I'll just wait at the bar. I think the bartender's really warming up to me anyway, right Joe?"

Grunts from the kitchen.

"But thank you for the offer. Really."

"Alright, suit yourself. But if you get bored, I'll be right over there cleaning up." What is wrong with me, Middy? Is it possible to be ruined by a woman? One who doesn't even know who you are? I mean wholly and entirely ruined, where no one else can even begin to compare? When all you want is her and nothing else will do? Because if so, Bluebird has officially ruined me, body and soul, she has ruined me.

The door opens again and this time it's a rough and tumble sort of guy with blonde hair and a visible gun on his hip along with another group of sailors. You look even rougher than your mugshot, Mr. Haynes. He's heading straight for the back room. Wonder what's going on back there...

"Joe!" A buzzer sounds and the door to the back is opening. Derek walks in while his compatriots fill the empty tables in the room. Are those guys with him or did they happen to get here at the same time? I should probably lie low, just in case.

Why are there children skating outside a seedy dive bar like this in the middle of the afternoon, don't they have school? Guess I can't be the one to talk, really. Did I ever tell you I used to skateboard, Middy? Haven't been on one since I was seventeen though, it was the night my mom almost died. I had gotten into a huge fight with her. She was mad that the police came by again, asking if she knew anything about some break-ins in the neighborhood. She said she didn't. But she knew it was me and my friends. We never took much, it was more for the thrill of being able to get in and out without anyone realizing it.

Anyway, I stormed out, jumped on my board, and didn't bother to look back. If I had, maybe I'd have seen her collapse. Maybe I could've stopped it, but I didn't. I skated away. I didn't even realize what had happened until four hours later when I finally looked at my phone and saw a dozen missed calls from Desmond. She was already in recovery by the time I got to the hospital.

I remember Desmond screaming at me. "Where the hell have you been?" He was in his uniform, which meant he'd had to be called out of something and I was doomed. He yelled about my loser friends, again. Told me I was wasting my life, again. The same stuff he always tried to tell me. "*Channel that energy into something productive.*" "*Why not join the military, like me?*" All the things I hated to hear him say. But then he changed tactics, he actually called me out on my own BS.

"*I seem to remember growing up with a kid that would climb every tree, building, and barricade he could, the one that had zero fear in the face of danger, that one that would stand up to every bully on the playground, even the ones twice his size. That's what this uniform is. It's standing up for the little guy. And you know, there's more to it than you think.*"

Then he went on about how it could open doors I couldn't even imagine existing, and there being a whole world out there that needed people like me. "*Good people with strong hearts,*" he said. And blast it if one of his speeches didn't finally sink through my thick skull.

I made a promise that night, to my mother and to myself, that I would be better. I would make something of my life. And Desmond was there every step of the way, he helped me get into West Point, helped me survive my plebe year and the next three after that, but then after my first tour he told me about the Zeta Defense Agency. I didn't re-enlist, I joined the Agency instead, and I haven't looked back since. I still regret hurting my mom that night twelve years ago, but at least she made it to my basic training graduation. And I work hard every day for her, to keep my promise.

Derek, finally. He's emerged—well, emerged might be too nice a term, more like got thrown out of the door. He's clearly drunk and screaming about cards. So I was right about the gambling. Super sleuth Killian strikes again.

A large man in a suit has followed behind him. "And don't come back here, Derek. That's it, you're done. Joe, Derek Haynes is barred from this establishment from now on. Hear me?"

"Yes, sir, Mr. Finch."

"Whatever! I don't need you rats, I've got a good gig going anyway now." And what, pray tell, would that gig be, Derek? Probably should follow our own little rat to his sewer.

"Thanks, Joe, see ya 'round."

More grunts from Joe.

"Aha! Good one, Joe, later!" Clearly he can speak, he just spoke perfectly good English to his boss, but me? No, I get unintelligible grunts. Whatever.

Alright, Mr. Haynes, let's see where you're headed. You can't be the mastermind of all of this, so where's your boss? Derek's just winding around the streets and oh, now he's pissing on the building. Not even in an alleyway. Right off the street. I can't imagine how this man could be capable of anything even remotely related to the Agency mole or Nebraska's death. But she seemed to think so, so on I go.

Sadie's phone rang, pulling her from the story. It was Jonas.

"Hey Jonas, is everything okay?" The man didn't make a habit of calling on weekends.

"Yes, fine, I hope I'm not distracting you from your plans."

What plans, Sadie thought. "No, just having a productive afternoon at home," she said as she sheepishly glanced over to the neglected project files sitting on top of her laptop. "What's up?"

"I was thinking about the project, and I wondered whether we should include something about pigeons. Or messenger birds to some extent. Kids like that kind of stuff, right?"

"Yeah, kids like animals, Jonas. I'll check it out."

"Thanks, and Sadie…" He paused. "I appreciate your effort and diligence on this project. Often times it's that extra effort that leads to extraordinary opportunities in the future. At least in my experience."

And Jonas was certainly an authority on extraordinary opportunities. He held one of the more distinguished careers of anyone at the Smithsonian. Born and raised in New York, he'd attended Cornell for his undergraduate, where he won the Rising Star award at the age of nineteen. He did his doctoral studies abroad while living with an indigenous Amazonian tribe in Brazil. That spurred his documentary, which earned him the Anthropology in Media award from the American Anthropology Association. And Jonas wasn't a one-trick pony in the anthropology circles, he also spent three years on a dig in central Mexico, unearthing the secrets of the Pyramids of the Sun and Moon outside of Mexico City. It was still astounding that the Smithsonian even had a chance at grabbing the great Dr. Jonas Andrews ten years ago, but somehow they did and he'd been with them ever since.

"I can only hope to have the kind of experiences you have enjoyed."

"Ha, if you only knew. Goodnight, Sadie."

"Goodnight, Jonas."

Sadie decided to open up her laptop and put in a bit more of that extra effort before turning in for the night.

Chapter 6

It was 5:30 in the morning, but Sadie couldn't sleep. She continued to toss and turn, thinking about the story. After forty minutes of lying there, she decided to get on with the day.

One advantage of being up before the sun was that in DC—a port city with a proclivity for "reflecting ponds"—there was never a dull sunrise location. The colors, reflected perfectly in the still expanse of water, made for a picturesque backdrop for relaxing outdoors with a good book.

She decided to head over to Lincoln Memorial, one of the best places for the sunrise, because as much hustle and bustle as there was in Washington DC at any given time, there never seemed to be many tourists out and about at 6:30 in the morning. In fact, the city was all but deserted in the early hours of Sunday. She was free to drink coffee in the sunshine and bask in the light of the locale's historical significance.

The idea of knowing where humanity is going only by knowing where it came from held a certain allure for Sadie that she couldn't quite describe. Having little to no knowledge of her own history made her thirst for the history of others around her. That's what drove her to want to work at the Smithsonian in the first place. She still remembered the first time she had set foot in the Natural History Museum.

It was third grade and she was on a class field trip with Mrs. Kresge, the teacher who originally encouraged her love of history and discovery. Sadie had been in awe of the giant elephant in the center of the room—at the time it seemed bigger than any animal she could've imagined. But with every turn through the museum, a new exhibit showed her something she had scarcely even dreamed could exist, let alone be on display for all to see.

The Egypt hall had been especially intriguing, seeing how ancient Egypt functioned as a society and how they left behind a record of what they did and who they were. No one was forgotten and no one would be erased, a legacy for time itself. Granted, at age eight she couldn't form those thoughts, but she recognized something bigger in the world than her.

Then came the Galapagos exhibit and Carole Baldwin. The young female scientist who was discovering new species and had an entire movie explaining why the Galapagos species were so special. It was after seeing her that Sadie realized she could be a researcher too. It didn't matter if Tony Pasquale made fun of her glasses or corrected her whenever she got something wrong in class. She was determined; there were still things to be discovered and stories to be told and just because she was a girl didn't mean she couldn't.

Whenever Sadie felt like she was falling into a rut, she would picture Tony's face when she won the science fair that year and he didn't. She laughed as she thought about it now, walking alongside the calm reflecting pool in the crisp November air.

"Little early for a tourist," a voice behind her echoed.

Sadie turned to see an older janitor emptying the trash cans for the day. "Oh, I'm not a tourist, just couldn't sleep is all," she replied.

"I'm sorry?" he said as he took off his headphones.

"I said, I'm not a tourist, I live close by. Just taking an early morning walk with my thoughts and looking for a good reading spot."

"Okay," he replied, "well, stay safe and remember to pick up after yourself." He replaced his headphones and went back to work.

Even the older generations are getting into technology these days, more and more of our communication is being cut short, Sadie thought as she continued on her way. Not many people were content to enjoy the sounds of nature, to find the peace that it can bring into one's life.

After a short walk to the Basin, tourists began appearing around her, crowding to capture their next 'gram-worthy cliché of a photograph.

"Miss, can you take our photo, please?" one of the tourists requested as he tapped Sadie on the shoulder.

"Sure." *I love taking photos of other people's families,* said her sarcastic inner voice. It was a nice enough looking family. Father, mother, son, daughter—probably a pet back home. One big happy family. Sadie felt that familiar sting at the back of her eyes, the one that made her tighten her jaw to maintain composure. She knew she shouldn't be upset with them, it wasn't their fault they had what she didn't. But that didn't make it any easier. *Push it down, Sadie.* "Here you go, I took a couple so you can pick your favorite."

"Thank you so much," the father responded, taking back his phone. "Lee, why aren't you smiling? Your mother doesn't have any nice pictures of you smiling, this is our family vacation…" His voice trailed off as they walked away.

Sadie found her favorite bench and pulled out the strange-looking e-reader, anxious to discover what Killian Quinn was up to next—a welcome mental distraction. She skimmed through a strange series of pages detailing the size, height, and clothing descriptions of passersby until she found where the part with Derek picked back up.

"Alright Derek, last night you had your fun, plenty of drinking and whatever was going on in that back room, but I could use a break in this case. Where's your boss already? Just give me something, anything other than debauchery." He just woke up in the early hours of 3 p.m.-well done, sir-and… did he really just swish his mouth with whiskey? Wow, this guy is a winner. I can only imagine the stench in his apartment. He's out the door already, slamming it open and scaring a cat away down the alleyway. Now he's laughing at the poor animal. Of course he is, that's what psychopaths do.

Looks like we're going somewhere other than the bar today then, exciting.

I follow him six blocks to the old train yard. Why is it always train yards and alleyways with these criminals? Can't they meet in the park or a coffee shop like normal people? What I wouldn't give for an espresso right about now. He's picking up rocks and skipping them down the tracks. God, I hope he's waiting for someone because this is boring, even for this moron.

I spoke too soon. A black Mercedes just rolled up in the nearby parking lot and two men are getting out of the car. One looks like your standard-issue bodyguard—leather jacket, gold necklace, goatee, and sunglasses. I wonder if there's a catalog they all shop from. *Bodyguards Quarterly*. "Hit Wear for the Modern Hitman." The other guy, though, he's the interesting one. Tall, older gentlemen with a dark buzz cut, scar over his left temple, fine Italian suit. Definitely the boss type.

This looks promising. Damn, too far to hear. Could really use a bionic ear device right about now. I'll just have to get closer.

Alright, Derek, who's your friend.

"I have a new assignment for you, Mr. Haynes." Scarface gets right to the point, I like it. "There is a... problem that has come up." Okay, a piece of paper is changing hands.

"A people problem you need me to solve?" Well, it's certainly not a math problem, moron. No one would trust you for that.

"Yes. I suspected this was going to have to be dealt with at some point but was asked to be... delicate. I no longer care. Find him, deal with him however you see fit."

"With pleasure, sir."

"Report back to me on the normal number when it's done."

"Yes, sir." Derek folds the sheet of paper up and puts it in his top coat pocket. I'll have to nick that later. Scarface is getting back in his fancy car and driving away. Derek starts going the other direction.

And we're back to the seedy dive bar near the docks. Time to settle in for a few more hours of vice and sin, Derek? It amazes me how many people find themselves at a place like this. At least there's plenty of people watching to be had. Guy sitting over there in the corner anxiously tapping his foot and constantly checking his phone. And this guy already approaching the bottom of his bottle, it's still happy hour, what problems are you trying to drink away, sir? Then there's the couple in the back booth. Young, don't even look like they belong here. He's got work boots on and a well-worn sweater, but she, well, she looks like she just stepped off campus of some hoity-toity private school. Ah, there it is, she's playing with the shiny new ring on her left hand. Adorable. Running off with the salt-of-the-earth type.

She does the same thing, ya know, 602. She has all these little quirks that are so subtle that you'd miss them if you weren't paying attention. Like when she gets really into a book, she bites the inside of her bottom lip. Or whenever she's about to walk into a place, she quickly tosses her hair. Like she's bracing herself for whatever social interaction is coming. Or the

Face she makes whenever she catches a glimpse of herself in the mirror. It's all the little things that sum up a person, and every little one of those quirks add up to the captivating woman that is 602. You better be looking after her, Middy. Watching over my Bluebird.

"Wow," Sadie remarked. "This guy's got it bad." She gazed out over the water, watching the cranes fly across it in the morning sun, the light reflected against their feathers. There was a certain serenity that came from being out so early in the morning. A little tufted titmouse bird landed on the branch over Sadie's bench. He puffed up his feathers, as if to wake himself up, before beginning a morning song to which he seemed entirely accustomed. Another titmouse found its place next to the first one. The pair sang in unison for a brief moment before flittering off. Loneliness began to prod at Sadie's mind again, and she returned to the book to prevent any further thoughts from creeping in.

Derek's out again, stumbling his way toward the pier. God, the temperature is dropping fast. I can already see my breath in the haze of the streetlights. He's turning into an alleyway two blocks down. I bet if I skirt around I can catch him from the other side.

...He's just standing there, leaning against the wall like he's waiting for something.

"You can come out now." Wait, what did he say?

"Killian, right? I know you've been follow-ing me since yesterday, rather serendipitous really that I should be given your picture this afternoon. Killian Quinn. Twenty-nine years of age. Zeta Defense Agent. Aww, and recently lost his partner of six years. Poor Nebraska, hope she didn't suffer too little." How in the world... Her name does not belong on your lips, you piece of filth.

"Then I guess we're all formally introduced, Derek Haynes, age thirty-five, the scum of society. Though, it seems you aren't as dim as I thought you were."

"There are a few advantages to knowing you're being followed. So, would you like the first strike? Come on, I like a challenge, I'll even put one hand behind my back." How is this the same drunk fool from last night? He's a lot taller up close, at least three inches above me.

Right hook.

It doesn't phase him. Great.

"My turn."

AUGHHH! Dammit, that hurt.

"*Try another approach, Rook. Don't run headfirst every time.*" Okay, Brask... but maybe sometimes... I'm running at the man, trying to get a low center of gravity to rush and lift him off the ground. A knee meets my face. Even the dirt tastes like fish. My head is spinning.

Derek grabs my legs and I'm being pulled back toward him. There has to be some sort of weapon around here. Reach, Killian, Find something, anything. Gun probably would come in handy right about now. One point For you, Middy. Aha, a pipe! One stamp on his instep and I'm Free. Okay, Find your Footing, Killian.

"Ha! I think you may have a size problem there, too cold For you out here?"

What is he talking about? Oh perfect. This metal pipe is only Four inches long. "It's not the size of the pipe in the Fight, it's the size of the Fight in the pipe."

"That made zero sense."

"Yeah, it... made more sense in my head. Whatever." Aim For the head... Direct hit. I can see the blood running down From his eyebrow. He pulls out a Sig Sauer P227 Tactical.

"Uh oh." This is clearly not going to be a mano a mano Fight. Cover, Killian, now! Bullets ricocheting off the dumpster behind me. Think, Killian! Maybe I can outrun him and circle back without him realizing it. I need a peek at that Folder, and it wouldn't hurt to leave him alive For now. He may be strong, but agile doesn't seem like his style. I bet I can lose him on the rooftops.

Up the nearest Fire escape. Adrenaline is a truly wonderful thing, I can literally Feel it pulsing through my veins. But there's racing Footsteps only yards behind me. Maybe Derek *is* agile after all.

Finally, the gap between us is growing, a little Further and—

"Dammit!" Out of rooftops, only a fifty-foot drop into an icy lake below. How did I get so turned around? "Just perfect."

"Aw, did you run out of rooftops to parkour over?" That mocking tone is probably one of the most annoying sounds I've ever heard. I'm really starting to hate this guy.

. "Well, ya know, you win some you lose some." Maybe if I can dive—phew, that's a long way down. Perhaps I can slide...

"That's a mighty big drop there. Way I see it, you only have two options. Option one, let me kill you, option two, let the fall do the job. I hear most people die on the way down from a jump; their hearts can't take it. Personally, I'd choose option one, but that's me being selfish. So what'll it be?" He's screwing a silencer on his Sig. He doesn't want to risk the dockworkers hearing, isn't that thoughtful of him. I can see my breath drifting skyward. Heart pounding. Am I really going to do this?

"Ya know, I think I'm going to have to trust my heart won't give out and go for option two. It's been fun though, keep in touch. We'll have to do this again sometime." Now do it, Killian, just jump! Gunshot. Pain, burning pain ripping through my arm.

What have I done?

This fall is taking longer than expected. Rolling, dark gray waves inching closer. Is this what it's like before you die?

Water hitting my feet like cinder blocks, cinder blocks made of ice. Bullets streaking through the water all around me.

Focus, Killian. God, it's cold, it feels like I have ice for veins. Every movement of every muscle hurts. Fairly certain I may turn to ice before I reach the shore. The human body can continue to function for about ten minutes in freezing temperatures. You can do this, Killian. It's not a long swim. Just keep swimming. You've done this before.

Did you know that, Middy? As a boy, I fell through the ice playing an especially competitive game of hockey with Desmond on the frozen lake near our house. I still remember the frigid fear that gripped me, the air escaping my lungs as quickly as the arctic water was flowing in, and the frantic search for an opening in the casket lid of ice. Dark, I know.

Damn it's cold, I can't feel my fingers.

It was only thanks to my brother Desmond, who was quick enough to tie off a rope and take the plunge himself, that I even survived to find myself in another icy lake now. Talk about your irony... Is that irony? I have no idea. Des never lets me forget that I cut his leg with my skates that night though, always complains how it still bothers him when it's cold out. Like, excuse me for trying to stay alive, sorry if that inconveniences you, big brother.

Almost there. I can't feel anything

anymore, not even the cold. That's probably a bad sign. Is the distance getting longer? How long has it been? Less than ten minutes, I hope.

Just.

Keep.

Moving...

Shore! Finally... God, it's even colder out of the water.

Just going to lie here for a minute, one minute will be enough to keep going, right? But you're not here to answer that question are you, Middy? No one is, just me.

Damn, I can still hear Desmond's voice from that night, "*No Killian, get up, we have to go home, you can't lie there, we have to get you warm! Get up!*" He's right, I have to get up. Still pushing me on and saving my life again, brother, and you probably have no idea. I don't even know if he's realized what I'm doing yet. When he does though, I'm sure there'll be a record-length lecture with my name on it.

When Sadie finally looked up, she realized it was already 11:30 a.m. and the Dupont Circle farmers' market she visited every Sunday morning would be ending soon. She quickly hailed a taxi for the two-mile trek. Killian's fate would have to wait.

Chapter 7

Sadie exited the cab and started to walk through the maze of tents selling fresh produce and flowers. Nostalgia continued to pull her back to this farmers' market. It harkened back to a time when neighbors bartered with each other over their products. And getting vegetables without walking under fluorescent lights was always a plus.

She wound her way through the different stalls, looking at vegetables, fruits, and flowers in every color of the rainbow, not to mention the local artisans displaying their wares. It would be easy to get lost in the beauty of it all. Especially on a day like today with not a cloud in the sky.

"Three for a dollar," Kitchi called out from the jewelry stall with a heartfelt smile. He was an older man who came to the farmers' market every week to sell his hand-carved, wooden sculptures. He also made the little wooden rings with animal carvings on them that Sadie had been regularly buying from him for two years.

"That's way too low, Kitchi," Sadie said, walking over to his stall. After the eleventh ring, Kitchi finally asked her why she was buying so many, noting she only had ten fingers. Once he found out she bought them for the kids in foster homes and at St. Anne's, he practically started giving them away—generous soul that he was. "At least let me give you ten dollars for the three."

"No, Kimi, I made these special for you this week." Kitchi had begun calling her by that name recently. He said it was because Sadie always looked like she had a secret only she knew, but Sadie had learned that wasn't the whole truth. His wife, who came with him from time to time, told her that, while they were never able to have children, Kitchi had always wanted a daughter named Kimi. "See, they all have the morning star, hope for a better tomorrow. And a bear from me, to remind them to be brave like Kitchi."

"Alright, well I'll let them know. And one of these days you'll have to come with me, Kitchi."

"Naw, they don't want some old man telling them stories," he said as he placed the rings in individual silk bags, most likely bought for the occasion.

"Of course they would! You need to teach this new generation, Kitchi, otherwise who knows how they'll turn out."

"If they turn out anything like you, Kimi, we're in for a better tomorrow than today. Take care now!"

"You too," Sadie responded as Kitchi went back to his whittling.

She continued to wander through the tents. Still, she felt like she could hear the story calling her from her purse. She began to read as she walked, disappearing back into the world of Killian Quinn.

Middy, you've got to meet me. The numbness is going away and, oh God, he definitely hit me, but I think it's okay. I can feel, alright, good. Just a graze. Sort of. Tie it off and keep going.

One foot in front of the other, Killian, you can do this. What I wouldn't give to be bulletproof. Ya know, when I was a kid, I used to dream of being Superman, being able to fly. I even had pajamas with the cape and everything. One time I put it on and walked out to the balcony of our third-story apartment and climbed through the bars, God, I must've only been four or five, but I hung outside of those bars feeling the air in my face, cape blowing in the wind. My mom saw and screamed for me to come back in. I remember thinking that was the angriest she'd ever been.

Her eyes made me sad. Bluebird's eyes remind me of my mom's, actually. Eyes that hold the kindest souls to walk this planet. But both hidden behind a wall, a wall built out of necessity from the world beating you down time and time again without relent. I wish I could fix it...

Just get down the street, Killian. Or this alley, that looks warm, there's a cozy steam vent and oh, a nice, puffy, black trash bag. Meet me here, I'm just near O'Malley's, buddy. My vision is getting a bit fuzzy, Petey, please hurry, I need...

"Wait, what, Petey? O'Malley's?" Sadie exclaimed. She looked up in the direction of O'Malley's. The Dupont Circle Farmers' Market was only a block away from the pub.

Enthralled by her reading, she hadn't noticed the black SUV pulling up next to her. Nor the two men getting out of it. It wasn't until they put a bag over her head, stuck a needle in her neck, and shoved her into the SUV that Sadie was even aware of their existence.

Her head began to swim and then her vision went black.

Chapter 7.5

Killian awoke to the stench of garbage surrounding him. He'd managed to make his way to O'Malley's. Almost. The pain in his arm, not to mention the presumable hypothermia, had caught up to him and he'd stumbled into the alley full of last night's bar trash and passed out. *Thank God for heating grates and short-lived DC cold fronts.* That grate probably saved Killian's life. His mind retraced his steps from the day before, especially his missteps. He'd let his emotions get the better of him, like Nebraska had warned him not to do. *Brask… I'm sorry*, he thought. *I have to be better.* He reeked of blood, sweat, and spoiled beer. He could only imagine the sight of him as he emerged from the alleyway; he hadn't shaved in days and his clothes were stained with everything imaginable. He squinted at the bright sun overhead. It was already midday.

Killian walked past the pub windows, only to see none other than Petey himself sitting at the bar, enjoying a pint and watching the Liverpool game.

"Are you serious right now?" Killian spat as he walked up to his friend. "I spent the night in an alley, half dead, I might add, waiting for you and you're here drinking a beer!"

"Killian, you're alright!" Petey leaped off the stool to embrace his friend, then stopped short when the smell hit him. "Maybe not, you smell like trash. And don't look much better."

"That's what happens when you almost freeze to death and pass out in the trash heap behind a bar." Killian turned his attention to the bartender. "Can I get a coffee, please? Black."

He turned back to Petey, who was surveying him with a bewildered expression. "So where were you, Petey? I needed you last night."

"Oh, yeah… the messages on the device. About that." Petey paused as Killian took the mug from the bartender and sipped, allowing the warmth of it to fill him. "I may not have it anymore."

"What!" Killian almost spat out his coffee. "What do you mean you don't have it anymore? Where is it?"

"Ha, funny story actually, you see—"

"Petey, short version."

"This is the short version, believe me, the long version is significantly more entertaining. Did you know that this city has three different speakeasy bars within a five-mile radius?"

"Petey!"

"Right, so I'm following your girl, yeah? Like you asked me to do, then her friend walked up and invited me to hang with them and, well, I didn't notice my backpack missing until the third bar."

Killian stared at his friend, dumbfounded. "And the device was in your backpack?"

"Yeah, but I got it back. Turns out your girl picked it up here before she left." Petey gulped down the rest of his beer. "Unfortunately, the device wasn't in it."

"So then where is it?" Killian retorted. Instead of answering, Petey pointed outside toward the Dupont

Circle Farmers' Market. That's when Killian saw her. Sadie Smith. The girl he was supposed to protect. The girl he'd spent the better part of four years following. The girl he'd eventually fallen for.

His Bluebird. She was right outside, following her normal Sunday routine. But this time, she was wholly engrossed in one of her stories. When Killian focused, he noticed it wasn't a book she was reading at all, it was the device.

"She has it?" he asked angrily. "How could you let it out of your sight?"

"Hey!" Petey snapped back, "I told you I was no good at this inconspicuous stuff. You're the agent guy, I'm the desk guy. And besides, could it be in safer hands? I mean, who's going to go after some random Smithsonian girl with what essentially looks like some hipster, retro Kindle?"

Killian glanced back at Sadie, guilt gnawing at his heart. He couldn't disagree with Petey, what were the odds that Domino had someone looking for the device? After four years of following Sadie himself, he knew that no one else was following her—a lesson learned the hard way. He let the muscles throughout his body start to relax.

That's when he noticed a black Yukon coming down the roadway. It was headed in Sadie's direction.

As Killian's focus switched to Sadie, she stopped and looked directly at the bar. As if she was looking right at him. He couldn't move. He wanted to. He wanted to run to her, to make sure she got out of the way, but a paralyzing fear rose within him.

The Yukon screeched to a halt.

He watched as two men got out, grabbed Sadie, and pulled her into the vehicle.

No! Killian forced his muscles to work again. He dropped his coffee and ran outside, but the SUV was gone.

Sadie was gone.

Petey ran up beside him. "Okay, so maybe I was wrong about that last part."

"You think?" Killian glared at his friend as he tried to formulate some sort of plan to get her back. "Petey! Please tell me you're still able to track Sadie's phone?"

A look of understanding came over Petey's face, along with a smile. "You know I can."

"Good. We're getting her back."

Chapter 8

Sadie awoke in a dark room. She tried to move but felt the pull of plastic against her wrists, chilled by the cold metal chair they were bound to. It was impossible to make anything out in the darkness, but she could hear water drops in the distance, some sort of a leak, and the whir of a large fan. The echo made the room feel massive. She took a deep breath. The air smelled used, like a pressurized plane that relies on recirculation. Her neck ached from where they had stuck her. *What time is it? And where am I?* she thought to herself, the panic starting to set in.

Her pulse quickened. She pulled at the restraints on her wrists. *Zip ties?* She knew how to get out of them from a self-defense class she took once. The instructor did not, however, get to the section covering what to do when they were attached to a metal chair behind your back. A now glaring gap in the course syllabus.

She heard muffled voices approaching from behind her, but she couldn't quite make them out. She strained to listen, hoping for any clue as to where she was or why she was there.

"Call the general, I think he may be interested to see what's currently on it. I want to have a chat with this girl."

The lights turned on, blinding Sadie for a moment as she heard the door slide open behind her. As she began to catch her bearings, she noticed the room wasn't nearly as big as it sounded, but rather completely encased in metal. In the reflection of the wall ten feet in front of her, she could see three figures entering the room. The metal was warped, but it was enough to make out one of them placing a gun on the console behind her.

"*Piacere ragazza,* so very nice to meet you. Wait, why is she facing the wall? That doesn't help anyone, turn her around, please." Two men appeared at Sadie's side, picking up her chair and turning her around to view the rest of the room. There were two security consoles, as best Sadie could tell based on the number of screens, between her and the door. "There we go, now we can see your beautiful face, *ragazza.* Thank you, men. You can go now."

"Where am I? Who are you? And what do you want with me?" Sadie demanded. She tried desperately at her restraints again.

"So many questions. All in due time, dear girl." The man spoke with a soft Italian accent, which explained his style: a three-piece suit with leather loafers. He took off his jacket and set it on the console next to his gun. As Sadie regarded him closer, she could tell he was older, mid-fifties perhaps? There was some gray scattered in his buzz-short hair and a scar over his left temple.

"But first, I would like to talk to you a moment," he said, pulling up another chair to face her. "You see, I have little information on you besides what we have gathered from your personal effects. Sarah Mercedes Smith from Washington DC, born June 20th, and you work at the Smithsonian, apparently. In fact, until you acquired this," he lifted the device Sadie had spent the better part of two days reading, "I did not even know you existed. So, I would like to know how it is that you came to acquire this particular device?"

"That's what this is about?" Sadie asked, not sure if that was a good thing or a bad thing. Two new men entered the room and sat down at the security consoles, both wearing black jackets with a patch on the arm. The man in the suit paused and looked at Sadie, letting a grin flash across his face.

"You don't even know what this is, do you?"

"No, I mean, it's some sort of e-reader thing, but honestly, I just found it yesterday… Saturday, if today isn't still Sunday."

The man laughed. "It is, in fact, still Sunday, Sunday evening actually. And this is not your typical e-reader. This device is very special to me. It was made by my mentor of sorts, a long time ago now. He was a brilliant scientist by the name of Charles Carter, whose sole desire in life was to 'unlock the secrets of the human mind,' as he put it. Even at the young age of twenty-one, I could tell this man was a genius. And you know what, he did it. Charles Carter figured out a way to channel another person's thoughts." The man began to pace as he spoke.

That can't be possible… Can it? Sadie wondered. *I have to get out of here.*

"He created a device to do exactly that, to lock onto a person and transcribe their thoughts. Quite astounding really. One device that could read anyone in the world. Well, I *thought* he had only created one—tragically damaged shortly before his death," the man said, rubbing the scar on the side of his face. "But as fate would have it, my old mentor had another trick up his sleeve. He apparently created a second one, this one. I'd heard stories of it, even seen sketches of it, but I'd never been able to hold it in my hands and use it until now. He outdid himself, really, this is fantastic. See the transcription is the tricky bit. If you don't get it precisely right, you get a jumbled mess of nonsense. And so far Charles Carter has been the only man to figure that part out."

While he was rambling on, Sadie subtly began to wiggle her hands free of the restraints behind her. Or at least attempt to.

"The ZDA has been trying to hide it from me for years."

Sadie's ears perked up. *Either this is one elaborate ruse or...* the implications started to race through her mind. If all of this were true, not only was it possible to tap into other people's thoughts, but you could literally read them on an e-reader. And there were other people who already knew about all of this and were using it regularly.

"But that is why it is so fortuitous that you have brought it to me. And today of all days, *bravissimo*." The man kissed his fingertips in the style of a French chef. "Thirty years ago I was supposed to present the original device to some very important people, who were disappointed, to say the least, that it was damaged." He regarded his left hand with more than a little disdain, and Sadie noticed that it was missing a pinky. "But now, just as I am to meet them again, you deliver it to me. So thank you for flaunting it around the city, you made this easy for me. See, these devices have a certain signature of sorts, and we have been picking up readings here and there over the years, but never as consistent as these last few days. You must have been very engrossed in this 'story,' eh?"

A red light started to flash from the security console on the left. "Umm, Mr. Soto, sir," said the man sitting in front of it. On the monitor, Sadie could only make out five dots in a circle at the top of a larger rectangle. "Someone is… well, he's waving at the camera, sir."

"What?" Mr. Soto strode over to the screen. "Oh. *Him*. Bring him in, we'll know if he has something up his sleeve," he said, waving the device in the air.

Does that mean…? Sadie's head began to pound with the possibilities.

The door slid open again and two guards strode into the room, carrying a man between them with a bag over his head.

"Killian Quinn," Mr. Soto said, "so nice to see you… alive."

Sadie jumped at the name and looked more closely at this newcomer. He wore a dark gray sweater with a black leather jacket and jeans, and she couldn't help but notice the wrap on his right arm, tied tight and soaked in blood.

"Get Derek on the phone, ask him why I am having to do the job I paid him to do. And stick Mr. Quinn over here," Soto instructed one of the guards as he gestured in Sadie's general direction.

Derek, Sadie thought, *not good. What have you gotten yourself into, Sadie?* She could feel her heart pounding through every vein in her body as the reality of the situation set in. *Focus, Sadie! You need to get out of here.*

One of the guards grabbed the spare chair and scooted it next to Sadie, pulling the hooded man along with him. He tied Killian Quinn to it in much the same fashion as Sadie herself had been tied. Once he was finished, he yanked the bag off Killian's head and left the room.

Sadie could now see Killian clearly, albeit just his profile. She had been reading his story for the better part of the weekend and realized she didn't have a clue what he looked like. She blinked more than a few times in an attempt to clear her eyes.

It can't be…

He had dark, curly hair with more than a five-o-clock shadow's worth of beard. Sadie studied the man, trying to see past the beard and dirt, looking for confirmation on what she already believed.

"Killian, at long last I get an introduction," Soto said with an obvious edge to his voice. He cracked his neck before taking a deep breath. It seemed as though frustration was getting the better of him. "So tell me, what brings you to my doorstep, and in decent enough health, it seems, despite my best efforts."

"Oh, don't beat yourself up, it's not for lack of trying. Good to meet you too, Scarface." Then Killian smiled.

It was the same smile. *James.* The man who saved the little boy at the Smithsonian. The man Sadie had lost herself in. The same man that left without explanation. A new anger flared inside her. *Calm down,* she told herself. *Not the time. Get out of here first.* She twisted and pulled at the restraints once more.

"Scarface?" Soto questioned.

"Oh I'm sorry, don't like that one? I have others if you'd rather, Tattered Temple, Italian Ignoramus, Maimed Man, Domino Dog."

Soto folded his arms. "Are you done?"

Killian paused. "Yes. Wait… Suited Scab. Okay, now I'm done. Go on with your threatening or monologuing, whatever you were doing. Don't mind me at all." He turned to Sadie. "Hi Sadie, sorry about this."

Her skin went cold. She became painfully aware of her heavy breathing and elevated heart rate. Her life was intertwined with this in more ways than one. "You. You ditched me? And now you're here and you're Killian?" she asked, more confused than ever.

"Yeah, sorry 'bout that, but suffice to say I'm here to get you out," he responded with a grin. That grin. That damn grin that made Sadie feel like everything was going to be okay now. But she knew better. She'd seen that grin on his face before. She knew not to trust it.

"And how do you plan to do that, Mr. Quinn?" asked Soto. "I imagine it would be difficult to escape when we can quite literally read your next move. Even for a distinguished Zeta Agent, like yourself." He set the device on the console to his right, patting it gingerly.

"Oh, incredibly difficult. Thankfully, I'm fantastic when it comes to not having a plan. Improvisation is kinda my thing. And I also have some very talented friends…" Killian looked over to Sadie and gave her a wink. He paused, as if expecting something to happen. The room remained silent for an extended beat.

"I'm sorry, was something supposed to happen there?" Soto looked to the other men in the room. "No? Okay, so as I was saying—"

The door behind him opened and another guard came running in. "Sir, Shawn Ambrose is here for you."

"Already?" Soto asked, almost frantically. "He's not

due for another hour! No matter." He turned, putting his jacket back on. "Looks like we're going to have to finish our little chat later. You." He pointed to the guard on his left. "Watch this," he said, handing over the CarterScott device, "he's bound to try something. I'll be back later, I have a few more questions for him." And with that, Soto left.

Silence fell over the room. Sadie looked back at Killian, trying to process all that had happened the last few minutes. As she studied him up and down, she again noticed the blood-soaked rag tied around his arm. "Wait, in the story you were shot. And hypothermic. But you're okay now?"

"Yeah, well it was just in the arm," Killian whispered, trying to shrug his shoulder. "And never doubt the warmth of an alleyway grate and the healing properties of a cup o' joe. So, about getting you out of here…"

"Hey! Quiet down you two," ordered the guard on the right as he stood up. He turned to his colleague. "I'm going to go grab a coffee. I have a feeling we'll be here all night at this rate. Want anything, Randy?"

"Actually yeah, I'll take a coffee. And just one sugar this time, whatever you did last time tasted like diabetes in a cup," replied the other guard.

"Yeah, yeah, yeah. You should learn to live a little, Randy." With his exit, that left only one guard in the room, who looked more concerned with his phone than anything.

Sadie's nerves were heightened, she wanted out and the man sitting next to her was her best hope. She'd seen, or rather read, his ability to get out of a scrape, surely he'd be able to get out of this one.

"So what's the plan?" she whispered cautiously, scared the guard would hear, but needing something to focus on, specifically something that would grant them freedom.

"No plan," Killian said plainly, while he eyed the remaining guard.

All Sadie's hopes deflated.

"What?" Her accusation echoed louder than she anticipated, but now anger was filling the void left by her hope. "What do you mean no plan?"

"That's the beauty of it. If I don't have a plan, they won't know what to expect." Killian winked at her again. *This can't be happening. I—*

The lights cut out.

Sadie heard sounds of a struggle. She could feel feet kicking the ground beside her chair followed by silence. Then a knife broke the ties that bound her wrists and a hand grasped hers, pulling her up and out the door.

By the time the emergency lights turned on, Sadie and Killian were already rushing down the corridor. Not only had Killian managed to break them out, but as Sadie looked down, she realized that he had also grabbed the device.

The pair wound corner after corner, running in circles, it seemed.

"Do you even know where you're going?" she asked incredulously. Granted, it was hard to tell where one was going in the maze of hallways lit only by the ominous red emergency lighting. Footsteps sounded around the next corner.

"Sure I do," Killian responded. "In here." He opened

the door beside them to usher Sadie into the next room. Not a room, per se, more of a small storage unit of sorts… A closet. It was a closet. Filled with brooms, mops, everything including a sink.

"This is a broom closet," Sadie said dryly. "You have no idea how to get out of here," she continued, frustration now building on top of the fear. *Why am I following this guy?* she thought to herself. "And how do I know I can even trust you? The other day you said your name was James."

"My middle name is James, so I didn't lie, and would you rather trust the guys with guns following us? Don't worry, I'll get us out of here, I'm fantastic at improvising, remember?" And there was that grin again. A crooked smile that slowly slid from his lips all the way to the corners of his big, blue eyes. "Shh, someone's coming." The footsteps passed by the door along with muffled voices.

"Do you know what's going on?" said one voice.

"Not a clue. Maybe they're doing maintenance again?" responded the other.

"I hate these old buildings. How do we get assigned to headquarters instead?"

"If I knew, think I'd be here stuck with your ugly mug?"

The voices trailed off as they continued down the hallway.

Killian and Sadie stood three inches from each other in utter silence for what felt like forever. She could feel his warm breath on her cheek, his strength in the hand that was still holding hers, the very smell of him was intoxicating and overwhelmed her senses. With his ear against the door, listening, Killian stared down at Sadie, the ferocity behind his eyes burning in the dim light. She hated this feeling, the vulnerability. She longed to trust this man, to let him in, but her mind knew better. *You know how this ends,* she told herself. *You've been here before.*

Once it was quiet outside the door, the pair cautiously exited the closet into a now empty hallway.

"So where to now, Killian James Quinn?"

Killian looked back at her, she could see the frustration on his face; the never-ending maze of hallways was beginning to grate on him too. Without a word, he tightened his grip on her hand and pulled her onward.

They continued running down the long, white corridor, passing door after door. The lights flickered back on and with them came a loud, wailing alarm.

"Door number two," Killian said, pulling Sadie into the closest room.

The hallway alarm now almost completely muffled. She took in the space in front of her. It was a research lab, easily one hundred feet long by one hundred feet wide, filled with over a dozen workstations. Sadie couldn't help but let her curiosity take over, leaving Killian staring through a small window in the middle of the door.

"Hey, Killian, look at this place," she said, walking among the different stations.

"We don't have time to—" Killian turned and finally looked at the room. "What in the…" he trailed off, running toward one of the computers. "Please turn on, please turn on. Yes!" The screen came to life.

While he started frantically combing through the computer, Sadie continued to walk through the lab. She saw more devices like the one that had brought her here, but slightly different. They were all larger, bulkier, it seemed. One was labeled D246, another A113. She passed one station displaying what looked like a hearing implant on a ceramic mannequin head. Next to that sat a small, white disk, about the size of a half dollar but octagonal. As she walked past, she could've sworn it began to glow. She turned back and picked it up. Sure enough, it glowed purple.

"Hey Killian, look at this thing, when you walk by it turns purple, do you think—"

"I can't believe this. They have everything." Killian gaped at the screen in front of him.

Sadie ran over, absentmindedly pocketing the small disk.

"They know every single Agent we have, they have files on each of us, even on our assignments. They know our archiving process, they know shipping patterns, they know everything! How?" He gazed up at Sadie with a look of confusion and betrayal on his face.

"I have zero idea what you're talking about. Shouldn't we get back to escaping?"

The door creaked open. Killian pulled Sadie down to hide behind the workstations as two men entered the room. As Killian reached up to turn off the screen, thankfully facing away from the door, she could hear slow and steady footsteps searching through the lab. Red dots blinked across the wall in front of them. *Guns. Great,* she thought.

Sadie instantly felt as though she'd entered a book, and not one of her comfortable historical fiction ones. It was something straight out of a spy novel by James

Patterson or Lee Child. She remembered all the time spent in her gray beanbag chair, staring out the window, envisioning herself in the stories she read, never imagining that she'd ever actually live them herself. And yet here she was, in a strange research facility, with a man she barely knew, hiding from men with guns, all thanks to reading a device she'd found under her couch. *And people say reading isn't dangerous.*

The footsteps drew closer and closer, red dots scanning the room for a sign of movement.

"Follow me," Killian mouthed. There was only one exit, so Killian and Sadie began the slow trek back to the door, hiding behind each subsequent workstation as the two guards moved around the room. Sadie could see the door now. It was so close, just one workstation away. But there was a guard hovering in front of it.

Killian moved to the last station, the guard standing on the other side. He gestured for Sadie to hold where she was as the guard turned and began walking in her direction.

Sadie pressed her back so hard against the workstation it was as if she was trying to become part of it. She tried to steel herself for what was coming. Her mind raced through every self-defense class, every story, every movie in her life as if to prepare for the worst-case scenario—her mind had terrible timing.

She sat frozen in fear while the armed guard moved closer and closer to her. The footsteps stopped, and she peeked around the corner to see the tip of a boot poking out from the other side of the workstation. She quickly shot back to her hiding place and closed her eyes tight, praying for this nightmare to be over.

"I think we're all clear," the guard called out right next to her.

The footsteps started to walk back toward to door.

Sadie finally let herself breathe. As her muscles began to relax, she leaned her head back against the workstation with more force than she intended, and it shook.

She froze… but the footsteps kept going.

Phew.

Then a pencil rolled off the desk and clattered onto the floor directly next to her. *Of course that would happen*, she thought to herself, acknowledging the irony of the situation. She stared at it with the fire and fury of a tempest, never had she hated a pencil so much in her life.

Sensing the beam of a red light on her forehead, Sadie looked up to find the guard staring down at her, the barrel of his gun inches from her face.

"We've got y—" At that moment, Killian ran up and jumped him from behind, forcing the gun to go flying as the two wrestled on the ground. The other guard came running to help as Killian choked out the first one.

"Get up!" the guard yelled at him, holding his rifle against Killian's head.

"Alright, alright, let's all calm down a bit. He's okay, he's fine, just taking a little nap," Killian said as he slowly stood at the guard's behest.

Sadie watched in horror, knowing she had to do something. As the guard bent down to check on his partner, one hand on the gun still pointed at Killian, she searched desperately for something that she could use as a weapon. She spied a hefty-looking coffee mug on the station not far from the guard. *Hope this* works, she thought as she grabbed it and slammed it down on the guard's skull in one swift move, shattering the ceramic mug to pieces.

He crumpled to the ground, motionless.

Sadie looked at Killian for approval, still holding the handle of the mug. She couldn't believe what she'd just done. She'd never knocked someone out before.

"That works too," Killian said as he grabbed a gun, earpiece, and walkie-talkie from one of the guards. He stood and cracked open one of the computer towers, pulling out the hard drive. "Okay, let's get out of here."

Now equipped to listen in on the search, it was easier to avoid the guards. They finally made it to a service staircase and ran downstairs, reaching the ground floor and exiting into a deserted main lobby. Through the glass walls, Sadie could see Petey outside in a van waiting for them.

Petey. The man whose backpack started this whole ordeal. Anger and confusion rose within Sadie, overwhelming the fear she'd felt moments ago.

"See, told you I'm good at improvising," Killian said as they ran toward the door. Shots began to ring out from behind them, and he quickly pulled Sadie to safety behind a support column. As he peeked around the corner, Mr. Soto emerged in the main entryway.

"Not leaving yet, are we, Agent Quinn?" Soto said as more guards rushed in behind him.

"Yeah, my ride's here, next time though," Killian called out. He pushed Sadie toward the door, turning back to return fire as they made their way to the exit.

Sadie had her fingers on the handle when an

excruciating pain erupted from within her head. She screamed and dropped to the floor, writhing in agony. Crying out for it to stop.

As shots continued to erupt through the air, Killian's warm arms lifted her from the ground, cradling her while he moved with haste. She pulled herself closer to his chest and the echoes of gunfire faded into the ceaseless pounding inside her head. The pain was almost too much to bear.

Once they were in the van it began to dull slightly, but Sadie could barely open her eyes. She heard the muffled sounds of voices. Killian and Petey were yelling at each other. And then she blacked out in the back of an unknown vehicle for the second time that day.

Chapter 9

It was 2 a.m. before Sadie awoke, now for the third time that day. Waking up in a foreign room was becoming far too much of a regular occurrence for her liking, and even with the pounding in her head, she made a mental note to stop doing it. Last she remembered, a splitting headache hit her like a ton of bricks and then nothing. Nothing until the dream that woke her up. It was the same dream she'd had over and over again since she was a child.

She was two years old. She'd spent the day running around the zoo and now stood on the Asia Trail watching the giant panda. The sun shone brightly and the breeze bristled through the bamboo stalks as all the tourists surrounded her with their disposable cameras that were so common in the early nineties. The panda was her favorite; Sadie held a blue balloon with a panda on it. Even in the dream, she could feel her cheeks ache from smiling so much throughout the day. The baby panda rolled into its mother's lap, grabbing for more bamboo. Sadie turned to her mom but realized she wasn't there. Time started to speed forward. The people came and went around her, the sky turned black, rain splashed onto the ground as lightning and thunder rippled through the air. Still Sadie waited for her mother to return for her. The world began to spin, grown-ups were yelling over her, she let the balloon go and watched it retreat into the sky until finally, high in the air, it popped. That's how it always ended. A pop to wake her up and remind her of her reality.

Sadie turned over and found herself facing an illuminated salt lamp on the nightstand underneath a framed picture of Petey smiling ear-to-ear beside some guy and a ticket that read *Comic-Con 2016–Nathan Fillion Photo Op*.

So this is Petey's place, she assumed. She regarded the rest of the room. The wall beside her was covered with posters of various sci-fi movies and games, from what Sadie could gather. Next to it, on his dresser, was a clear display box covering a life-size green and yellow helmet that Sadie didn't recognize.

On the other wall, above his desk, were three mounted swords. A katana, a fencing sword, and what looked like something out of *Lord of the Rings*. The room was meticulously clean and organized, save for the desk. Petey's dual monitors and computer tower, which seemed at least two feet tall, were surrounded by empty Red Bull cans, Cheetos bags, and what had once been milk and cereal in a clear glass but was now a gelatinous white block encasing a metal spoon.

Sadie got up and walked toward the door. She could hear voices from the other side.

"They had everything, Petey, there has to be a mole in the Agency, how else—"

"Hey, shh," Petey said as Sadie slid open the door.

"Hey guys." She blinked in the bright fluorescent lights, feeling slightly embarrassed to have intruded into their conversation.

"How ya doing? Here, sit down," Killian said as he pulled up a seat at the counter for her next to Petey.

The rest of Petey's apartment looked as meticulously curated as his room. The kitchen had little in the way of space or appliances, just a fridge, range, and a sink. But there was a coffee maker with fresh coffee gurgling inside it, if her sense of smell was accurate.

"I'm sorry, is that coffee?" she asked, wishing for it to be true.

"Yeah, I'll get you some." Petey rose to get her a cup, but Sadie beat him to it. Without another word, she walked right past Killian and Petey and poured herself a hot cup of the black liquid gift of the gods. No milk—today was not a day for frills. Then she took the seat at the kitchen bar next to Petey, downed her coffee, and stared at the two men whom she barely knew—beyond the fact that they had saved her life, presumably.

"So how are you feeling?" Killian asked, clearly unsure of what to say to someone who had been thrown into the deep end of a pool she didn't even know existed.

Sadie firmly placed the now empty mug onto the counter, ignoring Killian's question, and asked, "What in the world is going on? And why does my head feel like it's been hit by a battering ram?" She pushed the cup toward Petey, motioning for a refill. Killian and Petey just stared at each other, as though afraid to be the one to speak.

"This is all you, brother," Petey said, walking to the kitchen, "I'll get the coffee."

Killian shot Petey a look of utter exasperation. "So, I'm Killian, this is Petey, as you know. And, well, let's start with the easier question. The headache. Short answer, I have no idea. Maybe stress? You weren't hit or anything, so that's a plus."

"Great," Sadie said flatly, attempting to massage the pain away from her temples.

"Advil?" Petey proffered the blue and white bottle.

"Yes, please. And on to the next question. What is going on?"

"That's a bit of a bigger one," said Killian, handing Sadie a glass of water to go with her pills. He looked at Petey for some help on how to continue, but Petey shrugged his shoulders. "Alright, Band-Aid approach. We work for the Zeta Defense Agency. A covert organization tasked with protecting the people of America and their thoughts."

"Thoughts?" asked Sadie. "So you *can* read people's thoughts." She immediately felt naked and exposed. Her entire life had taught her to hide emotions, to keep things close to the chest. Now her world exploded at the very notion of having to protect her thoughts from people as well. *How many people can read thoughts? Are they reading mine now? Could they read the thoughts of my dreams too? Why can't I stop thinking of stupid questions?* All of these things began racing through Sadie's mind.

"Well not us, but we have technology that can," Killian said.

"Some people can naturally though," Petey interjected as he returned to his seat next to Sadie with her coffee and a plate of muffins. He grabbed one and took an enormous bite. "We call them Listeners."

Sadie and Killian stared at him as he continued chewing.

"Oh, I'm sorry. Did one of you want the blueberry

one?" Petey paused with the muffin halfway to his mouth. "It's the last one, but I'll go halfsies."

Sadie chuckled and Killian continued to stare at his friend.

"Seriously?" he asked, shaking his head in embarrassment. "Read the room."

Sadie looked at Killian, then Petey, then over to the muffins. "Actually, Petey, I think you're onto something," she said, glaring at Killian as if he had just hurt Petey in some way. She grabbed the chocolate muffin on top—sugar could always be counted on for comfort.

"Right," Killian continued. "So yes, some people can read thoughts naturally, and they're called Auritors, not Listeners. Only Petey says that."

"But Listeners is way easier to say," Petey responded as he continued to scarf down his muffin.

"Anyway," Killian went on, ignoring Petey's interruption, "Auritors are kind of rare so that's why the technology was developed, to be able to listen in to individuals. A scientist named Charles Carter discovered that all human thought exists on the same frequency spectrum called zeta waves. Hence the Zeta Defense Agency."

"And that's what these devices can register? So the government is listening to our thoughts," Sadie said.

"Not exactly. First of all, we're not actually part of the government, we technically color outside the lines. And we don't listen to everyone, we only have a handful of these." Killian pulled out the device that Sadie had been reading. She now regarded it with more than a little distaste. "And each of these can only be tuned to a single person at a time."

"That's what I've been reading then, on that thing, thoughts? Your thoughts, I'm guessing?"

"Yeah," Killian responded, shifting his gaze to the floor. It wasn't hard for Sadie to read the embarrassment spreading across his face. Her mind ran through everything she had seen on that device to figure out the source of his self-consciousness.

"So then what do you actually do at the Zeta Defense Agency, if not listen to people's thoughts?"

"See, when the technology was unveiled in the eighties, we weren't the only ones there. An operative from an organization known as Domino was there too. He stole one of the original prototypes, but it looks like they haven't been able to replicate it yet. There are theories that the one they stole was damaged somehow, but again we have very limited intel on their organization as a whole. This though," Killian said, gesturing to the device, "would've brought them much closer."

"Okay, so if they don't have the technology, then why are they such a threat?"

"Well, just because they don't have the technology doesn't mean they don't have their own Auritors. Once we started looking more into Domino, we discovered a network with ties to some of the nation's biggest influencers from economic and market drivers all the way up to government offices. Their sole goal is to use mind reading to shape the world and line their pockets to their advantage, by any means necessary. And the list of casualties in their quest isn't a short one. We're there to make sure that these *influencers* are protected from the unseen threat that is Domino."

"But if they're *unseen,* as you say, how can you tell who they are?" Sadie asked. "They just walk in and say to the person, 'Hey, I'm from Domino, I'm here to read your thoughts. Don't mind me.'"

"No, but that's where *our* Auritors come into play," Killian continued. "They can read anyone they're near and they stay close to our targets, keeping an ear out for anyone wishing to 'do harm,' so to speak. If they catch on to someone from Domino, we can then go in and remove them from the situation."

"Okay." Sadie looked down at her empty mug, as though the residue of coffee grounds would somehow spell out a rational translation of the words rattling inside her pulsating head. But no, just as the cup of golden nectar had disappeared, so too had any chance of her understanding. She rose and began pacing between the living room and the kitchen. "So your Auritors are there to protect important people from Domino, but if you guys aren't Auritors, then what do you do?"

Petey burst out laughing. "Baaahaha, what *do* we do, Killian?" he asked sarcastically as he reached for another muffin.

"Oh shut it, Petey," Killian snapped.

"I'm not trying to belittle your job or anything, but if these Auritors are so important and key to saving people or whatever, then what do they need more people for?"

"Well Auritors are rare, like I said, so that's why there are more people like us with the devices that are placed in positions to do the same thing."

"Then how did I end up with one that was 'tuned' or

whatever to you? Is that this whole mole problem you were talking about? …Or should I say thinking about?" Sadie may have been out of the loop, but she was determined to make sense of all of this. She'd read enough mysteries and adventure books in her life, and this was the closest she figured she'd ever get to living one.

"That's an excellent question. How did that happen, Petey?" Killian asked acerbically.

"Hey, look! I told you I wasn't good at this secret agent kind of stuff. I'm just an analyst," Petey started then looked over at Sadie. "I did tell him that, I promise. And you were there, I was minding my own business when Piper came over to me, right? And then things carried on, and is it my fault that I'm a gregarious person and make friends easily?"

"He is rather gregarious, Killian," Sadie said, laughing.

"And see, Sadie here, being the wonderful person she is, picked up the bag for me."

"Yes," Killian said, "but how did she end up with the device and you not realize it until—" He paused. "When did you even notice?"

"Sunday morning," Petey mumbled while taking another bite of muffin.

"Sunday morning! What were you doing all day Saturday?" Killian exploded.

"Look. Friday night is a bit of a blur, *but* I did remember making brunch plans with Piper on Saturday, that's how I got the bag back."

"Wait, you had brunch with Piper?" Sadie interjected.

"Yeah, we went to that Tyber Creek place, so good. The salmon benedict is fantastic."

"Wait, you went out with her friend?" Killian asked

his friend incredulously.

"Are you that shocked? You know the ladies can't get enough of this animal magnetism, I can't help it. And honestly, it was her idea, she's very persuasive."

"Oh that's true." Sadie began, "One time—"

A thundering knock at the door cut her off. Sadie immediately looked at the two men in panic.

"Killian, it's me, open up," came a voice from outside.

Killian ran to open it and a man wearing full military uniform walked in and immediately grabbed Killian in a giant bear hug. Killian, dwarfed by at least five inches, all but disappeared in the man's embrace.

"Are you okay?" the man asked, finally releasing Killian and giving him a once over. He was probably in his late thirties or early forties with salt and pepper hair that he wore combed over and held tight in military fashion.

"Yes, Des, I'm fine," Killian responded with a fond smile. *Clearly they're close*, Sadie thought.

"Good." The man smacked Killian on the side of the head. "What have I told you about getting yourself into trouble like that?"

"I know, I know, but did you go check that place out?" Killian placed himself on the other side of the man as if to prevent Sadie and Petey from being acknowledged.

"Yes, now look. I took a whole team to the address you gave me, we had to navigate around the local authorities, but everything checked out—no mysterious Domino labs," said the man. "We couldn't find anything like the place you described. Whatever was there is long gone now. We couldn't even find a trace."

"There has to be, though, I was there," Killian pleaded.

"Did you check every floor?"

"Yes and there wasn't—" The man turned away from Killian and stopped dead in his tracks, looking directly at Sadie. "Killian, what's going on here?"

"Know how I left out the details about how I found that place? Well, this is Sadie," Killian said.

"Killian, you know the rules about Penumbrials. Do you have any idea the danger that you've put yourselves in?"

"Desmond, please, just listen. I can explain." Killian shot a look back to Petey, nodding toward the living room, then guided Desmond into Petey's bedroom.

"Right, let's go over here, Sadie. This is more of a family dispute anyway," Petey said. Sadie followed him to the couch, regarding the room as if searching for a distraction. It was open concept with a large TV over the fireplace. Not to mention what looked like every gaming console ever invented.

"Wait," Sadie paused and turned to Petey, "did you say family dispute?"

"Yeah, that's Killian's big brother, Desmond. He's kind of in charge of the whole Zeta Defense Agency and the liaison, so to speak, between us and the contacts we have in the government. He's actually the one who hired Killian as a Zed."

"Zed?" Sadie raised an eyebrow.

"Yeah, because Zeta Defense Agency Agent is long and redundant. So it's like the Feds, except Z for, ya know, Zeta. Nut?" Petey offered her a walnut from the bowl on the living room table.

"No, thanks," Sadie responded as she got up and began

to pace in the living room, hoping a perspective change would help her reorient herself to the new information.

A bookcase filled almost the entire wall to her left. Petey had everything from sci-fi fantasy to the classic literature of Steinbeck and Fitzgerald. She browsed the list of authors and titles. "*The Complete Works of William Shakespeare* in gold leaf sandwiched between *The Hitchhiker's Guide to the Galaxy* and *Ready Player One?*"

"What? Just because I like sci-fi, I can't have a wide range of tastes? Tsk, judgmental much." Petey continued to crack nuts and then throw them up in front of him, attempting to catch them on their way down. "I also have all the works of Sir Arthur Conan Doyle and Edgar Allan Poe. I like reading, sue me."

"You are one interesting man, Mr... wait, what is your last name?"

"Jackson," he attempted to mumble.

"Really? Peter Jackson, like—"

"Yes, like the *Lord of the Rings* guy. So to avoid the whole discussion, I'm Petey, let's leave it at that. I will say he did a fantastic job with those movies, even if he did completely remove Glorfindel."

"Right. They must confuse you two a lot, right? Because there's such a resemblance?" Sadic couldn't help but laugh at the situation, until Petey gave her a look. She continued to peruse the bookshelf. "So as an analyst, does that still make you a Zed?"

"Me? Heck no. That's reserved for those fools crazy enough to run around and chase people that are most likely armed. I prefer to stay indoors, behind a computer, where it's safe. Killian on the other hand, he's a Zed through and through. Probably one of the best, honestly. I remember this one time, I had somehow been assigned to field duty for an op. Thankfully, I stayed in the van, but still, it was fieldwork and I was not amused.

"We got word that a Domino operative had infiltrated one of our safe houses and screwed up all of the security measures, hence why I was there, to try and reset them. So Killian goes running in, guns blazing, devil-may-care attitude, thinking he's going to take the guy down all by himself. Well, Killian being Killian actually does it. Two minutes later, he's running down the stairs with the guy in cuffs in front of him, claiming that he even managed to defuse the bomb they set up too! Then BOOM! The bomb he '*defused*' goes off, blows the whole place to pieces.

"Throws Killian and the Domino guy flat on their faces. Killian was fine, obviously, but then his partner Nebraska comes storming out of the van and rips into him. 'Rook! I told you to hold! But no, you had to run in like always and almost get yourself blown up!' But Killian is just sitting there staring at her.

"Then he stands up, dusts himself off, and says, 'Hey Brask, so I got the guy, but I think we're gonna need a new safe house. And you should answer that phone that's ringing, it's probably Des.'" Petey shook his head. "There was no phone ringing, it was just his ears. Then he walks toward the building, staring at the fire, and the entire back of his pants was gone. There he was, butt flappin' in the wind, but he couldn't care less. In his mind, he'd saved the day. Quintessential Killian. That's the level of crazy it takes to be a Zed." Petey's infectious laugh filled the living room and Sadie couldn't help but laugh along. At the same time, a realization of what type of world she had been thrust into started to form in her head.

"So Killian joined Zeta Defense Agency thanks to Desmond… how'd you get involved with them?"

"Ah, now that's a story. See, Killian was recruited, I sort of forced my way in," Petey said with a look of pride. "I'm a bit of a conspiracy theory fan. If it's denied by authorities, I'm interested. And in my pre-ZDA days I might not have had the cleanest of records. So if there was a question I had, I would figure out a way to get the answer."

"You were a hacker?"

"You say that like it's a bad thing," Petey said, taken aback.

Something clicked in Sadie's memory. "Oh wait! Hacker… Middy. That's you, right?"

"Middy! It's Midnight please." He rolled his eyes.

"Oh, sorry. No offense meant. That's how Killian referred to you on the device thing."

"What?! He called me Middy!" Petey turned in the direction of his bedroom. "It's MIDNIGHT. Get it right. For crying out loud, it's not even that long of a name. And Middy sounds… ridiculous!" He went back to cracking the nuts with an extra bit of force.

"So hacking…?" Sadie asked cautiously.

"Right. Yeah, it was a means to an end, and one of the conspiracy boards kept mentioning these covert societies acting in and around DC. Granted, the rumors were a bit grandiose even for my taste, but I was intrigued. I started to notice large amounts of data flowing on the dark web and followed it down the rabbit hole all the way to the

Zeta Defense Agency. Thankfully, instead of throwing me into some secret American gulag, they offered me a job. A job that came with a clean slate. So I've been on the straight and narrow ever since. Well, mostly. A guy's gotta have hobbies."

"Like hacking into an entire building's power grid to assist a crazy secret agent?" Sadie questioned with a smirk.

"Exactly."

Sadie's mind sorted through all of Petey's explanations. For every question he answered, three more popped into her head. "So how does the device work then?"

"That's a loaded question involving a lot of higher thinking, but here's the easiest way to explain it as I've been told: the device is like a radio. We all know about FM and AM radio bands, but the device essentially picks up another band, we'll call it ZM for zeta. The device can pick up that band, and just like a radio, you have to tune into a specific station, the device tunes into a specific person's broadcast, essentially."

"Okay… makes sense, I guess," Sadie said, trying to wrap her head around the idea.

"And that's why a device can only be tuned to one person at a time, just like a radio station, you can't listen to them all at once."

"And Listeners are the same?"

"Well, they can switch between 'stations' quicker than the device. I'm not a Listener, but from the ones that I've talked to, it's almost like being in a room full of conversations. You can listen to one easily, but you have to focus and drown everything else out. The really good Listeners have trained themselves to listen to multiple people at once, but it's about as hard as listening to two conversations at once. Possible, but takes a lot of mental effort."

"So Listeners have to train to hear people. Can anyone do it without training? How do you find them in the first place? I imagine you can't run a newspaper ad asking for people that can read minds."

"Ha! I wish. No, apparently most Listeners don't even know they can hear thoughts, they just think they're super intuitive. I imagine most of the Listeners we have working for us were recruited from industries that are known for that, like psychiatrists. Also why most of them give me the heebie-jeebies. I don't like people trying to shrink my head."

"Fair enough. And anyone can be read?"

"Almost everyone, there are Muffles, but—" Before Petey could finish, the door to his bedroom flung open.

"I don't want to hear another word about it, Killian," Desmond said as he charged toward the front door. "I told you I'd look through the notes and into your mole theory, but right now I need the Agency focused on finding the new location of Domino's lab. You have forty-eight hours to pick a replacement for 602, otherwise I will choose for you." Desmond turned to look at Sadie. "Ms. Smith, I'm sorry for everything that has happened to you and any role my brother played in it. I know this may sound difficult, but please try to forget what happened here today and I urge you to return to normal life as best you can. It does not do to dwell on things beyond our control."

He opened the door to exit then paused, without turning, and said, "And Mr. Jackson, don't think for a second that you are in the clear on this, I expect to see you at nine-hundred hours first thing tomorrow morning."

"When you say tomorrow morning, do you mean Tuesday morning? Because it's technically already Monday morning." Desmond merely turned his head a few centimeters to glare at Petey with as much indignation as one can manage with a side glance. "Right, so Monday it is then. I will see you in…" Petey looked down at his watch. "Six hours, sir."

And without a word, Desmond slammed the door and was gone.

Chapter 10

The early morning rain beat gently against the window of the car as Sadie looked out at the shop owners opening up for the day. Another cold front would be hitting them this week. Killian had borrowed Petey's car to take Sadie home and tried admirably to coax her out of her silence, but Sadie couldn't fathom the words that would even begin to explain her experiences of the last twenty-four hours.

"Sorry about Desmond, by the way, he's a good guy. Just a bit 'by the books,' you could say," Killian said as if with a heavy heart, knowing that he would soon turn over his protection duty to another, stripping 602 from his life.

"So he's replacing your job?" Sadie asked, still not sure how much she was supposed to be "forgetting" about this whole affair.

"Yeah… I guess I never finished explaining everything. Part of my job at the ZDA is protecting what we call Penumbrials. They're people who have a genetic mutation that makes them completely unreadable. By our tech and even Auritors. That makes them very valuable to Domino because they can be used as undetected agents in various situations."

"Oh… OH! Is that what Petey meant by 'Muffles'?" The dots were finally starting to connect in Sadie's mind.

"That's another Petey term. He says it's because their thoughts are too 'muffled' to hear," Killian rolled his eyes, "but please, stick with Penumbrials."

"Okay…" Sadie struggled to understand this new world of powered individuals. "It just doesn't sound like that great of an ability. At least when compared to someone that can actually hear the thoughts of another person."

"Well imagine a lock that literally no one in the world can pick. It would be the most sought after safe in the world. That's what happens when you tell a Penumbrial something; it's locked from prying minds and devices."

"So they're a drop box of information. It really doesn't sound that incredible." Sadie looked back out the window of the car, the streetlights blurred in the steady stream of rain. The sound of it hitting the roof of the car was enough to calm her senses after being on high alert for the better part of twenty-four hours.

"They normally have other talents too. Most of the time, Penumbrials have incredible memories. The best, safest USB drives on the planet. You can tell them anything and they'll always remember it." Killian kept glancing over at Sadie as if to make sure she was still okay, that her head hadn't exploded from information overload. Though Sadie felt it wasn't too far from that point.

"So they're pawns. And you as a Zed protect these pawns?" Sadie asked, turning to meet his gaze.

"Yes, when we learn of someone with the ability, we begin to surveil them to be sure Domino doesn't try to move in."

"But why would you assume that they'd even want to work for these Domino people, especially if, based on what you're saying, they're not so great?"

"They don't always have a choice. Domino has almost endless means and uses them to entice people to their initiative. When that doesn't work, they have no problem forcing the option, threatening their families."

"That's horrible!"

"That's why they're the bad guys," Killian said, pulling up to a stoplight. He looked at her with a grim expression across his face. She couldn't help but feel like there was more to this story, that there was something Killian wasn't telling her.

"Sadie," he continued, "have you ever felt like you could never really connect with people? Like somehow people always felt a sense of unease around you?"

Sadie paused. *What is that supposed to mean?* she thought. But if she was honest with herself, she knew exactly what he meant.

"Maybe. I don't know. How do you expect someone to answer that? No, there aren't many people I feel close to, besides Piper and maybe Allyn? But what does that matter?" she asked, trying to contain the emotions that inevitably followed whenever a subject like this came up.

When enough people leave your life, including the two people who are always supposed to be there, just get up and walk out, you tend to have a few trust issues.

Sadie thought back to all the times as a child when, after a few months, the family she was currently living with would call her social worker Carla Reynolds and say, "It's just not going to work out. It's not quite the right fit." Like the Josephs. They were a nice family, they had a little pug named Bob that Sadie absolutely adored.

She'd pretend to go out on expeditions in the backyard with Bob, digging up the secrets of the past. But she never felt wholly comfortable around Frank and Virginia Joseph. They often tried to start conversations at dinner, but everything felt so awkward. That's why it didn't surprise Sadie when Carla showed up to get her. That time, like every time, she sat in the back seat of Carla's car and apologized, as if it was her fault that Carla had to come to pick her up again. "It's okay," she would say. "It's not you, it was definitely them. You're a perfect you and that's all you can do." It was always her answer to everything. But that wasn't the *real* answer to everything.

Maybe this is.

"These Penumbrials, people always look at them like they have a secret, don't they?" Sadie asked cautiously, her mind already running with the idea. She looked down at her hands, tracing the lines of her fingers.

"Yes."

"Because they do." Her hands stopped at her ever-present pinky ring.

"Yes."

"And you protect them?" Off and on. Off and on. She couldn't stop taking her ring off and putting it back on again.

"I do."

"And you protect me," she said with finality as she left the ring on and looked up to meet Killian's soft gaze.

"I do."

Then she knew. She knew for certain that it was true. She was a Penumbrial. It wasn't her fault. It wasn't something she did that made her seem so cold to those potential foster parents. It was a genetic fluke. A roll of the proverbial dice that she was one of these individuals. An individual member of a group. She wasn't alone. There were others like her. There was an answer and it made her exceptional.

"I'm one of them." Sadie's voice rang out with a new-found contentment.

"Yes, and that's why this is all my fault, what's happened to you. It was my job to protect you, and I'm sorry to say that I've failed miserably." Killian turned back to the road ahead.

Sadie continued to look at him, trying to figure out the words that would soothe his guilt. She thought back to the device. Everything she'd read for the last few days. About the woman Killian was supposed to protect. About 602. About Bluebird.

"So Bluebird… that's… that's me then," Sadie said as she returned to twirling the ring on her pinky finger. She remembered the words she'd read just days before on the device. *"Body and soul, she has ruined me."* Those were Killian's thoughts, this man's thoughts, about her.

"Yeah…" Killian responded, flushed bright red with embarrassment. "Sorry if I made you feel uncomfortable." He started fiddling with the controls, attempting to turn on the windshield wipers. The rain had turned to sleet and began to collect in his view.

"No, it's flattering, kind of. Don't know that I've ever ruined anyone before." She considered Killian, the man that thought she was beautiful and brilliant. "So that coffee, you didn't ditch me for a better offer?"

"No! God, no!" he exclaimed. "That call was from

Desmond telling me they'd found my partner's body in a subway station."

"Oh… I'm sorry," Sadie said as she put her hand on his arm. She felt the electricity of their connection and quickly pulled her hand back. "Nebraska, right?"

"Yeah, they thought it was a mugging at first, but it wasn't. That's what started this whole thing. Trying to figure out who killed her. Who the mole in the ZDA is!" He slammed his hand on the steering wheel, making Sadie jump.

"And she never told you about any of this before…?" Sadie asked tentatively, unsure of how to say the words "before she died."

"No. That's what's so hard about all of this. Nebraska always played things close to the vest," Killian paused. "I didn't know any of her suspicions until after… after she was dead. She sent me a package with a letter explaining everything. I mean, I knew she was acting a bit withdrawn, but I figured it was her way of dealing with Oliver's death."

"Oliver?"

"Her boyfriend. He's the reason she started researching a mole in the first place. He died in a car accident shortly after his assigned Penumbrial was knocked off, and Nebraska couldn't believe he was at fault; she loved him. Hell, I'm probably the only person that knew that. And the only reason I ever found out was a complete fluke."

"A fluke?" Sadie frowned.

"Yeah, like I said, close to the vest. A few months back, I happened to catch Nebraska and Oliver in a back booth at Thirsty Bernie, sitting down to a cozy dinner.

So me being the pestering partner that I am, I walk over there fully intent on embarrassing her. She was visibly shaken, even tried to shoo me out of there. But Oliver, he was a cool guy, he just said, 'Nebs, it's done. He knows. But it's okay, Killian won't say anything.' She was so afraid of anyone finding out about them, some rule about intra-agency dating, but I would never betray Nebraska like that. Then Oliver smiled at her and it was like all her fear had melted away. They'd really found it; love." Killian looked over at Sadie. She could see a glint in his eye. Then that familiar grin flashed across his face, and an overwhelming sense of warmth and safety came over the car, as if to fight the cold that was outside. He looked away before Sadie could respond.

"But then he died two months later and Nebraska started spiraling in her own way. I should've pushed her more. I should've forced her to tell me." His jaw tensed as if set in stone. "I could've been there to help. I could've done something."

"Killian, it sounds like she made her choices. And as much as it hurts, there's nothing you can do now to change it. But you're trying to do right by her, and that's admirable."

"I'm trying. I… I'm sorry, this isn't your problem. I just don't understand how Desmond can ignore the signs."

"Well I'm no super-spy or anything, but didn't you take a hard drive from that place? Isn't that going to convince your brother?"

"Honestly, I didn't tell him about it. I left it with Petey to see what he can get off it. Apparently the rest of it is protected by firewalls and failsafes, or whatever it is the Petey always rambles on about." Killian sighed. "It's probably for the best that they reassign you. After all, I've put you in enough danger, and if I keep going with this, I don't know if I'll be able to do any better. I won't let you be in a situation like that ever again. I promise," he said as he pulled up to her apartment. He didn't look over at Sadie, he just gripped the steering wheel tighter, his knuckles going white.

"So I go back to normal life then? Pretend I know nothing about Penumbrials, Domino, or you?" she asked, pausing at the end, reflecting on what it would mean to say goodbye to him.

Killian sat silently staring at the road ahead as the snow began to fall. "Yeah, it would be the best thing for everyone. I'm really sorry to turn your life upside down. You should probably take a few days off, regain your footing, so to speak."

Footing, Sadie thought, *is that how he's going to try and explain what I need?* What she needed was to go back in time and never pick up that backpack or at least never turn on that damned device. She didn't need footing, she needed an undo button. "You're probably right, a few days off may be a good idea… Dammit, I can't! I have a project due and I totally forgot about it, again!"

The crushing thought of disappointing Stead and Jonas for a second time made her stomach twist into knots. "I have to turn in the report by this afternoon." She glanced down at her watch before looking back at Killian, who was still staring straight ahead. "Thank you for bringing me home and," Sadie hesitated for the briefest of moments, "for everything else." She undid her seatbelt and reached for the door. "I hope you find who you're looking for, Killian."

"Thank you," he said softly. "Take care of yourself, Sadie." He finally turned toward Sadie as her name passed his lips. For a moment, she could see the pain behind his sorrowful eyes. She knew that pain well, it was a regret that couldn't be fixed with a few words. Killian turned back to the road ahead.

Sadie got out, shut the door, and watched Killian Quinn drive out of her life as quickly as he had entered it.

Walking into her apartment, she found it exactly as she left it less than twenty-four hours ago, but somehow everything seemed different. Sadie sat down at her desk to finish the report. She stared blankly at the screen, the cursor blinking at the beginning of her next sentence, begging to be written. Then she realized it wasn't the room, the report, or even the world that had changed, but she herself.

Chapter 10.5

Bruno Soto walked into his office trembling. He cradled a bandaged hand with extra wrapping around where his fourth finger had previously been. He had disappointed the Council yet again. The two strikes on his hand left their mark as a reminder that he had only one last chance to redeem himself.

His office was set up differently than the lab they'd had to abandon. Hidden on the thirteenth floor of the Domino building at K Street and Vermont, he was able to have a little more freedom. The room was dimly lit with two Edison bulb lamps on either side of his desk. A few museum-style lights ran along the bookcases that lined three of the four walls in the room. They were filled to the brim with old leather-bound books and unusual antiquities he had acquired over the years. One of particular note was a silver sword of the Knights Templar from the seventeenth century. Its pommel depicted a Knight, presumably chasing after the Holy Grail. The irony that Bruno's own life had been spent chasing his proverbial Holy Grail was not lost on him.

The sword, having belonged to a French lieutenant, was placed on a stand between two Gothic-style gargoyle bookends, miniature replicas of the gargoyles that guarded the walls of Notre Dame herself. The books on either side were all by French authors, ranging from historical pieces about Joan of Arc to Alexandre Dumas's *The Three Musketeers*. Bruno had a place for everything and everything in its place, with the exception of two fingers, that is.

The phone on his desk buzzed and the rasping voice of a woman who had clearly spent her whole life smoking came over the speaker.

"Sir, the general is here for you."

"Send him in," responded Bruno, steeling himself. He would not show his pain to this man.

"We had a deal!" Desmond Kalani stormed into the office ranting. "You were supposed to leave Killian out of this!" He walked right up to Bruno, as close to face-to-face as he could get with a five-foot mahogany desk between them.

Bruno sat back in his chair, basking in the other man's rage. Throughout his life, he found his happiest moments were those when his actions had angered or otherwise hurt another living being. He was the child that grew up lighting ants on fire with glasses stolen from his father while he slept off another alcohol-induced coma. His upbringing was not one of glitz and glamour like Desmond Kalani's surely had been. He'd had to work his whole life, claw his way up from the gutter he came from to the prestige he now felt he had. And here he found power over this man, a man of good repute and dignity, but Bruno had him on the edge of a rope. Exactly where he liked his enemies.

"I never promised that he would not be harmed," Bruno replied. "I merely said we would avoid any unnecessary harm, but believe me, he put himself squarely in the path of it. In fact, he walked into our lab of his own accord as I recall."

"And the barrage of bullets you fired in his direction, were those necessary?" Desmond was visibly on the verge of unraveling.

"Yes." Bruno smiled.

"We're done," Desmond said and turned to leave, "I bought you time with the Zed Agents to clear out your lab, but now I'm done. I've sold enough dignity to you people, giving up information and colleagues I considered friends. But my brother? That's where I draw the line. I'm out."

"How is Kalia, by the way?" Bruno asked as Desmond reached the door. He could almost feel the disdain steaming from the man's entire body. Desmond's free hand, clenched in a fist, began to shake.

"Do not say her name," he spat through gritted teeth. He still gripped the doorknob with such ferocity it looked as if it would pop off if he lost control for even an instant.

"I hear she's responding well to her cancer treatments." Bruno gently rolled the pen laying on his desk. "It would be a shame if they came to an abrupt halt, wouldn't it?"

"You promised her treatments wouldn't stop if I gave you what you wanted. I did that already." Desmond turned to face Bruno, his eyes pleading with him.

"Yes, but you don't tell me when it ends, Desmond. Don't forget where your daughter would be without us. I seem to recall a doctor telling you to say your goodbyes before we stepped in. Now she's living happily in a predicted remission, only weeks of treatment left to go."

"What do you want?" asked Desmond. The question lingered in the air, creating a palpable tension between the two men.

"This Sarah Mercedes Smith. I find it interesting that we've never heard of her from your reports before. How did that happen exactly?" Bruno picked up his pen and lightly tapped it on his forehead.

"Sadie? She's no one of importance. A weak Penumbrial that only recently came across our information desk. Killian was assigned to watch over her, just in case, but she's nothing exceptional."

"A Penumbrial, really? Interesting." Bruno stood, keeping his bandaged hand hidden behind him. "I would very much like you to bring her back to me."

"Why?" Desmond inquired, the ire slowly receding from his face.

"You see, she made me look a fool in front of some very important people." Bruno rubbed the wrapped hand he held behind his back. "And I don't appreciate that. Bring me the girl, and Kalia lives a long and happy life. I promise our business will be concluded and the treatments will continue." He looked up at Desmond, attempting to stare the giant man down.

"And you leave Killian out of this?"

"You have my word, if he stays out of our way," Bruno said, his eyebrow twitching slightly. "We'll leave him be."

"Done." Desmond opened the door and stepped out.

"And General, do be quick about it," Bruno said with a grin as Desmond shut the door behind him. Bruno sat back in his chair, pleased with how the interaction had gone. He called on the intercom, "Miss Ross, get me

Derek on the phone, please." Not only had he secured the information he needed on this "Sadie" Smith, but he had also managed to coerce an asset into giving her up.

"I have Mr. Haynes on the line," called back Miss Ross.

"Derek, I have an assignment for you. Well, the same one. I need you to take care of Killian Quinn for me. Please be thorough this time. Killian has fouled my plans one too many times lately and I can't afford to have him ruin this next one." Bruno looked down at his hand. "Yes, yes, I don't care how you do it, just get it done." He hung up the phone and poured himself a double Scotch out of the decanter on his desk. A twenty-five-year Macallan he'd been aging for a few years himself. He saved it for special occasions. He may have lost a finger this weekend, but what he had found was far more valuable in his eyes: the rarest of beings—a Nox Auris.

Chapter 11

Sadie slid into work with nothing resembling "get-up-and-go." In fact, her overall demeanor was more akin to "stay-down-and-sleep," but her career wouldn't progress itself. For as long as she could remember, working at the Smithsonian had been her dream. She wasn't about to throw away her first big opportunity due to a silly thing like sleep. Not Sadie Smith. She would push herself toward her goal. That was one trait she always prided herself on: being able to accomplish anything she set her mind too. No subject was too lofty, no talent was left undiscovered, she wouldn't let anything or anyone keep her down. So, having only had one hour of sleep, she mustered what energy she could to drag herself to work. Her report was due to Stead before the end of the day. Challenge accepted.

By lunchtime, Sadie had managed to finish proofing the report and sent it off to Jonas for review. She leaned back in her chair to close her eyes for a moment, forgoing food for the blessed few minutes of rest that she could get instead.

"Turkey on rye with avocado, right?"

She awoke with a start to find Allyn standing before her desk, holding out a sandwich from the cart downstairs. "Sorry, I didn't mean to wake you. I saw that you didn't have anything for lunch, so I figured I'd bring you back something. You like turkey and avocado on rye, right?"

There were still good people in the world. People like Allyn. Over the last forty-eight hours of revelations, kidnapping, gunfire, and not to mention all manner of unsavory individuals, Allyn was a breath of fresh air.

"Yes," Sadie responded. "Thank you, Allyn. I didn't have time to grab anything this morning." She took the sandwich from him appreciatively and began unwrapping it as he sat down and unwrapped his own sandwich—bologna and mustard on white. He was a simple man, that Allyn, a man of not-so-discerning tastes.

"So busy weekend or just stayed up cramming for your report?" he asked as he bit into his sandwich, causing mustard to drop out the back onto his azure, Monday sweater vest. In fact, by the time he'd finish that bologna sandwich, most of the mustard would find its way onto his sweater. Still, Allyn smiled. Sadie looked at the man and couldn't help but call to mind the phrase, "Ignorance is bliss." Her own head was filled with thoughts of Domino, the Zeta Defense Agency, and Killian, despite her best efforts to "forget it all," as she'd been instructed.

She finished her sandwich and sat back, listening to Allyn's review of the indie film he'd seen over the weekend, and reached into her pocket, hoping to find a piece of gum. Instead, she found the little round device she'd pocketed at the lab and completely forgotten about. It still glowed purple in her hand as she fiddled with it, while Allyn continued his very one-sided conversation.

"Isn't lunchtime about over, Mr. Green?" a voice startled Sadie from her thoughts. It was Jonas, standing at the door. "I know Sadie is a great listener, but she has work to do too."

"Yes, that's right. Sorry, Sadie, I won't keep you." Allyn stood up and walked toward the door, attempting not to drop all of his wrappers and leftover sandwich bits. "Bye, Dr. Andrews."

"You know he gets flustered easily, Jonas, yet you still surprise him every time," Sadie said once Allyn had left, smiling as she placed the purple glowing disk on her desk. As it slid away from her, the hue began to fade. She stayed looking at it for a moment. *How odd.*

Jonas walked into Sadie's office and took a seat in front of her, pulling her back to the conversation.

"I know, but it's just so much fun." Jonas flashed her his most charming smile. "So your report…"

"Yes! Did you like it?" Sadie sat up a little straighter in her chair, her muscles tensed as she held her breath in anticipation.

"I did." She let out a sigh of relief. "Quite a few errors toward the end there, but I imagine that was done this morning in haste? That's the only explanation I can think of since you're normally an eagle eye when it comes to those sorts of things." Jonas regarded the device on her desk with subtle interest as Sadie tried unsuccessfully to push it under some papers while reaching for her water.

"Yeah, about that, I'm really sorry, this weekend got away from me and I had to finish it this morning." Sadie had let this project slip her mind twice already and was not pleased with herself on that fact. To be fair, she had been kidnapped, drugged, and discovered that not only were there secret societies operating with superpowers but also that she belonged to this select few. Though that wasn't something she could use to explain her tardiness or general sense of aloofness to the mentor sitting before her. She shook her head in an attempt to ground herself back in the present. "But do you think Stead will like it? That's the real question; if it's good enough for her."

"I think she will," Jonas said. "I fixed a few things and added a couple of others to bulk it up a bit, but I think it's ready. Go ahead and give it to her." He handed Sadie a printed and bound document while again glancing at the semi-hidden device on her desk.

"You bound it? How do you find the time, Jonas?" She regarded the laminated and finessed report, complete with cover page.

"I have my ways. So," Jonas said, leaning forward to grab the circular device, "what's this little thing?" He toyed with the now completely dull, white disk, inspecting it from every angle.

"Oh…" Sadie paused, filled instantly with the anxiety of how to explain what it was since, in all honesty, she wasn't sure herself. All she knew was that it changed to purple when she held it. And she was certainly not about to disclose the full details of her eventful weekend. "I'm not sure, one of the kids left it on that tour last week I think. I'm just holding onto it until the teacher gets back to me."

Sadie hated lying, it physically hurt every time she did, but growing up in the system she quickly learned that playing things close to the vest was always the better option. Until she knew what this thing was, she was not going to bring other people into a world she still wasn't sure about.

"Ah, probably a new fidget spinner or something."

Jonas quickly tossed it at Sadie, as if waiting to see her reaction to the thing. It started glowing purple immediately and she pushed it back into her jacket pocket. "Well, you have the report. I emailed it to you as well. And I'd suggest getting it to Stead sooner rather than later," he said as he rose from his chair. "Then get some rest, looks like you could use it."

"Right. Thanks…" Sadie got up and grabbed the report. "I'll take it to her now."

"Let me know how it goes. Honestly, sometimes it feels like no one can understand what goes on in that head of hers." Jonas hung back as Sadie walked down the hall, and she turned back to see him giving her a thumbs up from the doorway.

Sadie prepared herself for the conversation with Stead as she approached her office. While Stead had never said anything directly to make Sadie feel as though she had it out for her, Sadie always felt like she was on Stead's radar.

The first time Sadie met the woman, she had stretched out her hand in greeting and Stead merely stared at her for what felt like an eternity before saying a word. She stared Sadie up and down, as if to size her up, then coldly commented on the bit of mustard on Sadie's face from lunch before she turned and walked away. That's also the reason Sadie hadn't eaten mustard ever since, "The condiment of betrayal," she called it. But after that day, Sadie feared any interaction with the woman. That's why she was so surprised, not to mention terrified, when Stead put her in charge of this new display.

As she arrived at Stead's office, the door was open,

but the room was vacant. *Perfect,* Sadie thought to herself, *I can leave the report on her desk and get out of here.* She went to put the report down on her desk, but a framed picture caught the corner of her eye. The photo appeared to be from the late seventies or early eighties based on the discoloration, the clothes, and the questionable hairstyles. It was Stead, at least it looked like her, albeit much younger. She was standing with two friends outside of the Smithsonian. One, a young man with a medium build, glasses, and dark hair blown out on top and short on the sides. Even in the faded photo, Sadie could still see his piercing, light eyes. She couldn't tell if they were blue or green, but they definitely stood out. The woman on the other side of Stead had long, dark hair, skin that looked like Autumn leaves, and a smile that made the world seem right, like anything was possible. They were all so happy, even Stead with her blown-out, blonde Farrah Fawcett hair and a smile, an honest-to-God smile. It was hard to imagine Valerie Stead ever being that happy, but here was the proof of it.

"Can I help you?" Stead asked from the doorway, her tone sharp.

"I'm so sorry." Sadie turned quickly, knocking over half of the items on Stead's desk. *Oh God, not now, of course I'd make a fool of myself,* she thought, trying to pick everything back up, including the picture of the three young people which now had a massive crack in the glass. "I-I'm sorry," Sadie stammered as she handed the frame back to Stead. "I didn't mean to, I'll replace the frame."

"It's alright, it's not the frame that matters, after all, only the memories associated with the picture. There are more frames in the world," Stead stated calmly as she placed the photo back on the desk where it was and sat down. Sadie turned to leave when Stead stopped her. "Did you have something for me?"

"Yes. On your desk, I mean, here," Sadie said, passing over the report she'd forgotten she was still holding. "My report on the new display. Dr. Andrews has reviewed it as well and we think it'll be a strong display. We're fairly certain we can hit the deadline of ninety days."

"Fairly certain?" Stead raised an eyebrow while she flipped through the report.

"We are certain, ma'am." Sadie couldn't help but continue looking at the broken picture frame. "Ma'am, I'd really like to replace the frame, if you'd let me. It's such a nice photo and it deserves a proper frame."

"If you wish, you may, but you don't have to trouble yourself. It was old anyway," Stead said, staring at the photo like it had been taken a lifetime ago. For a second, it looked like a fragment of her icy facade began to melt.

"Ms. Stead, can I ask you about the photo?" The unexpected jolt of courage to continue the conversation even surprised Sadie as the words fell from her mouth. But she couldn't let go of the opportunity to know more about this woman who had once been so happy but now seemed permanently stoic at the best of times. The irony wasn't lost on Sadie. She herself had shied away from plenty of happy situations for fear of them turning out badly, most recently Killian. But Stead's cautionary tale was beginning to write itself in Sadie's mind. She had to know what happened.

Stead continued to focus on the photo but didn't

object to Sadie's request, so she continued, "That was taken out front of the Smithsonian, wasn't it? Is that when you first started working here?"

"Yes, it was 1979 and I had just started working here. This was my very best friend, Ally, and her boyfriend at the time. We were thick as thieves, the three of us, we called ourselves 'the three musketeers.' Ally and I met in college and were best friends for fifteen years. We thought we had the world at our fingertips when this photo was taken…" Stead seemed to have been transported to another time and place altogether from Sadie's point of view. For a brief moment, Sadie could see the real person that was under her hard shell. Maybe she wasn't so bad after all.

"But that was a lifetime ago," she continued. And like that, the cold, hard Stead was back. "I'll review your report this week and get back to you by Friday. Thank you, Ms. Smith."

"You're welcome, have a good day, ma'am," Sadie said as she turned to leave the office, now with a better understanding of the woman that ran the Smithsonian.

"Ms. Smith," Stead called out. "Is this yours?" She proffered the small disk to Sadie. It glowed a vibrant purple in Stead's hand.

Sadie stopped. All she could do was gaze at the glowing purple device. *No way…* she thought. *Is she…* Sadie looked up to see Stead staring back at her.

"Yes, I'm sorry, it must've fallen out of my pocket when I was picking everything up." Sadie rushed back to grab it and the color didn't change. "Thank you." She could feel Stead's gaze upon her as she walked out of her office.

Does that mean Stead is like me? Sadie thought as she slowly walked back to her own office. *How many Muffles,* as Petey had called them, *are there?* She made it back to her desk and sat down. Her head was starting to ache. Not a sharp pain, just a dull hum in the back of her skull. Killian was right about one thing, she needed to process all of this and "find her footing."

For Sadie, there was only one place that made her feel grounded and thankfully it was only a short walk away.

Chapter 12

In the Albert Einstein Planetarium—Sadie's favorite spot for thinking—the presentation began. She sat alone in the dark, watching as the stars swirled from stationary points to lines stretching across the sky and the universe spun before her. The Earth shrank away to reveal the solar system, the Sun burning so brightly it illuminated the empty room. Its light burst and began to flare out as the galaxy came into view. The blue and purple haze of the Milky Way continued to condense until eventually giving way to the wildest imaginings of the universe.

Ever since her childhood, this was the only place that guaranteed a good view of the stars she loved so much. It was Sadie's way to re-center herself when life threw curveballs her way, and the past weekend had certainly been a curveball.

Dark Universe played backdrop to the thoughts that swirled around her like the Milky Way itself. Would she be able to return to any semblance of normal life after knowing what she could do? Did having this new ability change her view of herself? Would she ever see Killian again?

Stop it, Sadie, she continued to tell herself. There was no denying the connection she felt to the man, but she wasn't about to let herself slip beyond the safety and security of her wall. Not again. Not for a man she barely knew. Regardless of those eyes or that smile that seemed capable of melting stone.

"Hey, Bluebird."

"Oh sh—Killian?" she exclaimed. Killian plopped himself down in the seat next to her. "What are you doing here? Wait, how did you even get in here? This whole museum is closed—"

"For repairs, I know. But it wasn't that hard to get into. And you're in here, aren't you breaking the rules too?" There was that stupid grin again.

"Yes, but I work here. It's different. How'd you know I was in here anyway?"

"This is your spot. Figured after the weekend we had that you'd come here. I wanted to check on you…" Sadie saw the genuine concern fade from his face, replaced with a look of deep sorrow. She knew as well as he that they wouldn't be seeing each other again.

"I think I'm about as okay as you would expect… How have others reacted to it?"

"Honestly, I don't think anyone has ever learned about the ZDA quite like you."

"Leave it to me to be the different one." Sadie laughed in a half-hearted attempt to lighten the mood. She could feel Killian staring at her like she was a wounded gazelle, and she wasn't one to let others pity her.

"Yeah, this really is all on you, isn't it?" Killian jokingly responded. "I'm off the hook?"

"Yep. I'll take this one," she said, looking back up at the stars overhead.

"I don't know how I'll ever repay you."

"I'm sure we'll think of something."

Killian leaned forward, patting both his jacket and pants pockets. "How about some gum?"

"Gum, really? Is that all the gratitude you can—" Sadie looked over to see the zebra-printed pack of gum in Killian's hand. "Wait, is that Fruit Stripe? That's my favorite."

"I know." He shot her a grin again. *Damn that grin.*

"Right, see now, this isn't fair," she said with a smirk as she took a piece of gum. "You even know my favorite gum, but I still know next to nothing about you beyond your terrible taste in nicknames."

"Wait, what's wrong with my nicknaming ability?" Killian frowned as he took a piece for himself.

"Scarface? That's a rip-off. And Bluebird, where did that come from?"

"Okay, Scarface was a good one, first of all," he said, turning his entire body to face Sadie with a look of consternation on his face. "And secondly, Bluebird originated from the first day I was assigned to you." His point made, he calmly settled back into his seat to stare back up at the stars.

"And when was that exactly?" she asked coyly, trying to get as much information as she could.

"Roughly four years ago. You were on the subway and came to the rescue of this redheaded kid against some dumb teenagers."

"I remember that! Kids can be cruel."

"But you got the better of them anyway. And you were wearing this t-shirt with a bluebird on it, so it kind of stuck."

She considered this for a minute. "Alright, I'll allow it then. But the jury is still out on your naming ability.

So what else can you tell me about yourself, Killian James Quinn?"

"What do you want to know?"

"Anything." Really, Sadie would have been thankful for any amount of information to put them on a level playing field. A series of rapid-fire questions popped into her mind. "Favorite color?"

"Green."

"Favorite food?"

"Italian."

"Favorite movie?"

"Oh, now that's not fair. There are so many genres out there, how can someone choose just one?" he pleaded with an incredulous look.

"Okay, okay, if you could only have three movies to watch for the rest of your life, what would they be?"

"*Godfather: Part II*, it's the better choice, let's be honest. *Ace Ventura: Pet Detective*. And, hmmm…" Killian gazed off into the stars that circulated on-screen above them, as if this was some monumental, life-changing answer. "*10 Things I Hate About You*."

"Really? The first two I could see, but then you go and throw a chick-flick in there?"

"What's wrong with that? It's a classic! Julia Styles and Heath Ledger do Shakespeare in a modern-day high school? That's good entertainment right there."

Sadie laughed, allowing herself to forget about the rest of the world, if only for a few seconds. "Alright then, good answer."

"What? Didn't think I was a well-rounded secret agent?" That same winning smile spanned his face.

"No, no, not that. I will give you that. You're a surprise, to say the least." Sadie focused back on the presentation to save herself from being drawn in by that damn grin again.

"So, is there anything else you want to know besides the superfluous?"

"Really? Okay... tell me about your family then." Sadie turned to look him directly in the eyes.

"My family?" Killian asked with one eyebrow raised.

"Yeah. I mean, I've met Desmond. Any other siblings?"

"Oh he was enough, believe me. About as overbearing an older brother as you can get... But he meant well. I never knew my dad and Desmond's dad was always busy with the military. Our mom tried her best, but she worked hard to support us both, so Desmond kind of took over the parenting in his own weird way. Don't get me wrong, he'd still give me noogies and tease me no end, but at the end of the day, I know he'll always be there for me. Stubborn as a mule—he'd fight a mountain if it threatened me. But hey, that's big brothers, right?"

"Yeah..." She dropped her gaze. "Big brothers."

"Oh... that's right. I'm sorry, Sadie."

"No, no, it's okay." *No, it's not*, a voice said in the back of her mind. "I'm used to it." *No, you're not.* "Yes, the orphan thing is a downer, but you push through it." *No, you don't.*

"Really?" Killian looked at Sadie with concern. She realized she was going to that place again, the poor little orphan place she hated to find herself.

"The way I see it," she continued, gesturing to the curved screen, "if the universe can continue to spin amid the likes of black holes and exploding stars, I can keep on breathing and moving forward. Regardless of parental status, or even being kidnapped and learning of secret societies and abilities." She tried to smile, to reassure Killian she was okay. To reassure herself that she was okay.

Killian was quiet for a moment, looking up at the spinning universe as the narrator highlighted various objects in the night sky. "My brother says that too… 'just keep breathing.' He says if you can breathe, you can move forward. It's when you hold your breath that the world moves on without you."

"Your brother sounds like a smart guy."

Killian turned to study Sadie's face. There was a heat to his gaze, she could feel it fixated on her. Part of her wanted so badly to turn and give into that heat, to give into him. But the other part, the part that had been burned before, wouldn't let her. He broke the silence first.

"But what if you don't want to move forward? What if you just want it all to freeze in a single moment?"

Sadie gave in and their eyes locked. She could almost feel the pain hidden behind those soft sapphires. The air was still between them. Her heart thumped a strong, steady beat as if solely charged by the electricity in the air. She took a deep breath and looked away. "I don't think we have much choice in that matter. Things change, move forward, it is the way it is."

"I guess you're right…" Killian lay back in his seat with a barely audible sigh.

"So the *Agency*, tell me more about it."

"Honestly, the less you know the better, as they say…"

"But don't they also say a little knowledge is a dangerous thing? I'm fairly certain *The More You Know* is a more apropos motto right now."

"Maybe, but if—"

A door opened in the far west corner of the room. Sadie immediately sunk further into the chair, eyes focused on the corner, as Killian slid down between rows of seats.

"Who's in here?" a voice called out. Sadie let out a sigh of relief.

"Hey Ron, it's okay. It's just me," she called back in response. Ron was the security guard. He'd been at the Smithsonian for as long as she could remember. He also had a sweet spot for Sadie and gave her access to the planetarium even while the entire National Air and Space Museum was under renovation.

"Oh, Miss Sadie. Phew. You had me scared for a moment. Thought I heard voices. Must be this darned hearing aid of mine. I'm sorry, but the night crew is here, Miss Sadie. I'm going to have to ask you to shut everything down now."

"No worries, Ron. I'll take care of it and meet you outside in a minute."

"Thanks, Miss," Ron said as he left, the heavy door slamming behind him.

Sadie looked around for Killian, but she couldn't find him. One more thing to add to his list of ongoing abilities: the disappearing act.

"That was close."

She almost jumped out of her skin as Killian appeared next to the door that Ron had just exited.

"You've got to stop scaring me like that. How'd you get all the way down there?" she asked as she turned off the projector.

"I am very, very sneaky," he said in a thick Spanish accent. When Sadie looked back at him with confusion, Killian shook his head before continuing. "But really, at this point it's instinctual to put myself between you and potential danger…"

"Well I'll try to avoid potential danger from now on and you can stop scaring me, deal?"

"Deal, Bluebird…"

Killian stared at the ground as the pair left the planetarium. They came to a stop in the museum foyer, and Sadie found herself tracing the lines of tile, not knowing how to say goodbye, not wanting to.

It was her turn to break the silence this time. "So, I'll see you around maybe?"

"Maybe. Hopefully at some point. But for now, it's best if I let the new guy take over. I can't be responsible for any more 'potential danger' in your life, Sadie. I just can't," he said.

The sound of her name on his lips was almost too much for Sadie to handle. She felt the tenderness, the sorrow, the worry in those last few words. She wanted to console him, to hold him close and tell him that everything would be okay. But she couldn't. She didn't know if it would all be okay. She didn't know how to open herself to that vulnerability. Not with Killian.

A voice called out from across the foyer and she let go of Killian's hand, "Walk you out, Miss Sadie?"

Sadie turned to see Ron standing not too far off from

them. "No, it's okay, Ron. I'll be fine. Thank you though." She waved goodbye before turning back to Killian, but he was gone. She was alone again.

Chapter 12.5

"Michael, I have some news for you," Desmond said as Agent Michael Patel took a seat in his office early Tuesday morning.

It was a simple room, exactly what you would expect from a man that had spent the better part of his life in the military. Utilitarian black metal cabinets stood in stark contrast to the white walls. The front wall and door were made of glass, so the office was completely visible from the bullpen area below. It was equipped with a switch to change to frosted glass, should Desmond need to. He had a two-seater couch along the far wall and leather chairs that sat in front of his plain, black desk, which was meticulously organized with an inbox, outbox, computer screen, and roster book.

Desmond didn't bother with frivolous decor. What he did have, though, were two personal objects on the desk. One was a *hei matau koru*, a combination of a swirling whale tale and hook, that his grandfather had carved by hand from the bones of a beached whale in Hana, Maui. It symbolized family, strength, and a connection to his past, or at least that's how Desmond explained it. The other was a photo of his daughter, Kalia, and her mother, Naomi, taken on their family vacation three years ago. Any sort of vacation from the Agency was a rarity in Desmond's life. It was only to the beaches in

Rodanthe, North Carolina, but Kalia loved horses and it was a dream come true to watch them running wild and free on the coast. Desmond had never seen his daughter so happy and having that little face, so full of excitement and wonder, on his desk every day reminded him of what was truly important in life.

Michael stared at the *hei matau koru* as he waited for Desmond to continue. Every Agent that walked into this office stared at the small carving, but none dared to ask about it. Desmond was an amiable albeit demanding man and kept most people at the Zeta Defense Agency at a distance. Not because he didn't enjoy their company, but because he was taught from a young age that duty came first, and if your men were going to respect you, they had to see you command that respect.

Desmond took a deep breath. "I'd like to assign you to field work, on a trial basis."

"Really, sir?!" Michael could barely contain his excitement. "I mean, yes, sir, whatever you need me to do. I'm ready, sir."

"Great, we have a Penumbrial that needs a new Agent assigned to her protection duty. Her previous Zed played a little fast and loose with the rules and she almost got hurt in the process. So I need you to keep an eye on her for me. Make sure trouble doesn't find her and that she doesn't go looking for it. Can you do that for me, Mike?"

"Michael," the Agent mumbled under his breath.

"I'm sorry?" Desmond asked, as if to give the man a chance to reassert himself.

"Nothing, sir. I won't let you down, sir," Michael said as he left the office.

"I'm sure you won't." It pained Desmond to do this to the poor man. All Michael wanted was a chance, but Desmond knew his best opportunity to turn Sadie over to Soto without arousing suspicion was to put the most inexperienced Agent on her guard duty.

∞

Desmond stopped in front of his home in Bethesda, a quaint, two-story Tudor-style house with a bright blue door. Even from the driveway, he could hear his little girl squeal with delight as she and her mom danced to Disney music. He walked in to find them twirling around the kitchen singing "I am Moana!"

"Daddy!" Kalia shrieked with excitement. "Come play with us, you can be Maui!" She ran up and handed him a spatula to hold. "Here's your hook!"

"My hook," he said, dropping his bags by the door and scooping his daughter into his arms. "Well then, I'm going to be a great hawk and fly you all around the ocean."

Moana was Kalia's favorite because, as she said, "They look like me, you, and Mommy!" They had probably watched the movie together at least five hundred times in the last couple of years. Whenever Kalia went in for treatment, that's the movie she would want to watch. Desmond knew every word verbatim, but any time he heard the songs, his heart hurt because he associated it with his daughter's sickness.

"Oh no, it's Ta'ka!" Desmond said as he and Kalia crashed onto the couch. "I'm hit, I'm done. Continue without me, Moana."

"Nooooo, Daddy," she said. "That's not how it goes."

"No? How about this?" he asked as he began tickling her incessantly. "Is that how it goes?" Kalia's childish laughter filled the entire house until she started coughing. A reminder that Desmond's perfect little girl was still sick. No amount of laughter would stop that from being true.

"Okay," Naomi said, coming into the room. "Time for all the little princesses to get ready for bath time. Your father can come kiss you goodnight once you're in bed."

"Daughter of the Chief," Kalia corrected, rolling off the couch. "Thanks, Daddy." She craned on her tiptoes to give her father a kiss on the cheek. It still amazed Desmond how much someone so small could overwhelm every sense in his body and take total control of his heart.

"See you soon, pumpkin-eater." Desmond stood and walked toward his office.

"I saved you a plate for dinner, it's on the table," Naomi called out.

"I'm okay, thanks, I've got some work to do," he called back, already opening the office door. "Let me know when she's ready."

Desmond's home office wasn't that dissimilar to his one at the ZDA—utilitarian design at its finest. But there was one significant difference. The room was filled with mementos that his daughter Kalia had made for him over the years: a macaroni masterpiece of a whale, a miniature clay sculpture of a bottle and a hamburger, and a flower that she had picked for him at school last week. It could never be said that Desmond wasn't a family man—maybe that's what made his betrayal that much more difficult to swallow.

His father Eli had instilled a sense of duty in him, to family and to responsibility. Even after Desmond's parents split when he was six years old, Eli continued to support the family monetarily, though work took most of his time. Before Desmond learned about Eli's true work at the Agency, he had resented that he took second place in his father's life. But it wasn't until thirteen years ago, when Eli was dying, that they ever discussed it. The night Desmond spoke to his father for the last time.

"I know you resent our relationship—" Eli had begun on that cool September night as Desmond sat at his father's bedside.

"Dad, it's okay—"

"Don't interrupt me. It's understandable. I put too many things ahead of you and your mother, and it wasn't right. You two were the best things that ever happened to me, Desmond. And I put my work ahead of that. I'm sorry. Know that if I could do things differently, I would, and don't go making the same mistakes. You have a responsibility to the Agency, to the people, as we all do. But don't let it be at the expense of your own life. Find someone that makes you happy and never let her go. Family first, always remember that."

Eli would never know how soon his son came to understand those words; he'd passed away that night in his sleep.

Two weeks later, Desmond found himself flying his father's remains to Hawaii for the burial ceremony in Hana, Maui. He hadn't been to the island since he was a boy, again for a funeral, that time his grandfather's. He hadn't known much about the man, or the rest of his

Hawaiian family, for the matter. Eli joined the military as a young man and left the island, never really looking back. On Desmond's first visit to Hawaii at the age of ten, he began to learn about his heritage and his family, the one his father had left behind. Desmond always had every intention of going back, but life got in the way, as it usually does. So it wasn't until sixteen years later that he stepped foot on the island of his ancestors to bury another family member.

After the ceremony, Desmond found the nearest purveyor of spirits on this island. Still in his dress blues, Desmond and his late father were military men after all, he walked into a little place called the Umbrella Tree Bar and came face-to-face with the beautiful and enigmatic Naomi.

"What can I get for you, soldier?" she said with a joie-de-vivre that Desmond had rarely encountered in his twenty-six years. She had long, straight, black hair tied into a braid that wrapped around to rest on her collarbone. Desmond found himself trailing the line of her hair to the necklace she wore—a wooden carving of a fish hook that blended into a whale tail. He thought back to the *hei matau koru* that he'd found in a box among his father's belongings along with a note addressed to him that read only, *Carved by your grandfather.* The piece was inscribed with the phrase, "*hele mua ka ʻohana,*" meaning family comes first.

"Hey there, you still with us?" Naomi's voice called Desmond back to the Umbrella Tree Bar.

"Um… Yeah, sorry. Zoned out for a minute. What did you ask?"

"What can I get for you?" She looked at Desmond with a curiosity and kindness that he needed in his life at that moment.

"Alcohol. Whatever you've got."

"We've got plenty," she replied and selected a cold beer from the fridge behind her, cracking it open. "So leave or assignment?"

"Funeral," he replied flatly. Even though he wasn't close with his father, in fact Eli Kalani had been close with very few in his life, Desmond still felt a twinge of pain at the word as it echoed in his head.

Naomi paused, Desmond's beer still in her hand. "You're Kalani's son, aren't you?"

"So you knew him then?"

"I knew the family." She grabbed two glasses from beneath the bar along with a bottle of bourbon from the top shelf. After pouring both, she raised hers to the sky. "To Eli Kalani."

"To my father," Desmond echoed solemnly.

"You know your grandfather is the reason I'm here today? When I was a child, I snuck out of the house to follow my big brother to the beach for a late-night surfing session. I was only seven or eight at the time, but I wanted to do everything he did. He didn't know I had followed him, or that I brought a board along with me. I could barely carry the thing, let alone ride it by myself, but I was determined to try.

"When the waves inevitably swept the board away from me, I was pulled along by the leash on my ankle and I couldn't get my footing. Your grandfather happened to be on the beach that night and must've heard me struggling in the waves because, at sixty-two years of age, that man dove into the ocean to pull out a scared little girl and save her life. He carved this for me the next week, to remind me to be brave enough to ask for help, especially from family members. I've worn it every day since. I never met your father, but if he's anything like his father, he was a great man. So here's to the Kalani family." She raised the glass again and finished it off.

"Thank you," Desmond responded. He knew the type of man his father was, a Guardian through and through, but learning that this was a family legacy made Desmond feel like it was in their blood to protect people. It was his responsibility.

"Ya know, all this funeral and family talk can get a bit heavy. And life can become hard trying to get through it, but there's one thing my family has always said, 'just keep breathing.' When you feel you can't go on, take a breath. Then another. Focus on that and anything is possible."

Those words were etched into the corners of Desmond's mind that night. He proceeded to spend the remainder of the evening talking with Naomi. By the end, Desmond found himself smiling, and not just that, but genuinely happy for the first time in a long while. Naomi had uncovered a bright spot of hope left inside of him. At the end of his two weeks in Hawaii, he was determined not to let that happiness slip away.

He couldn't avoid his responsibilities at home any longer but begged Naomi to come back with him to DC. Being the free spirit she was, she agreed. Six months later the pair were married. In the thirteen years they'd been together, her words continued to pick Desmond up when he felt the world caving in on him. Desmond knew the truth; *he* wasn't the source of strength. It was Naomi's words, her bold smile, her unwavering faith in him that was the true strengthening force in his life. And he would do anything to keep a firm hold on that force.

When Desmond and his wife had Kalia, he made a promise to them and to himself that he would never let anything take first place in his life, not even his work with the Agency. Family first. That was his mantra and that was what had led to the predicament he found himself in. When faced with the possibility of losing his daughter, he had lost all hope. He became a broken man, full of rage at his helplessness. Desmond prided himself on fixing problems, but he was unable to fix the problem of saving the person he loved most in the world.

That was, until Domino. When they'd received a letter accepting Kalia onto the medical trial, they never questioned the source. They were overjoyed. Their prayers had finally been answered. It wasn't until three months later when Desmond learned the truth about Domino's involvement and he began to tear apart inside. It started small at first. Diverting a few archival runs to Domino's lab. Then siphoning off funds earmarked for expansion into Soto's account instead. It was a small price to pay for Kalia's life. No one at the ZDA was really getting hurt by it, no one besides Desmond, who could feel his soul slip with each act. Then they started asking for more detailed information, intel about the Agents that worked at the ZDA and the assets they protected. He had managed to delude himself into believing that Soto wasn't going to hurt anyone, that the man could be reasoned with, and maybe, once Kalia was better, Desmond could turn the tables on him and shut down his whole operation. Cripple Domino from the inside like they'd attempted to do to the ZDA.

It wasn't until the first asset went missing that Desmond realized how naïve he'd been. When the two Agents assigned to protect the asset died unexpectedly, he was already too deep in an ocean of deceit to do anything about it. He couldn't keep his head above water anymore. The only thing keeping him from letting the water rush in and drag him down to its darkest depths was his daughter. She was the light in his shadows. Her smiling face that greeted him every night when he arrived home from work, the goodnight kisses. She was getting better, there was no denying it. As Desmond's life slipped away from him, his wife and daughter found new life every day. He deemed it an acceptable cost, his soul for their happiness.

Desmond poured himself a bourbon and swirled the glass in his hand as he stared into the lit fireplace in his office. His mind drifted to the awful things he'd already done. *So many things. I'm sorry...* He reached for the red ball that sat next to a photograph of himself with Killian. *Killian,* he thought, *that was too close.* He squeezed the ball in his hand. *Can we hold on for just a few more days, brother?* As he watched the flames dance in the grate, leaping out as if to grab him and pull him into the fire, he felt the fissure inside of him growing wider. Was he willing to trade the life of one woman, this Sadie Smith, to have his daughter's life secured and finally be rid of Domino?

A knock at the door pulled him back to reality. "*Ku'u lei*," Naomi stood in the doorway, "our princess is waiting for you."

The last few years had left their mark on Naomi, but there was no telling Desmond that. Every time he saw her, he fell in love with her all over again. Gray might have teased at her temples and frown lines creased her forehead, but her smile still held true. That only made his guilt that much worse, knowing she still stood by him, unaware of the damage his decisions had wreaked.

"I'll be right there, love." Desmond turned back toward the fireplace, swirling his bourbon once more.

"Hey, are you okay?" Naomi asked, walking closer to him. "You seem like you've been somewhere else for a while now. What's going on?"

"Yes, I'm okay." He tried to smile, put on his brave face for her. He wasn't sure it would work this time. She knew. At least, she knew *something*. Naomi understood Desmond better than most and there was little that escaped her attention. It hadn't taken her long into their marriage to get the truth of the ZDA out of him. Still, Desmond was always careful to keep the details to a minimum, especially after Kalia was diagnosed. Naomi didn't need any additional stress in her life after that. He was grateful to have someone understand, even if it was in a limited sense.

"I'll be okay."

She noticed the ball in his hand. "So Killian got himself into trouble again?"

"When doesn't he?" Desmond chuckled. "It's bigger this time."

"You know Killian, he always manages to get himself into trouble, but somehow he finds his way out of it too."

"Yeah, because I'm there for him."

"You don't give him enough credit, Des." She gently folded her arms around her husband from behind. The warmth of her body was a welcome consolation. "Don't forget who raised him, who took him from delinquent to Agent. He's got a good heart, Desmond, and you've taught him well. Have a little faith in him."

It's not my faith in him I'm worried about, Desmond thought. *It's my faith in me.* He drained the rest of his glass and put his hands on Naomi's. She was right; he had been somewhere else. They hadn't really talked in months. He was going to change that.

"Daddy, you didn't come say goodnight." Kalia stood in the doorway, holding her teddy bear. So small, so innocent. Desmond's whole life was in that room. In that moment, he made his decision.

"Oh, I'm sorry, love. Let's get you back into bed." If it meant his family would be safe for good, his soul could handle one more tear. At least, that's what he hoped.

Chapter 13

The days seemed to drag on for Sadie. Her weekend had been like something out of a book, and her love of stories compelled her to continue living in that world. A world of mystery, intrigue, and treachery. But instead Sadie found herself cataloging volumes and proofing the work of other associates at the Smithsonian—things she once loved to do. She didn't hate it, but the back of her mind ached for Killian and his life of adventure.

She'd spent the better part of the week looking over her shoulder for him, but he wasn't there. Gone was the man with dark, wavy hair and light blue eyes. The man that wore reckless abandon like a tailored three-piece suit.

Not worth it, Sadie, she told herself. *He's in another domain altogether.*

An intra-office message popped up on her computer screen.

"Coffee break?" It was Allyn. He'd been trying all week to get Sadie out of her slump, this was just the latest attempt. She could use a break, though, and maybe caffeine would help the dull headache that had been pulsing in the back of her head since Monday evening. It seemed that no matter what she did, there was a constant buzzing in the base of her skull that wouldn't go away. She assumed it was stress from the weekend—a break would do her good.

"Sure," she responded, gathering her purse and phone.

"*Great, meet you downstairs.*" Allyn, reliably kind as ever. He would give the shirt off his back to anyone that asked. Granted, it would more likely be a sweater vest, but the principle applies.

∞

"So we wager all but two of our points on this last bonus question thinking even if we're wrong, which is unlikely, we'll still win. And the question, get this, the question is, 'How many crystals were in Darth Maul's two-bladed lightsaber in *The Phantom Menace* according to current canon? And so Bobby, he says four, and I was like, 'No, no, no, that's according to Legends, but according to the *current* movie cannon, it's definitely six!' And we go back and forth because the whole table agrees with dumb Bobby, but at the last minute I steal his piece of paper with the answer and replace it with mine that says six and turn it in. And we won! It was amazing! Best trivia night. Ever!" Allyn laughed and threw himself back in his chair in triumph. Every Thursday brought a detailed regaling of Wednesday night trivia.

"Good for you," Sadie said. "Stick to your guns." She tried to smile and gave a slight chuckle, but the persistent headache seemed to be worse in the packed coffee shop.

"So..." he said with a look of empathy on his face. Sadie knew she wasn't her usual self and could tell Allyn didn't know what to do to help, but he was trying and for that she was thankful. "Any word back from Stead yet on your report for the display?"

"No, nothing yet. She probably ripped it all apart and gave it back to Jonas to fix," Sadie said with a dry laugh.

Out of the corner of her eye, she noticed a man in a suit observing her while he waited for his coffee. Then he sat down at a nearby table with a newspaper and his drink.

"I'm sure it was great and she's just not had a chance to read it yet," Allyn said.

But Sadie barely heard his platitude, she was busy watching the suited man a few tables behind him. The one sitting alone reading yesterday's paper—the one she suspected was watching her too. He had dark brown hair, cut short on the side and gelled back on top. His black suit and pristine white shirt were perfectly ironed, his black leather Oxfords buffed and polished to the point of reflecting light. He dropped his glasses down slightly while reading the paper and glanced up in Sadie's direction every so often. When he noticed her looking back at him, he readjusted himself in his seat to hide more fully behind the newspaper.

"…no idea how smart you really are, do you?" Allyn's voice called Sadie back to the conversation.

"What did you say?" she asked.

"Hm? The report, I bet you have no idea how good it was. Are you okay?" Allyn asked, looking around. "Is there something going on behind me?"

"I'll be right back," she said, getting up from the table and walking toward the man. It was a crowded shop, making it difficult to get to him, but not so crowded that he had anywhere to hide.

"Hi, I'm Sadie, but I'm guessing you already know that."

"Hmm, I'm sorry? How would I know that, ma'am?" He turned back to his paper.

She continued, "Desmond said he'd be reassigning

Agent Quinn. You must be the new Zed. You're supposed to protect me, right?"

"I think you have me confused with someone else," the man looked around nervously.

"So if I were to run out into the street, in front of a car, you'd do nothing?"

"I would advise anyone against that, ma'am. But please don't."

"How long have you worked at the Agency then, Mr...? Do I get to know your name?" She sat across from him, moved his coffee, put her elbow on the table, and rested her head on her hand. She was determined not to leave without answers. Maybe there *was* a way to get back into Killian's world.

"I don't think that would be wise, Ms. Smith," said the man, moving his coffee cup back to where it was.

Sadie smirked at the slip he'd just made. She'd never given him her last name. "I don't really care what would be wise, sir. If you're going to be following me and clearly know everything there is to know about me, like Killian apparently did, I think it's only fair I at least know your name," she said, moving his coffee to the side again. His nostrils flared as he went to grab his cup, but she moved it and held onto this time. Maybe it was the tension headache, maybe it was the desire to re-enter their world, but Sadie was not going to be pushed around anymore. If anything, she found herself doing the pushing. She picked up the man's coffee and smelled it. "Mmm, cappuccino with coconut milk, and is that cinnamon I smell? Nice choice."

He twitched, almost imperceptibly, but Sadie caught

it. She had him. She slowly raised the cup to her lips.

"Michael," he said curtly, reaching for the cup before she could actually take a sip from it.

"Now was that so hard, Mike?" asked Sadie as she relinquished the coffee back to him.

"Michael," he repeated

"What?"

"My name is Michael, not Mike. Mikes are what you talk into." He set his drink back down exactly where it was before, even turning it to face the same direction, and returned to his paper.

"Okay then. That's a start." Sadie glanced back at Allyn, trying to mind his own business as he cleaned up the coffee he'd inevitably spilled on the table. She wanted to stay, to push this new Zed even more, but looking at Allyn there alone reminded her of who she was. She couldn't let him sit there much longer. Sadie turned back to Michael.

"I have to get to work, but I'm sure we'll be seeing plenty of each other in the future. Take care, Mike," she said before rising and heading back to her table.

Allyn looked up at her, eyes wide. "What was that about?"

"Nothing. Let's get back to work," she said and ushered him out the door. At the last minute, she turned to wave goodbye to Michael, making a mental note that she would do everything she could to get closer to that man. She'd had a taste of adventure and she wanted more.

Chapter 13.5

Killian paced in Petey's room, playing with the memorabilia that covered the walls and surfaces. He grabbed a toy pistol, pretending to shoot the invisible enemies surrounding him and simultaneously setting off a barrage of sounds from the toy.

"Careful with that," Petey snapped. "It's a classic! A Kenner blaster from the eighties, it's almost an exact replica of the blaster Harrison used in *A New Hope*, complete with working soundboard. There are only a handful of those in the world."

"Sorry," Killian responded, gingerly putting the pistol back on its stand, and continued his personal tour of Petey's room until he found an odd-shaped squeeze ball. He sat on Petey's bed, throwing the ball at the ceiling while his friend typed furiously at the computer.

"What is taking so long?" Killian grumbled. "We've been at this for two nights in a row. How was I able to read everything on that hard drive at the lab, but now when we want to dive into it, we can't get in?"

"Because it was a network-encrypted drive. When it was on their network, it was a free flow of information, now that connection has been severed, it's locked up tighter than Fort Knox. If you would like to give it a go, please, be my guest."

Killian sighed then continued throwing the ball

at the ceiling.

"Because that doesn't make concentrating on this any more difficult," Petey spat, clearly frustrated. "And please don't throw that at the ceiling, it's not a ball, it's a Holy Hand Grenade replica."

"I'm sorry, but with the lab gone, that hard drive is our only connection to these people. There has to be something on there that gives us a clue as to who the mole is."

"I know, buddy, and I'm trying. But they apparently have some amazing coders on their side too. Try taking your mind off of it."

A difficult request for Killian. He tossed the ball in front of him, a habit he'd had since he was a kid. It used to annoy Desmond to no end. They had lived in a modest house in Baltimore, small and thin walled. Killian started throwing the ball as a way to think when the weather kept them inside. One particular night, Desmond hit his tipping point.

"Would you stop it with the damn ball?" he had yelled as he ripped into Killian's room.

"What's your problem with it, fart face, I'm in *my* room."

"Because, donkey breath, I can hear it in mine and I'm trying to study! I've got a final in the morning," Desmond said, snatching the ball mid-air.

"Why bother, you know you're going into the army like your dad anyway. What's the point of school?" Ten-year-old Killian had thrown himself back on his bed.

"It takes more than brawn to succeed in the military." Desmond chucked the ball at Killian and pulled him in for a noogie. "*And* life, for that matter."

"Easy for you to say, you've got it all. You're huge, you get all A's and, bonus, everyone loves you. Your life is easy."

"Yeah, my life is pretty good. But it's not perfect, I have a really annoying little brother to deal with," Desmond said, picking up the ball again and tossing it in the air himself.

"Whatever, I'm the best little brother you could have and you know it!" Killian exclaimed, climbing on top of Desmond in an effort to steal the ball back.

"Oh do I?" He stood up, playing keep-away for a minute, then finally acquiescing and passing the ball back to Killian. "Yeah, I guess you're alright," he said, turning to leave.

"Hey, Des…" Killian threw the ball toward Desmond.
"Yeah?"
"How d'ya do it?"
"Do what, kid?"
"Get everyone to like you? Especially the girls…"
"Is this what the ball throwing is about? Does my little bro have his eye on a girl?" Desmond came back and sat next to his little brother.

"Maybe, but I don't think she even knows I exist."

"Well, thankfully you're talking to a master silver tongue, and because I like you, just this once I'll impart my vast knowledge of the female species," he said as he pitched the ball to Killian again.

They continued passing that ball back and forth almost until morning as Desmond taught Killian about love and life. Killian relishing every minute with his big brother. All the while they kept throwing that ball, a tradition that had lasted through their adult lives. Any time either of them had a problem, tossing a ball was their way of working it out.

Petey's alarm clock went off.

"I'm sorry." Petey stood up. "It's 8 a.m., we've gotta get to work and it's still processing. I'll keep going on it tonight though."

"Yeah…" Killian caught the ball for the last time as his phone dinged with an email alert.

Killian Quinn, you are hereby put on administrative leave. Effective Immediately.

"What!"

"What's up?" Petey asked as he put his customary work hoodie on for the day.

"They're putting me on leave? Effective today!" Killian looked at his phone in disbelief. "Why would Desmond put me on leave and not even say anything?"

"I don't know, man, but I wouldn't mess with it. We pulled a lot of crap last week and I'm just glad we didn't get fired. Take the rest of the week, clear your head. Maybe it'll give us a chance to get this unlocked and we can go to Des first thing Monday with clear evidence?"

"Yeah, maybe you're right," Killian said as the two walked out of Petey's apartment.

"Go take a break, I don't think you've done anything for yourself in years. Play tourist for the day or something. And I'll call you if I get anywhere with the drive."

"Thanks," Killian said, and Petey left him standing on the street outside the apartment. He was right though, Killian hadn't had a day off in years, albeit by choice. As the years passed while watching Bluebird, Killian had found it harder and harder to pull himself away from her.

Killian's "day off" ended up turning into an opportunity for his disappointment and anger to fester. He'd spent the better part of the afternoon at a pub before he stormed into the bullpen at the ZDA. Petey stopped him in his tracks.

"Killian, man, you can't go in there right now, take a beat," he said, trying to hold the smaller man back.

"Move, Petey, this doesn't concern you," Killian said, stumbling forward.

"Have you been drinking?"

"Yes, but I don't see why that's important."

"Come on, you don't want to talk to Des like this. Let's go get some coffee and talk it out."

"No! No more talking, I want to talk to Desmond, to my perfect big brother." Killian stared straight into Petey's eyes. "Now move, Analyst Jackson," he said with all the rage of a wild animal.

"It's your grave." Petey shrugged, stepping aside.

Killian crashed into Desmond's office. "Administrative leave! You're kicking me out? Now?" He was quickly followed by Desmond's secretary, Casey.

"I'm sorry, sir, I tried to stop him," she said.

"It's okay, Casey. Killian, calm down," Desmond replied, flipping the switch on his desk to turn the glass from clear to frosted. Casey closed the door behind her as she left, still looking at Desmond apologetically.

"I won't calm down, I get that you took me off guarding Sadie, but come on, I'm the closest one to this problem. I knew Nebraska better than anyone. She left that letter to me. She trusted *me* to finish this."

"Have you been drinking, Killian?" Desmond asked. Even through blurred vision, Killian could see the disappointed look on his brother's face. Killian didn't care.

"I need to be out there, working," he continued, ignoring Desmond's comment. "And what does it matter if I've been drinking? It's not important! What is important is that there is still a mole out there—"

"There is no mole!" Desmond roared. He was not a man prone to losing his temper, so when he did, it was serious. "Killian, I've had teams poring over the information you got from Nebraska and I'm sorry to say, but there's nothing there. It's all circumstantial. Nebraska was a great Agent, but none of us are perfect."

"You can't be serious. There's no way you can explain away everything she found. If you had read—" Killian stopped before he could implicate himself in the theft of the prototype CarterScott device. He couldn't risk the one last safety net she'd left him. He felt trapped. *Why won't he believe me? For once!* Killian thought as he paced the office like a caged lion, hungry for answers.

"I did read Nebraska's notes, Killian. Including her letter to you about Oliver. She was obviously distraught over his death. And now you're following in her footsteps!"

"At least one of us is! You *know* there had to be something more there!" Killian screamed.

"*Kokami*, Killian! You can find patterns in anything if you look hard enough." Desmond picked up a box of paperclips on his desk and slammed them on the floor in front of Killian. "There! I bet if you looked long enough you would find a pattern because you're looking for one. Sometimes things just happen. What happened to Nebraska was horrible, but unfortunately she was in the wrong place at the wrong time. I don't want you going down the same path."

Killian collapsed onto the couch with his head in his hands. "It's not fair, Des, she was the best of us. How could some lowlife just kill her for the change in her pocket?" He broke down.

"It's an unfortunate part of the world in which we live, brother." Desmond came and sat next to him, putting an arm on his shoulder. "Go home, Killian. Reset yourself mentally, come back better than ever."

"Maybe you're right." Killian's head was swimming, not just because of the booze, but with the implications of Nebraska being wrong. It meant that not only had he gone on a wild goose chase, but he'd inadvertently put Sadie in harm's way for no reason. This whole time he had justified his actions on the basis of finishing what Nebraska had started, but if she was wrong? Then he was the same old Rookie that ran into danger without thinking. And this time it had almost cost him more than he ever imagined. He would never let Sadie fall into that danger again.

Killian started for the door. "Thanks, Desmond, for trying."

"You know I'm always here for you, little brother." Desmond grabbed a ball from his desk, the one he'd brought from home, the same one they always tossed whenever there was a problem at work, and threw it to Killian. It was Killian's turn to hold on to it now.

"Thanks. Damn, Des, you've squashed it. You been

stressed out or something?" He knew the answer already. Even with Kalia doing better, he knew Desmond still worried about her constantly.

"Or something," Desmond scoffed.

"You've gotta be careful with this thing, I think it's older than some of our newest recruits." Killian tossed it around a few times. "By the way, who did you assign to watch over Sadie?" he asked as he grabbed the door handle.

"Agent Patel," Desmond said, sitting back at his desk.

"Mike?" Killian screamed.

"I believe he prefers Michael."

"Whatever! The guy that literally counts the number of Cheerios in his breakfast bowl each morning? That's who you assigned to watch over Sadie? He's the worst!" Killian marched back to Desmond's desk, anger rekindled.

"He may be eccentric, but he's one of the most conscientious and fastidious Agents we have. And that's what she needs right now, someone that won't interfere with her life." Desmond looked at him pointedly.

"But he's useless in the field!"

"That's not true, Killian, he's had the same training that you have. He knows how to handle himself and I have full confidence in him. Now go home, take the week to relax. And leave Sadie Smith alone. You know she's safer for it right now. Forget about her."

Forget about her, Killian thought to himself. How could he ever forget about her? He'd spent the better part of four years watching her, protecting her, learning everything there was to know about her, and he was supposed to forget about her, just like that? Like turning off a switch? It wasn't that easy.

Killian left Desmond's office without another word. But he wouldn't be going home.

∞

Michael Patel sat in his black Lincoln Continental, listening to the Jonas Brothers on the radio. He didn't like to admit to people that he enjoyed pop music, but it was a guilty pleasure.

He'd only been assigned to 602 for twelve hours and had already broken as many protocols, but no matter how bad of a mood he was in, an upbeat tempo and light-hearted lyrics always made it better.

Truth be told, 602 was Michael's first Penumbrial assignment. Until today, he'd been an analyst that longed for the field. He'd passed every physical test the ZDA had to offer but had a problem on the firing range. His nervous anxiety made firing a weapon difficult for him, but he still continued to apply for field work. Maybe that's why he'd been so surprised that Desmond had assigned him to his first field duty. He would take this job more seriously than any other he'd ever had, which was proving to be a problem when Ms. Smith continued to break protocol.

His phone buzzed on the seat next to him. It was a video call from his mother back in Chicago.

"Hi Mom," he said, turning down the music as his mother's face appeared on the screen.

"Michael, how are you, Beta?" She frowned. "You look thin, are you eating?"

"Yes, Mom, it's just the lighting. It's dark and I'm in the car." He turned the light on. "See, is that better?"

"You shouldn't be video conferencing when you drive, Beta, it's not safe."

"I'm not driving, I'm parked, it's okay," he said, glancing back up to 602's apartment. Her light was still on so she hadn't gone to sleep yet.

"How about food, Beta. Are you eating well? You're not eating those O pasta things out of a can still, are you?"

"They're SpaghettiOs, Aavi." Whenever he spent more than five minutes speaking to his parents, his accent started creeping back. While Michael had only recently moved from Chicago, he and his parents were originally from Mumbai and had emigrated to America in the eighties when Michael was only nine years old. "And yes, I'm still eating them. I'm a grown man, I can eat what I want." The very mention of the sodium-ridden, processed Italian treat made Michael's stomach rumble. He hadn't eaten since lunch and now he wanted SpaghettiOs. He found a calmness in their uniformity. He tried alphabet soup once, but it wasn't the same. He swore he could taste the difference in each letter. Granted, it could've been that he had attempted to eat them in alphabetical order so the As were distinctly warmer, and thereby tastier, than the Zs.

"Ask how his promotion is going," Michael's father said from off camera.

"Your father wants to know how the promotion is going," his mother asked.

"Yes, I heard him. It's going well, Baba," Michael replied as his father came into view. He still wore the mustache that he'd sported since the seventies.

"Good boy! You do us proud," his father said.

"Kavita's mother called me today, Beta, you remember Kavita, right?"

"Yes, Mummy, I do." Kavita was the daughter of one of his mother's friends. While his parents had agreed to give up the notion of an arranged marriage, claiming to be more modern, it didn't stop Michael's mother from strongly suggesting her own "perfect match" for her son.

"Well, she said Kavita will actually be visiting New York next week, you should go meet up with her."

Michael sighed. "New York isn't close to DC. It's over four hours away."

"You could make a weekend of it then," she said, unphased by this minor obstacle.

"I'll let you know, Mu—" A whack on the passenger window surprised Michael and he let out a rather girlish scream. "I have to go. Love you, talk later." He hung up the phone and looked out the window. "Agent Quinn!"

Killian Quinn stood outside Michael's passenger door with a black hoodie pulled over his head. "Let me in, Mike."

"It's Michael," he said under his breath as he unlocked the car door. "What are you doing here? You're not assigned to 602 anymore, you can't be here, it's against proto—"

"Yeah, yeah, I know, against protocol," Killian interjected. "I just wanted to check in and see how you're doing, this being your first field assignment and all."

"Oh, okay," Michael said, not quite believing it but appreciating the salvation from his overbearing parents. As Killian sat inside the car and closed the door, Michael was thankful he already had the music turned down.

"It's going well. She got home about an hour ago, I did a perimeter check, all clear."

"Good, good, and the secondary perimeter check?"

"Secondary perimeter check?" Michael asked anxiously. Had he messed up yet another protocol?

"Yeah, the second perimeter check. Supposed to be done thirty minutes after the first. You didn't do it?"

"No, I-I didn't know about a second perimeter check."

"You better go do it now. You always have to do two because, ya know, Domino would expect the first, but not the second," Killian said, tapping his temple.

"Right, good thinking. I'll be right back. Watch 602 for me?" Michael asked, hopping out of the vehicle.

"Of course! Go, I'll watch her."

"And you're not going to tell anyone back at headquarters what happened, right? That I missed the second perimeter check?"

"Oh, course not, we're brothers in arms now. We watch out for each other." Killian winked.

"Thanks!" Michael ran off into the night, humming the theme song to *X Company*, with a white-knuckle grip on the gun that still rested in its holster. He was determined not to make another mistake, there wouldn't be another chance at field work and he would not mess this one up.

Chapter 14

Sadie sat on her couch, trying to make some headway on her 1,100-page novel, which was proving difficult after the real-life adventure that she'd found herself in. And she kept getting distracted by the small, purple disk. She turned it over and over again in her hands, thinking back to her interaction with Stead. *How many more Penumbrials are there? Do any of them know,* she thought to herself.

A knock at the door put her senses on high alert. She pocketed the device and reached for the bat she now kept hidden behind her couch. It might have seemed silly to others but having some sort of a weapon offset the unease she felt after last weekend's affair.

Sadie inched quietly toward the door, bat in hand, and looked through the peephole. It was Killian Quinn.

She opened the door and exclaimed, "Killian! What are you doing here?" She immediately became aware of the ripped hoodie and pajama bottoms she was wearing, hoping she hadn't spilled anything on them recently.

"Hey," he said, pushing past her to switch the lights off.

"Sure, come on in. Are you okay?" Sadie watched him with concern.

"I'm fine, I just don't want anyone to know I'm here." He began turning off every light in the apartment except the front entry light, which couldn't be seen from the window.

"What are you doing? Why do you smell like beer and wet dog?" she asked suspiciously.

"Not important. Why does everyone keep asking me that? And I'm turning the lights off because the new Agent assigned to protect you is downstairs and I don't want him to know that I'm up here."

"Michael? Are you not supposed to be here?"

"Wait, you've met him?"

"Yeah, yesterday, we had coffee."

Killian stopped in his tracks to turn and look at Sadie, dumbfounded. "How'd you…"

"I picked him out. It wasn't that hard, I've got a thing for faces and had already noticed him watching me so I went up to him and said hi."

"Sadie, he could've been a Domino operative, why would you do something so reckless?" Anger and disappointment echoed in that last word.

Reckless? Sadie thought, a heat rising within her.

"Oh, *I'm* the reckless one? You were the one that turned yourself into them with zero plan. And if you thought about it for two seconds, you'd realize that I knew he wasn't Domino, because if he had been, he could've grabbed me at any point in the day. They kidnapped me in the middle of a crowded farmers' market, remember? I don't think they're ones for stealth," she snapped, concerned that this wasn't obvious to Killian, the supposed super spy. She knew it was harsh, especially as his mentor had echoed the same sentiment, but in true Sadie form, she found herself trying to push him away.

"Now, why are you here and why can't Michael know about it?" she asked and stood back, arms crossed.

"Because I don't trust Mike," Killian said in hushed tones as he squatted down against the far wall.

"Wait, you think he's the mole?" Sadie now whispered too as she joined him on the floor.

"No," Killian shook his head, "that guy can't even step on a crack, I don't think he's capable of being the mastermind behind all of this. I just don't trust that he's going to keep you safe."

"Why not? Hasn't he had all the same training you have? Don't all the Zeds, according to Petey?"

"They don't know the whole story." As soon as those words left Killian's lips, Sadie could tell from his face that he'd said too much.

"What do you mean?"

He sighed. "What I'm about to tell you… Petey and Mike, they don't know. I'm not even supposed to know. I only found out because Desmond is my brother. The ZDA isn't just another agency that 'colors outside the lines,' that's just what we're told. The Agency was started in the eighties, true, but the roots go much deeper. We're an offshoot of an organization that dates back centuries. It was only at the advent of the CarterScott device that they decided they needed more help and the ZDA was formed—a task force dedicated to stopping the misuse of the tech by Domino, but for all intents and purposes, kept in the dark about the rest of the organization." Killian looked at Sadie as if he was trying to impress the seriousness of this information upon her.

She sat in silence, unsure of what to think. "Who's they? The people that decided all of this."

"The Guardians."

"The Guardians, really?" she said with an air of disbelief at having yet another codename to learn. "And what are their abilities?"

"It's not like that. I mean, yes, they have abilities; their ranks are made up of Auritors and Penumbrials. But their influence is more," Killian used air quotes, "'*far-reaching*,' as Desmond put it."

"And you've met these Guardians?"

"Only one. Desmond."

"Your brother?" Sadie asked even more incredulously.

"Yes. Sadie, I don't think you understand what I'm telling you." His eyes pleaded with her to understand. "You love history, right? This is the motherlode of historical revelations. Desmond, my brother, is part of a secret organization—"

"You're part of a secret organization," she interjected.

"Yes," he paused, "but mine is a drop in the bucket. I've tried to get more information from Desmond... he won't bring it up again. He may head the ZDA, but even he answers to someone, some guy called the Regent, but I've never seen him."

"Okay, so then how is Desmond a Guardian? I thought he was the government liaison."

"He is, but he's also a Guardian. Ugh, you're making this too confusing, Sadie," Killian said with frustration. "Desmond's family has been involved for generations. His father started the ZDA in the eighties after the CarterScott device was invented and immediately stolen. The ZDA's sole purpose was to flush out the stolen device and track down the part of Domino that took it, protecting the people we know about in the process. But based on how Desmond talks about this purpose, there has to be more to it. I don't know what it has to do with last weekend, maybe it doesn't connect at all. But I do know that Michael doesn't have a clue about what he's up against like I do. There's more to Domino and I can't let you drop into harm's way again." Killian sat back, as if some giant weight had just been lifted off his shoulders. As if he'd been carrying that around for years without having anyone that he could open up to.

Sadie, on the other hand, felt as if the world had just been placed on hers. It was enough that the last week had introduced her to the concept of mind readers, but now the threat she already thought was too much to handle just grew. A chill shot down her spine and she instinctively pulled her hoodie tighter, attempting to hide from her own fear. Something in the pocket dug into her side.

"Oh! What about this thing?" she said as she pulled the small disk out of her pocket.

"What is it?" Killian asked, taking it from her, the hue disappearing from it as he did.

"I grabbed it at the lab. It glows purple, but only when I hold it. Well, me and my boss."

Killian raised an eyebrow. "Your boss? At the museum?"

"Yeah, could the glowing mean she's a Penumbrial, like me?"

"Probably. We have something similar to this at the ZDA, but not this small." Killian inspected the device before throwing it up in the air repeatedly. "Pretty handy little thing." He tossed it back to Sadie.

"So have you heard the name Valerie Stead as a

Penumbrial before?"

"Not that I know of, but I don't make a habit of memorizing every name in our database." Killian turned his head to look at Sadie. Now only inches from his face, she could feel the heat coming off of him as his eyes locked on hers, searching for something. "Are you sure you're okay?"

Sadie didn't know how to answer. No, she wasn't okay, but she would never tell him that. She wanted to, she wanted to throw off all these anxieties and let him hold her. To feel safe in someone's arms, his arms. But every interaction they had was tainted with the thought it could be their last. He was supposed to be out of her life. She was supposed to "forget" about him. She was supposed to be left alone. *Why make it harder on either of us with stupid emotion*, she thought to herself.

"Yes, Killian. I'm fine," Sadie responded with as much confidence as she could feign. Now he was the one who looked skeptical.

A knock at the door interrupted their conversation, and Killian moved himself between Sadie and the door so fast, she barely had time to react before he was there. She knew he was protective, but she hadn't seen him behave quite so instinctually.

"Stay back," he said as he started toward the door, grabbing a knife from his boot.

"Ms. Smith, it's Michael. Are you okay?" a voice asked from outside. Sadie breathed a sigh of relief as Killian double-checked through the peephole.

"Yes, Michael. I'm fine." She moved to open the door, but Killian stopped her, pleading with his eyes not to let

Michael in. "It's okay, Killian," she whispered. "I trust him." She opened the door.

"I saw your light go off but during my perimeter check I could hear voices. Are you okay, is anyone else here? Agent Quinn, by chance?" Sadie shot a look behind the door where Killian was standing.

"Hey, Mike," Killian said as he came out.

"Thank goodness it's you." Michael let out a heavy sigh of relief and put away his gun. "When you weren't in the car and I saw the lights flick off, I thought maybe you'd come to check too."

"That's right, I did," Killian said as he looked at Sadie and winked, flooring her with that devilish smirk. That look would be frozen in Sadie's mind forever. *Stop it, Sadie, not an option.*

"…But looks like we're all good here." Killian broke the silence, clearly attempting to say goodbye to Michael.

"Ten-four, sir. Sorry for the interruption, Ms. Smith, we'll be going now," Michael said, turning to leave. He paused to allow Killian to go first.

"Not a problem, gentlemen." Sadie let out a little laugh before fixing her gaze on Killian. "Goodnight."

"Goodnight, Bluebird," Killian said, whispering the last part, and something in his voice felt like home to Sadie. She didn't know if it was the soft timbre, the confidence that he projected, or the fact that he had opened up to her on a level that few had ever done before. All she knew was that she wanted to see him again.

"That was a close call, wasn't it, sir?" Michael said as the pair walked down the hall.

"You know you don't need to call me sir. We're both

senior Agents, Mike." Killian clapped him on the back as they turned the corner.

"Michael," he mumbled under his breath.

Chapter 15

Sadie ran out the door, almost getting her bag caught in the hinge. Overnight, a storm had rolled through the east coast, bringing even colder temperatures with it—another freeze in November. A layer of ice covered everything, including the steps outside of her apartment. She slipped, her coffee went flying, and she almost face-planted onto the concrete, but a hand grabbed her at the last minute.

Killian, Sadie thought as she looked up, expecting to see the man that was always in the right place at the right time. "Oh, hey, Mike," she said as she brushed off her skirt and leggings, trying to hide her disappointment.

"Michael, ma'am," he replied, offering her a napkin for her coffee. "Are you alright?"

"Yes, I'm fine." She looked down, noticing the coffee stain on her jacket. "Just peachy. Hey, how about giving me a lift to work?"

"Umm, that's against protocol, ma'am, I'd advi—" he began nervously.

"Yes, yes, you'd advise against it. But look, it's freezing cold and now I've spilled the only saving grace of my day. I appreciate the save here, but I could use a ride to work so that I can grab another coffee before our Friday morning meeting. So please?" Sadie gave him the most pitiful puppy dog eyes she could muster as she started inching toward the black Lincoln parked in front of her apartment.

Michael took a deep breath and looked as if he were about to say no. He hesitated. "Alright, fine. But only this once."

"Great!" She opened the door to the Lincoln.

"Wait, how did you know that this was my car?" Michael asked.

"Mike, look at you, you're about as by-the-book as an agent could be. Of course you'd drive a black, nondescript Lincoln. And it's the fanciest car on this block."

"Mich—never mind…" he mumbled as he got into the car and began to drive.

The pair sat quietly for the first few minutes of the twenty-minute drive to the Smithsonian, save for the NPR Michael had turned on to break the awkward silence. Latest news included a piece about Senator Ellison from Virginia announcing his campaign for President. Then something about a factory explosion in Russia over the weekend, with the death toll already rising to forty-three. The broadcaster, bereft of emotion on the subject, moved on to rising gas prices, which made Sadie glad for public transportation that eliminated the necessity of a car. The distance from her apartment to the Smithsonian may have only been five miles, but DC traffic in the morning always added to the commute. Another reason Sadie was glad not to own a car.

Michael's was impeccably kept. Everything meticulous and pragmatic, everything, that is, except for the Garfield bobblehead taped to his dashboard.

"So," Sadie said, trying to break the tension and drown out the drone of NPR. "How long have you been with the ZDA?"

Michael stayed quiet, glancing over at Sadie and then immediately returning his eyes to the road.

"Are you really going to ignore me the whole time?"

"It's against protocol, ma'am."

"We're the only two people in the car, who cares?"

Michael continued to look straight ahead.

"Come on. Give me something here," her headache-induced irritability getting the best of her. She stared at the little Garfield bobblehead. "So you're a Garfield fan? Do you too hate Mondays?" Sadie waited for a response before giving up and staring out the window, watching the people of DC go about their daily lives, blissfully ignorant of Domino and the Guardians and their abilities to read minds.

Her thoughts drifted back to Killian as she found them doing often as of late. His regard for Bluebird, for her, echoed in her mind. *"Eyes that hold the kindest of souls..."* No one had ever thought that about her before, at least if they did, they certainly hadn't told her. *I can't really bite my lip every time I read, can I?* Killian had taken the time to notice all of her little habits and eccentricities, to notice her.

"Actually, I just really like lasagna," Michael said, after far too long of a pause.

"Hey! There he is, he talks. I like lasagna too. We're getting somewhere now. And see, no one died because you answered a question." Sadie smiled, feeling as though she had just unlocked the secret of the pyramids. It was small, but it was a start. She wanted to know more about this world of agencies and abilities that she now found herself a part of, and if Michael was her only way in, she'd use him.

They didn't talk for the rest of the ride, but Sadie didn't mind. She had at least opened the lines of communication and her headache-ridden, caffeine-deprived brain wasn't up for much more. Her headache hadn't stopped since Monday evening, maybe that was why she'd woken up late this cold Friday morning.

As she got out of the car, she turned back to Michael. "Same coffee later? Your coconut milk cappuccino with cinnamon is on me today. Thanks for the ride."

Sadie smiled, pleased that she'd made headway with the nervous Agent. She started up the stairs, but a figure caught the corner of her eye and she heard someone shout, "Quinn!"

She turned to look, expecting Killian, but all she saw was an old man walking his dog.

"Come on, Quinn, it's freezing, just go already," the man said, tugging at the gray Great Dane's leash. Saddened, Sadie continued walking into the Smithsonian with a little less enthusiasm than she used to.

The Friday morning status meeting rolled on without too much discomfort for Sadie. Either Stead still hadn't read the report or considered it bad enough that she wouldn't be moving forward with the display, at least not with Sadie at its helm. Sadie tried to catch her after the meeting to inquire about it, but Stead left promptly and, as it appeared to a paranoid Sadie, had avoided any interaction with her beyond a few blank stares during the meeting.

"You feeling okay?" Allyn asked as the meeting adjourned. "You don't look so good."

"Thanks for the brutal honesty, Allyn," Sadie said with a chuckle.

"No, that's not what I meant, you don't look bad, you always look good, great even, I mean," he stammered. "You don't seem yourself today."

"It's okay, I'm just giving you a hard time. I haven't been sleeping well this week and this headache is not going away. I was hoping coffee would help, but the watery tar from the cafeteria isn't cutting it." She held out a cup of coffee with visible grounds floating on top.

"I can go to the coffee shop down the street and get something for you if you want?" He smiled with genuine sympathy. "I was thinking about going myself anyway, so it's really no trouble."

"No that's alright, thank you though."

"Ms. Smith, a word," Jonas called out from down the hall. Whenever he called Sadie "Ms. Smith" it either meant something had gone terribly wrong or that it was about to.

"I'm sorry, I have to go. Coffee next time?" she said to Allyn but turned before waiting for an answer.

"Roger, roger!" Allyn replied in his best robot voice, then trailed off, mumbling as Sadie walked away.

Sadie hurried down the hall toward Jonas's office. "Everything okay?" she asked as she stepped inside.

"Have a seat, please," Jonas said. He sat behind his desk, typing away at the computer with a furrowed brow.

Uh oh, Sadie thought, *this can't be good.*

After what felt like an eternity, Jonas finally looked up from his screen. "So I spoke with Stead, and don't look so nervous, it's nothing terrible. You can breathe." Jonas laughed as Sadie exhaled, realizing she had actually been holding her breath, waiting for the other shoe to drop. "We're going to push back the display a few months. It's nothing to do with your report. As a matter of fact, she really liked it, she and the rest of the board just think that this project deserves a little more time put into it."

Sadie was both relieved and disappointed at the same time. She'd finally had an opportunity to work on her own project, and it felt like someone just took it away from her. Not that she could blame them, she'd dropped the ball on this one. She kicked herself again for losing sight of her priorities. "Do I still get to work on it, though?" she asked cautiously.

"Of course! You're still going to be involved, but Stead wants us to focus elsewhere for the time being and come back to this in a few months once she's had a chance to get some 'other pieces lined up,' as she says. Don't worry, this is not a reflection on you at all."

Sadie sat there, running through the implications of what Stead could possibly have in mind for Sadie to "focus elsewhere." As she considered the possibilities, she couldn't help but think more about Stead herself. What had happened to the smiling young woman in the photo on her desk? How had she gone from someone so happy to the Stead today? The woman that Sadie had never seen laughing, never even seen so much as a smile. A frigid woman, so severe that her employees lived in utter fear, because she obviously cared more about a building than the people in it.

"Are you okay?" Jonas asked gently.

"Hmm?" Sadie was pulled from the torrent of her thoughts. "Yeah, sorry, just thinking."

"Honestly, Sadie, I think it might be a good thing that this project is being pushed back, I'm worried about you. You were late twice this week, you look exhausted, and you seem like you're somewhere else entirely," he said, standing up, walking to the other side of his desk, and leaning against it as he put his arm on Sadie's shoulder.

"Do I really look that bad? Why does everyone keep saying that?" She laughed, but it was starting to worry her. "I just haven't been sleeping well this week. I think it's time for a new pillow or something, my head has been killing me and I'm guessing it's my neck. Or the stress of waiting for Stead's response." She smiled while rubbing the back of her neck.

"Well try to rest up this weekend. If you need to cut out early today, you can. You don't have to worry about the report anymore; take some you time. Go out with friends, go to the park, get some sunshine. Try to turn that brain of yours off for a bit. And don't stay cooped up all weekend." He gave Sadie one of his signature smiles that made her feel like everything was going to be okay. "And Sadie, be careful."

"Thanks, Jonas," Sadie said as she left the office. *Maybe he's right*, she thought, *I need a distraction.*

∞

Sadie walked to the coffee shop down the street, thinking about what she could do for the weekend. She ordered her drink on autopilot but thankfully remembered to order Michael's too. They called out her name and she picked up her two coffees, turning to survey the crowded room until she found the one person she wanted to see.

"One coconut cappuccino with cinnamon, as promised," she said as she sat down at the small table where Michael sat "reading" his paper. He didn't reach for the coffee so she put it on the table near him.

"Thanks." He grabbed the cup and turned the sleeve so the logo lined up with the lid.

"So," Sadie continued, "tell me about yourself, where are you from? And before you say it's against protocol, remember this morning we had that nice conversation about Garfield and no one died? This is a safe space." She smiled, imploring him to answer the question.

Michael looked around his paper at her, deciding whether to respond or not. "I moved here from Chicago," he finally relinquished.

"Very cool. I've heard Chicago is a pretty amazing city. Never been there personally, but they say the food is great." Sadie waited for him to ask her something in return, but he went back to his paper, occasionally glancing up to survey the room. "I'm from here. DC, I mean. Born and raised, at least according to my birth certificate."

"I know," he replied, tapping on his smartphone. At least he had acknowledged that a conversation was happening.

"Right, that probably would be in whatever little dossier you have on me… Did it tell you that I have a very special skill?" she asked, grabbing the coaster out from under her coffee cup.

Michael looked up then, ever so slightly raising one eyebrow. "Yes, ma'am, that's why I'm here, you're a Penumbrial."

"Not that skill, I don't even know what good that one is. My real skill is this," Sadie said as she placed the coaster halfway off the table then, using one hand, flipped it into the air and caught it. "Ta-da!"

"Well done?" he said, raising his tone at the end as if it were a question.

"Oh come on, that's a pretty neat trick. Especially since I'm sleep deprived and only running on two sips of coffee at this point. Why don't you give it a shot if you think it's that easy?" She handed him the coaster with a taunting look.

Michael glanced around the coffee shop before putting down the paper and taking the coaster from Sadie. He did the same thing, placed it halfway off the table, flipped it, and caught it.

"Look at you, special agent man, now see if you can do it with two," she said, grabbing another coaster off a neighboring table.

"Two, like stacked on top of each other?" Michael asked incredulously.

"Yep, here, like this." Then she proceeded to place the second one on top of the other, positioned them halfway off the table, and flipped both in the air, catching them with one hand.

"Alright, alright, I can do that," Michael said confidently. "So just tap and—" The two coasters flew across the table and hit an older woman in the back of her head. Sadie burst out laughing as Michael looked up, completely flustered. "Oh, I'm sorry, ma'am. I didn't mean to." He was mortified.

"It's okay, Michael," Sadie said with a smirk as she bent over to pick up the closest coaster on the floor.

Just as Michael began to beam at her in response, Sadie's headache intensified. She turned her head, rubbing her neck to assuage the pain. It wasn't the worst headache she'd ever felt, but it was definitely worse than it had been the rest of the week. The buzzing in the base of her skull grew louder and the pain throbbed from the top of her neck to her forehead, just above her eyes.

"Are you okay, ma'am?" Michael asked, placing his hand on her shoulder.

"Yeah, I think I wrenched my neck or something. Thanks for playing, but I'm gonna head back to work. I've got some Ibuprofen at my desk."

"Okay, well if you need anything, let me know," he said, handing over her bag and coffee.

"Thanks." Sadie stumbled out the coffee shop and walked the two blocks back to the Smithsonian. Her headache intensified with each step.

∞

Allyn walked in on Sadie dumping her bag out onto her desk as she stood amid the destroyed contents of her drawers, anxiously looking for something.

"You okay?" he asked tentatively.

"I'm fine," she snapped. Allyn jumped and started backing toward the door. "I'm sorry," she continued, softer this time, "I thought I had some Advil or something in here, but I can't find it."

"Oh, here. I have Excedrin Migraine. I always keep it on hand," he said as he proffered two pills.

"Thank you, Allyn!" Sadie smiled gratefully and swallowed them down.

"It's no trouble. I get ocular migraines a lot, I think it's from staring at screens so much. That and focusing so closely on rock striations. They're crazy things, the migraines I mean, not the striations. My vision starts to fill up with these little psychedelic triangles that spread like windshield wipers on a car…" Allyn gently hit his palm against his forehead. "And you don't want to hear about these. I'm sorry. I always talk too much."

"No, it's okay. I think it's already helping, strangely enough." Her headache *was* starting to subside, it wasn't completely gone, but she could open her eyes normally again. *Pills shouldn't work that fast,* she thought, *maybe this is psychosomatic? Wouldn't that be perfect.* She shrugged off the thought, thankful the headache was finally starting to dull. That's when her phone started to buzz—a text from Piper.

Hey, going to O'Malley's again tonight with some people, including Petey ;) You down?

Petey! Sadie thought. She immediately replied back.

Yeah, totally!

She continued her text conversation, leaving Allyn hovering awkwardly. He fiddled with the hand lens he always kept in his pocket while he waited for Sadie to look up from her phone.

"Oh, I'm sorry, Allyn," she said. "That was rude of me. Thanks again for the Excedrin. I owe you."

"No problem at all. Hey, that's what I'm here for,

to hand out the goods," he said, changing his voice and pointing both thumbs at himself in a Fonzie fashion.

Sadie laughed, nudging his arm with hers. "I think I'm actually going to take Jonas up on his offer head out a little early, cover for me with everyone else?" She started packing up her bag, anxious to get home and change before heading out to meet Piper at O'Malley's. Hopefully she would be able to get some information out of Petey about Killian.

"Sure, I'll see you Monday." Allyn rubbed the place where her arm had been, a smile spreading across his face as he followed her out of her office.

"Thanks! Have a good weekend," she called out, running down the hall and passing Jonas, who gave her a knowing smile.

Once on the elevator, she turned to see both Jonas and Allyn waving goodbye as the doors closed.

Chapter 15.5

Killian sat on the bench at the corner of 10th Street and Constitution, watching the sun set behind the Natural History Museum and waiting for Sadie to leave for the night. He hadn't seen Michael Patel anywhere, so either he was better than even Killian expected, or he was already slacking on the job. Either way, Killian was glad to be there. While he sat, he recalled all the hours he'd spent waiting for this woman in the last four years. As uncomfortable as the bus bench was, nothing would compare to the three months he'd spent in Alaska last year because she received a fellowship opportunity to study whales. It was cold and dark, and then there was Sven. Sven, the scientist that got a little too cozy to Sadie. Killian still felt bad for what happened to that guy.

One Friday night, toward the end of the three months, Killian had followed Sadie and Sven out on one of their expeditions. Nebraska hadn't thought it necessary for him to follow them at every point once they'd run background checks on all of the scientists at the base, but he'd insisted on it after seeing Sven and Sadie together. Killian was convinced Sven was secretly a Domino operative trying to get close to Sadie to use her as an asset. It didn't help that the background check on Sven had revealed a long-term girlfriend back in Iceland, making Killian dislike the guy almost immediately.

For the two whale enthusiasts, it must have been a perfect night. Killian could hear the sounds loud and clear over their speaker even from fifty feet away. He'd also brought along a long-range bionic listening device, just in case, so he could hear every word they said to each other.

"Can you believe how active they are tonight?" Sadie had asked.

"It's great! These are the best recordings we've had yet," Sven replied in his thick Icelandic accent. He looked over at Sadie, handing her a tin mug. "Hot cocoa?"

What, no marshmallows, Sven? Killian thought to himself. *Should've brought the mini ones, they're her favorite.*

"Sure, thanks," she said, tucking escaped wisps of hair back into her beanie. "It feels even colder than normal."

"Here, scooch on over closer to me," he said and put his arm around her.

Through his binoculars, Killian could see how Sven was staring at her. He gently brushed some snow off of her bright red nose. Killian would never forget how Sadie looked that night, her caramel skin in stark contrast to the white fur snowsuit she was wearing, her dark brown hair poking out from under her beanie and hood. Her glasses looked almost frozen to her face and her nose had grown red in protest of the freezing temperatures. She was one of the most beautiful women he'd ever seen, and she had no idea he even existed.

Maybe that's why it hurt Killian so much when Sven leaned in for a kiss. Nebraska had warned him he was getting too close to her, but he protested in the name of duty, protecting the Penumbrial. Deep down, he knew it was more than that. His insides began to burn with jealousy as he watched the pair together. Above them, the aurora borealis came to life. It was as if every star in the known universe had come out to see the show, creating a perfect canvas for nature to paint upon. Green washed across the sky in a swell, then blue made its mark, before a pink hue hinted at the corners, anxious to join in. The competing blue and green colors that danced above him seemed to echo the tumult in Killian's heart. He didn't wait for Sven and Sadie; he gathered his things and began the three-kilometer trek back to the base at Point Barrow, allowing the northern lights to be his only guide.

When the pair finally arrived back at base three hours later, Killian was waiting for Sven near his bunk. Jealousy coursed through his veins as he let his suspicions grow into action. Sadie went to bed and the moment Sven rounded the corner before his cabin, Killian grabbed him.

"I know what you are," Killian spat. "I'm not going to let you hurt her, Domino scum."

"Woah, let's calm down, who… what?" Sven stammered, trying to make sense of the situation. "I think you have the wrong guy. Who's Domino?"

"Don't lie to me!" Killian yelled, slamming his knife into the wall next to Sven's head. "What do you want with, Sadie?"

"I-I don't know what you want." Sven began to cry. "Just please don't hurt me. I don't know who Domino is and I don't want anything with Sadie. I have a girlfriend, okay, back in Iceland. I didn't mean to cheat on her, it just sort of happened. But Sadie means nothing to me, please don't tell my girlfriend. If you let me go, I promise I won't tell anyone you were here, just please don't hurt me," he said, and as he took a long, wide-eyed look at the knife, he wet himself.

Killian stared down at the frightened man, realizing he was wrong. This was no Domino operative. He was a scumbag for sure, but he didn't work for Domino. Killian had let his emotions get the better of him again.

"Leave," was all Killian said as he released Sven and watched him run away into the bunk.

The next day Sven packed up and left without even a word to Sadie. That was the moment when Killian recognized he'd gotten too close. He would never regret protecting her, but he was ashamed of how his actions that night had impacted her, how it must have made her feel as though another person she had gotten close to up and abandoned her without warning. She left Iceland two weeks later, never knowing what happened to Sven, never knowing it wasn't her fault.

Killian continued to watch the passersby along Constitution Avenue. A few were leaving the museum through the rear entrance, but most were tourists taking photos of the buildings around the Smithsonian. For some reason, tourists loved taking pictures of the John F. Kennedy Department of Justice sign, as if they were somehow going to snap a photo of something nefarious happening in the windows and discover the truth of the Kennedy assassination.

He turned and looked back at the Smithsonian exit, hoping to see either Michael or Sadie. Instead, he saw the security guard walk out and lock the doors. He had missed her altogether.

Killian felt the barrel of a gun press into his side,

forcing him to inhale sharply. His senses heightened. His pulse quickened. A familiar, mocking voice accompanied the gun.

"I was hoping I'd find you here," said Derek as he sat down next to Killian on the bench.

"Derek, displeasure as always." Killian glanced down at the Sig Sauer P227 Tactical with a suppressor now pressed into his side. "Sadie isn't here, you missed her." *I missed her.*

"Oh, I'm not here for her." Derek smirked. Killian breathed a small sigh of relief before Derek continued, "She's someone else's project tonight."

Tonight, Killian thought. *What's happening tonight?* He had to deal with Derek and find Sadie. But there were too many people around to risk collateral damage.

"Where's your car?" Derek demanded. "You're driving us somewhere special."

"Oh good," Killian said as Derek pulled him up, and he led the two of them over to his car. *There's one problem solved. Hold on, Sadie, I'll be there as soon as I can.*

Derek directed them to the same Ivy City train yard Killian had followed him to last weekend. Made sense, really. It was secluded, empty, save for the occasional hobo or coyote, and the local residents were used to the sounds of gunshots at this point. Killian could almost feel his Kimber Eclipse Target II screaming out for him from the glovebox, unfortunately there was no way he could get to it with Derek in the passenger seat. He'd have to face him unarmed. Again.

They got out of the car, Derek's gun still squarely pointed at Killian, and began walking toward the back end of the yard between the parked train cars.

"You know, you really disappointed me last time," Derek said with an air of smugness. "Jumping into the lake like that. I thought you had taken the fun from me, but looks like you've got more up your sleeve than I thought."

"Glad to be of service," Killian responded. He started running through scenarios in his mind. The last time he faced off against Derek, the surprise had put him at a disadvantage. This time he had to be smarter. *Think, Killian,* he told himself. Derek Haynes had a good three inches and fifty pounds on him. He'd have to find higher ground.

He glanced around at his options as Derek continued rambling on about "Domino's latest plan." *Why do they always monologue?* Killian thought. "*Focus, Rook,*" he could hear Nebraska's voice in his head. He took note of the dirt and gravel mix below his feet; the ladders running up the sides of the train cars would provide an opportunity to gain ground. There was a rope not too far off. *Maybe I could reach it,* he thought. He just needed to think of a distraction.

"Only wish I had been the one to do the old bird in, to see the look on her face when the great Nebraska Hill died."

"What did you say?" All Killian's plans flew out the window at the mention of his partner's name. His brain set afire with the echoes of his last conversation with Derek. "I thought you killed her. You said she died begging."

"That's just what I heard from the guy who did it, who lured her into the Dupont Underground to watch her die." Derek sneered as he inched closer and closer to Killian, keeping the gun pointed directly at his head.

A train horn sounded in the background, and Killian took advantage of the split-second distraction to reach down and throw the mix of sand and gravel into Derek's eyes. He ran at Derek, slamming him into the train car behind, and beat his arm against the corner. The gun fell to the ground with a heavy thud. Killian followed up with a punch to the gut before starting a beating on Derek's face.

With a loud grunt, Derek finally blocked a punch and began his counterattack. His fist found the bullet hole from their last encounter and continued to barrage the spot, reopening the barely healed wound.

Killian's body screamed in agony; he let go of his hold on Derek and the world swam around him as his mind tried to force itself away from the pain. As he staggered back, Derek delivered a crushing blow to his jaw and grabbed him in a headlock.

"Want to know who did it?" Derek asked.

Killian could taste blood in his mouth but was helpless to release himself from the larger man's hold. His foot found purchase on a nearby rail as Derek whispered into his ear, "Desmond Kalani."

The implications exploded in Killian's mind. Every interaction he'd had with his brother in the last few days played over and over in his head. The denial, the caginess, the reassignment. Killian refused to believe it. He shoved his suspicions down, deep into the recesses of his subconscious. *Not Desmond, not possible*, he thought.

"No!" Killian screamed out. He threw his feet at the

ladder in front of him, using the force to push back on Derek and flip out of the hold. "You're lying!" he bellowed, whipping around to continue his assault. He didn't stop until his energy was spent.

Derek leaned against the opposite train car covered in blood, his eyes already swelling shut. He laughed as he spat blood out on the dusty ground.

"That all you got? Thought your brother would've taught you better than that. Or maybe he was too busy with his sick kid to help you recently. What was her name again? Cleo, Karla, oh, that's right, Kalia." Derek taunted.

Kalia's name on Derek's lips was like poison to Killian. *How does he know about Kalia?*

The ground began to tremble. The train they had heard earlier was getting closer.

"Come on, let's finish this," said Derek as he lurched forward off the railway car.

Killian mustered everything he could for a final push. He ran headlong into battle, not just against Derek but against the possibility of Desmond being the mole. The man he'd looked up to since he was a child, the man that had shaped the course of his life in ways unimaginable, the man he called brother. Desmond could never betray Killian or the Agency. It wasn't possible.

The rage fueled him, channeling every ounce of anger into each punch. A crack echoed from Derek's face as Killian's fist connected with his nose. They toppled to the floor, and blood mixed with dirt as the two men grappled with each other across the empty train track, the shaking beneath them growing steadily.

His energy began to flag again and Killian rolled away,

staggering to his feet to see Derek barely able to stand in front of him. In the corner of his eye, the train appeared.

It was speeding toward them.

The horn screamed danger.

Derek regained his footing and looked up at Killian. He smiled through the dirt and blood coating his face.

With one final kick, Killian launched him onto the tracks of the oncoming train and was immediately blown back by the speed of the locomotive, which muffled the sound of Derek's last scream.

He lay in the dirt, vibrating with the rhythm of the train in the ground beneath him. *I just need a minute*, he told himself. His head was still spinning from the fight and the ramifications of Desmond's potential betrayal. He didn't want to admit it, but it made sense. It explained how Domino had time to clear out their lab, how Domino knew so much about the Agency's assets, how Nebraska was killed. What it didn't explain was why. *No, it can't be Desmond, can it? But how else did Derek know about Kalia being sick?* Killian frantically reexamined everything he thought he knew about his brother. *There has to be a reason for it all. A reason that explains Desmond's innocence. A reason for… Sadie!* The thought hit his mind with enough percussive force to send him shooting upright. *Something is happening tonight.* He needed to find Sadie, now. He picked up his phone.

"Petey, it's me. Where are you? Meet me outside in ten minutes. They're coming for Sadie."

Killian skidded to a stop in front of O'Malley's to find Petey already waiting outside, glued to his phone.

"Alright, her tracking is still on. She's not far, but she's on the move. Just take my phone," Petey said, handing it to Killian and finally looking up. "Damn, Killian, are you okay?"

"Yeah, I'm fine. Had an issue I had to deal with first. Let's go." Killian moved back toward his car.

"Well, I'm kind of here with som—"

"Hey, babe!" Piper Montgomery stood at the entry-way, holding the door to O'Malley's open. "Are you coming back in for the next round?"

"Babe?" Killian questioned incredulously.

"Ha, what can I say. I told you, I've got that animal magnetism," Petey replied as Piper growled seductively from the door. "I'll be right in, Shmoops."

Killian shook his head. "I'm gonna be sick... Wait, was Sadie here too?"

"Oh, you know Sadie? I'm Piper, by the way, her BFF," Piper said, walking over with her hand outstretched. As she came closer to Killian, she quickly withdrew it. "Ew, why are you so bloody?"

"Where's Sadie?" Killian insisted, ignoring Piper's question. He stared at her with all the intensity he could muster. This was taking too long. The only thing that mattered was making sure Sadie was safe.

"Right... Yeah, we rode together, but then some big guy in a uniform stopped us before we went in. She knew him though. Told me it was cool." Piper thought for a moment. "I think she called him Donald or Demetrie, or something like that."

"Desmond?" Killian asked.

"Yeah! That's it. Desmond. I think she ended up

leaving with him… She never came in and that was like ten minutes ago."

Killian looked at Petey in complete horror. It was the final piece of evidence he couldn't explain away. He couldn't think of any reason Desmond would need Sadie. She had Michael protecting her. Killian felt a crack appearing in his armor, threatening to shatter the strength he'd absorbed from his brother. In that moment, he knew. He knew in his heart-of-hearts that Desmond was behind it and Sadie was now in peril. He thought of every moment he'd spent with this woman in the last four years. He had to do something. He would not lose her too. The hairs on the back of Killian's neck stood to attention as he stared at his friend, "Petey, it's Desmond. He's the mole."

Chapter 16

Sadie watched the view shift from neighborhood to industrial district out the window of Desmond's Road Ranger. She trusted the man. Why shouldn't she? He was Killian's brother, the one person he trusted more than anyone in the world, and Sadie trusted Killian. Forty minutes ago, when Desmond caught Sadie outside of O'Malley's asking to talk, she didn't think anything of it. When he said he wanted to bring her into headquarters to explain everything, she agreed. But now, as the car stopped in what seemed to be a completely deserted part of town in the dark of night, her internal instincts started to sound a red alert.

"So you said you wanted you to tell me more about the Agency and everything that's going on?" she asked cautiously as Desmond let her out of the car.

"Yes," he said, "Killian made me realize that you already know about us now, so maybe you'd want to come work with us." He locked the car and began walking. "Follow me, the entrance is just up ahead."

"I mean, yeah, that would be incredible." She'd done it, she'd found her way into this world for good. Sadie ignored the small alarm still sounding in the back of her mind. "Is Killian coming?"

"He's actually taking a few days off. He's been through so much lately." Desmond sighed. "But time heals all wounds. And I'm happy you'll be joining us, I'm sure Killian will be too." The very idea made Sadie blush. Even in the midst of living an adventure story, she felt butterflies erupt inside of her. *Stupid girl.*

The pair continued to walk across the gravel-laden lot toward a derelict hangar. She didn't know much about the area but could guess this particular stretch was home to an old plane manufacturer turned scrapyard. In the light of the moon, she could make out giant heaps of metal and trash.

This would be a perfect place to hide an agency, she thought, *or dispose of someone… Stop it, Sadie, you're being ridiculous,* she continued to tell herself. But that alarm kept finding its way to the forefront of Sadie's mind.

As they got further away from the car, and any sign of civilization for that matter, she noticed her headache begin to subside. The buzzing was gone, replaced with only the sound of the wind howling through the discarded metal.

"So tell me more about Killian," Sadie prodded, wanting to distract herself from her surroundings.

"What about him? He's my little brother and like all little brothers, sometimes you love them and sometimes you want to wring their necks in frustration." Desmond continued walking. He seemed to be picking up the pace. As if he wanted the walk and this conversation to be over as quickly as possible.

I'm so sorry, brother.

"What was that?" she asked.

"Little brothers, sometimes you love them, sometimes not so much," Desmond repeated.

"Yeah, no, after that. You said, 'I'm so sorry, brother.' Sorry for what?"

Desmond stopped short and turned back to face Sadie. His eyes focused on her with such ferocity that it felt as though he was trying to decipher some hidden secret on her face.

"I didn't say anything…"

Out loud…

Sadie froze. She definitely heard Desmond say the full sentence, but his mouth didn't move. Her eyes widened in terror at the thought.

You can hear me, can't you?

She nodded, almost in slow motion as realization dawned on both of them.

Oh God, that's why they wanted her.

"Desmond, what's going on? Who wanted me?" Sadie's gaze darted around the scrapyard. She felt like a caged animal being brought to the slaughter. Desmond didn't answer as he paced in front of her, and a heat formed behind her eyes, a lump growing in her throat. *Keep it together, Sadie.*

She can't be.

"You can't be. The last one was thirty years ago," Desmond mumbled to himself.

And she was the first in almost three hundred years. This can't be—I can't let this happen.

"We have to get out of here," Desmond said quickly, grabbing Sadie's arm, pulling her back toward the car.

"No, what? Tell me what's going on, Desmond," Sadie demanded, fighting the tears welling up behind her eyes. She pulled her arm from the man's grip, trying to back away, but into what, she had no idea. She didn't want to be here anymore. She'd made the wrong choice. Again. She'd trusted and been burned. Now all she wanted was to be back home next to Redy, reading books in her big gray beanbag with a glass of red wine in her hand and a blanket over her feet.

"Sadie, listen to me," Desmond begged, "I'll explain everything, I promise. But first, we need to get out of here. I've done something awful."

A lot of awful things

"But I'm not going to let anything happen to you, okay? Now please, just trust me, and let's get out of here," he said, trying to usher her toward the car. She could hear a raw edge to his voice.

"Awful things… what awful things?" she asked, visibly shaking.

The sound of footsteps distracted them. From behind the wing of a long-trashed biplane, a shadowy figure emerged. Desmond moved to place himself between Sadie and the figure.

"Answer her question, Des, what awful things have you done?"

Killian walked into the light.

Sadie immediately rushed out from behind Desmond but stopped short. She stood frozen between the two brothers, scared to trust anyone in this world.

"Killian, I promise. I'll tell you everything, but we have to get out of here now. They're coming," Desmond pleaded.

"Who's coming?" Killian asked.

"Domino. That's why we need to get out of here."

"Domino? So it is true then. You're the mole."

Sadie could see Killian's composure crumbling by the second. Desmond hung his head.

There are no words. Nothing can change what I've done. Nebraska...

"Nebraska... why are you thinking about her?" Sadie asked. Her mind exploded with thoughts and apologies from Desmond, like he was screaming. She could almost hear the fissure inside of him rip open. Sadie realized the truth.

"It was you, wasn't it?" she whispered. Desmond leaned against the rusty shell of a car behind him, holding his head in his hands. She looked back at Killian and saw the anger erupt in his eyes.

"No! You didn't!" Killian roared as he ran over to his brother and started beating his arm. Then he pleaded, grabbing Desmond's coat collar as tears streamed down his face, "Tell me it wasn't you, Des, tell me it's not true! Tell me you didn't kill Nebraska." He looked up at his big brother. His eyes searched, begged for a contradiction, but nothing came.

"I'm sorry," Desmond said as he clutched his little brother's shoulders. "I didn't mean to, it was just—"

Desmond was interrupted by a pair of headlights that illuminated the derelict hangar.

A figure stepped in front of the beams, casting a heinous shadow on the corrugated walls, and Killian leaped back to stand in front of Sadie as if on instinct. Bruno Soto walked out of the darkness, clapping. "Bravo, Desmond, quite the performance. It almost seemed like you were about to have a change of heart and run out on our deal."

"It wasn't an act, Soto, the deal's off," Desmond said, striding forward to position himself in front of Killian and closer to Soto and his men.

A shot rang out, around the metallic hangar. The smoke rose from Soto's gun. "Uh, uh, uh, not so close, General. Are you sure about breaking our agreement? I mean, we have to think of poor little Kalia, after all."

"Don't you dare say her name," Desmond growled. He took another step toward Soto but subsequently backed off with his hands up when one of Soto's three men pointed their weapon at his head.

"What is he talking about, Des, what about Kalia?" Killian said, looking back and forth between Soto and Desmond.

"Nothing, Killian, stay out of this," Desmond hissed. Sweat dripped down his forehead, stopping at his eyebrow. He looked at Sadie.

If the moment presents itself, grab Killian and run... I'll try to hold them off as long as I can.

"Soto, your deal is with me. Let the boy go."

"You didn't tell him, Desmond? You didn't tell your brother that you have been working for me all these months because we're the ones saving your daughter's life?" Bruno shook his finger. "Tsk, tsk, bad big brother."

"That's what they have on you? Why didn't you tell me, Des? We could've figured this out together." Killian's voice trembled. "We could've taken them down together."

"And Kalia would be dead, Killian. I did what I had to do. Now shut up and let me get you out of here." Desmond attempted to lunge for Soto, but he was met with the butt of a gun, sacking him in the gut. He fell to his knees as Soto's man loomed above him, rifle poised to shoot.

"Oh, Desmond, he isn't leaving here," Soto said with feigned sorrow as a smile crossed his face. "Neither of you are. And the girl, well, based on your attempt to double-cross me, you have clearly realized the truth. She is a Nox Auris." Soto bent forward, leaning tauntingly close to Desmond's face. "So she will be coming with us."

"A Nox Auris…" Killian said with surprise as he turned back to look at Sadie, who had been so engrossed in the action taking place in front of her, she'd almost forgotten she was part of all of this. "But that means—"

"Yes, yes, she's very special," Soto cut him off impatiently. "Not only is she a Penumbrial, but she's also an Auritor. A nifty little trick, one I think would prove useful in our research. Especially having lost the device. Perhaps you have it still, Agent Quinn?"

Desmond looked back at Sadie, the agony of guilt spread across his face.

I'm so sorry, Sadie. I'm going to try and get you out of here. Please tell Killian that I'm sorry for everything, but I have faith that he will be better than me. And I'm so proud of him.

"Soto, please," Desmond attempted to stand, "we can talk about this—"

"Enough!" Bruno Soto pointed his gun directly at Desmond's forehead.

He fired.

Desmond Kalani's body dropped to the floor, his blood mixing with the dirt as it washed onto the gravel below. Sadie saw the pupils in Desmond's eyes dilate for the last time, frozen in a look of horror. She stood motionless, unable to process what had happened.

The world moved at half the speed. Killian unraveled. He ran to his brother's side, screaming out in pain. Sadie would always have that image etched into her mind: Desmond's body on the ground with his eyes still open, Killian hunched over him, refusing to accept the truth. All the while, Soto stood there, smiling as he blew the smoke away from the barrel of his gun.

She had never seen a dead body before, let alone one of someone she knew. Someone she'd watched die. She looked up at Soto. All she could see was evil.

"Right. Come along, Ms. Smith. We have matters to attend to," Soto said and two of his men walked toward her.

"No!" Killian cried out as he pulled himself to his feet. Sadie saw the look in his eyes and knew he wouldn't let Soto get away, not even with the guns of all three of Soto's men pointed squarely at him, ready to fire. She couldn't watch him die too. Not Killian. She would not let him be put down like a dog in the dirt.

"Wait!" she screamed and threw herself in front of him. "You need me, right?" Sadie stared at Soto, trying to formulate a plan in her head while divining his. She discreetly placed her hand on Killian's right hip, hoping he wore his gun on that side.

"Yes," Soto replied cautiously, eyeing her, attempting to figure out if she knew what she was doing or not.

More than you know.

Sadie heard his voice slither into the back of her mind. She despised having his vile thoughts in her head, but right now, she needed the advantage. "Well if you want me to go with you, then you can't hurt him," she said with as much confidence as she could muster.

I want him dead!
No. Calm, Bruno. Reason.

Soto paced in front of his men. Having holstered his gun, he now held his hands behind his back. "Are you sure you're on the right side of all of this?"

"Right side?" Sadie asked, grasping Killian's gun.

And here we go.

"Yes, you've heard their pitch, but we've not had a chance to talk about the opportunities that are available to you within Domino. The things we could teach you about your abilities," Soto continued while inching closer and closer to her.

"I'll never work for Domino," she said adamantly, her hand tightening around the weapon. Her legs felt as if they'd give out if not for her locked knees. *How did I get myself into this mess?* Sadie cried in her own mind.

Like you have a choice, silly girl.

"You may change your mind yet," Soto said. "I can be very persuasive."

And all I need is that brain of yours intact, no consciousness required.

Sadie knew what she had to do.

She pulled the gun from the holster and held it below her chin as she stepped away from Killian and the group of Domino assailants. Soto jumped forward, betraying his concern for her, or at least her mind and abilities.

"What was that about an intact brain?" *What am I doing?* Sadie screamed inside. She felt the weight of the weapon in her hand. She'd never held a gun before. It was smooth, heavier than she expected. The touch of its icy metal against her skin was in stark contrast to the fire of destruction she knew it was capable of igniting. She could feel it shaking in her grip as the barrel grazed her neck. Every heartbeat pulsed her muscles closer to the trigger.

"Stand down!" Soto ordered as his men all moved their aim away from Killian and pointed it at the now-armed Sadie.

Clever girl. So you've already learned to read thoughts. Good.

"Killian walks out of here, I go with you, deal?" *Am I really doing this?* she thought to herself. She looked over at Killian; terror and betrayal flashed across his face. A face she barely knew, but one she was somehow willing to give everything for. She wished she could tell him it was going to be alright, that she would figure a way out of this, that she knew, if given the chance, he'd be there to save her again. But she couldn't, she could only look at him and hope beyond hope that he would understand.

Say I agree to this, what assurance do I have that Agent Quinn here won't follow us?

"Tie him up," Sadie responded.

"What!" Killian exclaimed. "Sadie, what are you doing?"

"I'm trying to save your life, okay?" she said then turned back to face Soto. "I'm sure even a Zed would need at least a few minutes to get out of restraints? But you can't harm him." Soto paused, looking between Sadie, Killian, and his men.

Clearly. He's like a cockroach that won't die, no matter how many times you try to squash him.

"Fine." Soto finally broke the silence. "You come with us willingly, we let him live. *Capisce*?" Sadie nodded.

Soto's men moved in on Killian and tied his wrists through the doorframe of the derelict car near his brother's still-warm body. One of them found and grabbed the CarterScott device out of Killian's pocket while he was at it. The three men returned to Soto's side. "Alright, we've held up our end, do we have a deal, Ms. Smith?"

"Deal," she said, lowering Killian's gun away from her chin with relief. She hated guns and just holding one made every fiber of her being shout in protest.

Soto grabbed the device while the other two men made their way over to Sadie. She gave Killian a desperate look. "I'm sorry, it was the only way."

"Today really is turning out to be a good day." Soto smirked, glancing down at Desmond's body. "Maybe not so much for you and yours though, Quinn."

"I will find you and I will get her back, you scum," Killian snarled. "You'll pay for this."

"Hmm," Soto said as he walked over to Killian, "see, here is the issue. I can already hear what's running through that precious little mind of yours." Soto looked over to Sadie. "You're not the only one with a gift, girl." He fired a shot at Killian's leg. Killian screamed out in agony.

Sadie still held the gun in her hand and she aimed for Soto. "Liar!" She pulled the trigger.

The shot rang out, bouncing across the metal surfaces surrounding them.

Soto stood, unharmed. One of his men had managed to aim the gun away at the last moment.

Two seconds too late. She'd missed.

Soto's men disarmed her quickly.

"Tsk, tsk, tsk, Ms. Smith. So close. At least now Agent Quinn will only be stuck with a leg wound, instead of the alternative, had he actually tried that silly escape plan." Soto marched over to Sadie, pulling her face close to his. She could feel the heat of his breath on her ear. "Don't ever try that again."

I don't need all *of you in working order.*

Soto caressed the side of her jaw, inhaling her scent, and an immediate desire to crawl out of her own skin consumed Sadie. His smile seemed to taunt her as he pulled away and walked toward his car. "And to be clear, I didn't break my word. The boy will be fine as long as someone finds him soon enough." His Cheshire cat grin sent a cold wave of revulsion down Sadie's spine. "Gentlemen, please help our guest into the car."

Sadie wanted to run to Killian, to help him, to do anything. Instead, she was forced toward Soto's car. The world felt like it was closing in on her. She'd wanted adventure, but she'd found death. She'd found herself being carted away while the man she was falling for writhed in pain on the ground. She thought she had done the right thing this time. She thought wrong.

Sadie bucked against the two men trying to force her into submission, desperate for freedom. She managed to scratch one of their faces, and he let out a monstrous scream as he grabbed his bloody wound. The other man slammed her head down into the doorframe of the car. Nerves in her face exploded in anguish. Tiny black dots appeared in her vision, growing to crowd out the reality of her situation as Soto's men forced her hands together behind her back, squeezing her wrists together in an unnatural way that felt as if they were about to break. She could still see Killian fighting against his restraints, attempting to stand on his wounded leg, oblivious to the pain. He screamed out for her, she could hear him calling her name. There was nothing she could do.

An almost silent shot zipped out from the darkness.

One of Soto's men dropped.

Then another.

Suddenly, tiny beams of light appeared all around them, red lasers pointed squarely at Soto and his one remaining man. He began firing back into the void, unable to see his target, but not caring. He fell, leaving only Soto, who held his hands up in quick surrender.

Ten armed men in full tactical gear surrounded Soto, his car, and Sadie. As they moved in on Soto, Sadie scrambled over to Killian and knelt beside him. "Are you okay?" she asked, quickly removing her jacket to create a makeshift tourniquet.

"What were you thinking?" demanded Killian.

"I was thinking of a way to keep you safe."

"By putting a gun to your head?" His expression hardened into one of fear and anger.

"Yes. Now, are you okay?" she asked again, forcefully this time as she pulled her jacket tight around his leg.

"Ah, dammit! Yes, I'm okay," Killian said. "But please, don't you ever do that again."

"I don't plan on it." She looked up from the tourniquet to see his beaming face. In one look, it seemed like he was burrowing into her soul. He'd found his home in Sadie's heart, but she forced herself to look away.

"Now, who are these guys? More Zeds?"

"No. I have no idea who they are," Killian said as one of the men in tactical gear ran over to them, silently assessing the situation.

"We need a medic," he called into the slim radio headset he was wearing.

A voice crackled in response, "Area secure, sir."

"All clear, Madam Regent," the man called back as he stared down at Killian and Sadie.

The pair exchanged a shocked look. Sadie recalled the conversation they'd had the night before, about the Guardians, about the Regent.

"Regent?" she asked.

"Madam?" Killian responded, a quizzical look on his face.

A black, unmarked van entered the scene. The back door slid open. Out walked Valerie Stead.

Chapter 17

"I want Soto in interrogation by the time I get back to the Library. I'd like a word with him." Valerie Stead somehow managed to seem even colder and more in control than she was at the Smithsonian. She looked over at Desmond, taking a moment of silence for him. In that instant, Sadie caught a fleeting glimpse of emotion rushing across her face; she *did* still have feelings.

"Sadie, are you okay?" Stead turned to her. She almost reached out to Sadie's bloodied forehead, but then returned her hand to a resting position behind her.

"Yes, I—what are you doing here, Ms. Stead?" Sadie stammered. She started to wrack her brain for clues. She was desperate to reorient herself in this new world.

"I know you must have questions. And I plan on answering them all in time. For now, why don't you go over to the van there and get yourself checked out by the medics, you're bleeding," she said, attempting some semblance of a sympathetic tone. "And I'd like a word with Agent Quinn—Killian, here."

One of the uniformed men cut the restraints off of Killian and helped Sadie up, guiding her toward the van. The whole area was awash with activity. Medics were running over to attend to Killian. Several agents were loading Soto's injured men into the back of another van that had pulled up, while their colleague pushed Soto into a Lincoln.

"Ma'am," the medic said to Sadie. "Have a seat here, please." He checked Sadie's vitals, handed her an ice pack for her forehead, and attached a number of devices to her fingers. Sadie ignored them all, she was numb to everything going on around her. The world dissipated into hushed tones and time seemed to slow as she thought about the day and its ramifications. Desmond's lifeless face, the sound of Soto's thoughts lingering in her head, Killian's scream of utter anguish.

In the distance, Killian and Stead were having what looked like a heated conversation. Instinctively, Sadie tried to listen, but no thoughts entered her mind. She tried to remember what she had done to hear Desmond and Soto, but it had just sort of happened. Petey was right; it took training to switch, training Sadie now wanted more than anything. Whether she was ready or not, she was fully immersed in this world.

The medic finished up with her, and Stead walked over to Sadie as Killian was loaded into the other medical van. "Is she cleared, Malcolm?" she asked.

"Yes, ma'am, a little shaken, but medically she seems fine. I would recommend watching that head wound, though, for signs of a concussion. But I think we're good, she's a tough one," Malcolm responded. He was a cordial enough man, very straightforward with his tasks, but he had a kindness to him. He too wore full tactical gear, which was slightly off-putting to Sadie as she regarded him properly for the first time.

"Good, please see that Agent Quinn is brought down to the G Level Infirmary," she said before turning back to Sadie. "Ms. Smith, I'd like a word. Mind taking a walk with me?"

Sadie looked over at Killian in the back of the van. He gave her a wave.

"Sure… Is Killian going to be okay?" she asked, rising to her feet. Her concern for him more important than anything else at that moment.

"He'll be fine. Don't worry. I'll take you to see him as soon as the doctors check him out," Stead said. She gestured away from the bustling scene as people began to clean up the mess Soto and his men had made. Sadie saw them place a sheet over Desmond's body before lifting it onto a stretcher. She didn't know him well, but she still felt an ache of sadness over his loss.

Sadie turned to follow Stead. The pair walked a short distance away from the hustle of the derelict hangar until they came upon a car that seemed to be a newer addition to the scrapyard compared to the other vehicles Sadie had seen that were completely devoured by rust. She sat on the hood of the car, waiting for Stead to say something. She wasn't about to be the first one to speak for fear of chasing off whatever information Stead seemed willing to share.

"I know this must all be very confusing for you, Ms. Smith," Stead began.

"Sadie is fine, really." She stuck her hands into her pockets, trying to warm them up, and felt the small glowing disk that she'd forgotten was there.

"Sadie it is then." Stead pulled out a handkerchief and wiped down a section of the vehicle to lean against. She looked entirely uncomfortable with the situation, straightening out her shirt and blazer before clearing her throat to continue. "Let me start by asking how much you know already about Killian and our endeavors, so to speak?" Her gaze fixed on the activity back at the hangar.

Sadie was hesitant to answer. The Guardians were supposed to be the good guys. But one of them just tried to turn her over to Domino. *How do I know she's any different?*

"Very little, I would imagine," she finally answered.

"It's okay, Sadie. I was already made aware of last weekend's events. I know you know enough about the Zeta Defense Agency to have questions." Stead glanced over at Sadie, as if urging her to go on. "So please, tell me what you know so I can fill in the blanks where possible."

Sadie fidgeted with the device in her pocket. "Okay, can you tell me what this is then?" She handed the disk to Stead—again, the purple glow remained.

Stead regarded it carefully, turning it around in her hand. "I was wondering when you were going to ask about this. If this is what I believe it is, it's a marker for Penumbrials. It glows purple when someone's thoughts are blocked. Hence why it glows purple when you hold it."

"And you. So you're a Penumbrial?" Sadie took the device back.

Stead nodded. "I am."

Somehow this reassured Sadie. There was a common ground, an admission of abilities by both parties that gave her confidence to continue the talk. Conversations went both ways, and Sadie wanted more answers. "Okay. So here's what I know. I know that the Zeta Defense was formed back in the eighties after Charles Carter created a device that could read thoughts, and then there's

Domino, who want to use that device and ones like it for unscrupulous means. And I know that there are people out there with special abilities called Muffles and Listeners." She tried to gauge Stead's reactions as best she could from the partial view of her face that was lit by the hangar.

"You've been talking to Mr. Jackson, haven't you?"

"Yes, ma'am," she replied. "Guess I should say Penumbrials and Auritors then." Stead breathed a soft sigh of relief and Sadie could see the woman's shoulders begin to relax. "I also know about the Guardians." Stead straightened again. "I know that Desmond was one of them, and that the ZDA is just a part of your organization. I know that they have a Regent that's in charge of the entire operation. And now I'm assuming that's you… Madam Regent."

Stead turned slightly, revealing a wry smile that had spread across her face. "And I'm guessing Killian was the source of this information? Desmond always did have a soft spot for the boy." Her gaze fixed on a point in the distance, instead of toward Sadie. "And how do you see yourself fitting into all of this?"

"I'd like to be part of it, Ms. Stead," Sadie said, fidgeting with the ring on her pinky.

"Please, call me Valerie." Sadie flushed at the thought of calling this icy woman she'd referred to only as ma'am and Ms. Stead, her boss for almost four years, so casually by her first name. Valerie could sense the shift too, it seemed, as she quickly continued, "And I'm afraid you already are part of it, my dear. You always have been." She looked down at the ring Sadie was playing with. "How long have you had that ring?"

"Oh this? As long as I can remember. It was the only thing I had when… when child services picked me up." Sadie felt that familiar heat gathering behind her eyes, the same heat she felt every time she thought about that day. She pushed it back down.

"May I see it?" Valerie asked and Sadie handed it over to her. Valerie turned it around in her fingers and read the small inscription. "*Praesidio in Statera*. Do you know what that means?"

"Protect the balance. I've looked it up before, but never found anything relating to it online."

"You wouldn't. *Praesidio in Statera* is the motto of the Guardians, has been for over two thousand years."

Wait, what? Two thousand years? Sadie knew that the Guardians were old, but not millennia old. And what was a secret society's motto doing on a ring she'd always owned?

"I know, it's a lot to take in," Valerie continued. "I'll explain everything in due time. For now, know that you are safe with us and you have a family here. This ring is a gift and a promise that you will always have a place with the Guardians." Valerie rested her hand on Sadie's shoulder, then after thinking about it, removed it abruptly.

"It's because I'm a Nox Auris or whatever, isn't it?" Sadie had read enough about history and warring societies to know that if one side considered something of use and ultimate power, the other side had to think the same.

"Regardless of your abilities, or even lack thereof, Sarah Mercedes Smith, you will always have a place with us." Valerie looked at Sadie with such genuine concern, Sadie was taken aback. She'd never seen such emotion on her boss's face before. In fact, if she thought about it, she hadn't seen that level of concern for her in very many people at all over the years. It was gentle and fierce at the same time. "But now that you mention it, we should talk about what it means to be a Nox Auris."

"It means I can read and not be read, right?"

"Yes, but it means more than that. It means you are a beacon that both sides of this war will want to use and even exploit. You can't let that happen, Sadie. You must stay true to yourself, to your beliefs. There are some, even inside the Guardians, who don't always have the best intentions. Some believe that the end justifies the means. For now, we can work with you, train you, hone your abilities. Then if you decide you want to help, there is always work to be done. Domino has never stopped trying to configure the world to their benefit, and the Guardians have never stopped trying to rebalance the scales. *Praesidio in Statera,*" Valerie said as she handed the ring back to Sadie before standing to leave.

Sadie sat in silence, staring at the ring she spun between her fingers. She thought about what Valerie was saying, the "gift" she'd been left. Then she thought about her life as she knew it, her apartment with the big gray beanbag chair, the stack of books that would remain untouched if she decided to take Valerie up on her offer. The days spent reading, just her and Redy on a rainy Saturday afternoon, would be over. She'd be walking through a new door to a new life. How would she explain this to Piper? What would it mean for her career? *The Smithsonian.* Sadie hadn't thought about it, but how was Valerie the head of a secret organization when she was at the museum so much?

"Wait, how are you the Guardian Regent and still in charge of the Smithsonian? You're always there!" Sadie exclaimed.

"Yes, about that... Has anyone mentioned the 'Library' to you at all yet?"

She furrowed her brow. "Library? No..."

Valerie smiled. "Good, this is always my favorite part. Let's go for a drive."

∞

When Valerie parked in front of the Smithsonian, Sadie looked at her with confusion. When they entered the building and walked to one of the many service elevators that Sadie had used more times than she could even count, her suspicion grew. "Valerie, what are we doing here? And what does the Smithsonian have to do with the 'Library?'" If anything, she would've assumed they'd be heading to the Library of Congress, not the Smithsonian.

Valerie didn't say a word. Instead, she quietly took Sadie's hand and waved it over the Smithsonian logo that adorned the top of the button panel. When she did, the logo flipped open to reveal a keyhole. "I told you that ring was a gift and a promise. It's also a clever key." She took the ring and placed it inside the small hole. A lever popped out from the center and Valerie rotated it three times. The elevator began to glide down. Past the basement level one. Level two. Level three. But still it continued downward after the level indicator went blank.

It finally came to a stop and the doors opened to reveal a balcony. An eight-story high balcony that overlooked a single room, bigger than any Sadie had ever seen in her life. It stretched easily five hundred feet across and looked like it went on for at least a mile. The whole place was filled with rows and rows of bookcases. Sadie could almost smell the history. She gaped at Valerie with shock, amazement, and no small amount of disbelief.

A drone flew directly over Sadie's head then dipped down in between one of the many shelves. It selected a single book, removed it, and flew away with a haste and precision that could only come from robotics.

"This was downstairs this whole time?" Sadie exclaimed. Valerie just smiled.

"What is it? What are all those books?"

"This is the Library. And the current headquarters of the Guardians. Millenniums of records of human thought are stored here. Before Charles Carter and his device, we Guardians recorded our experiences the old-fashioned way." She had an air of pride about her as she looked out over the books. "Every great leader and thinker that came into contact with an Auritor has a book down there. We still use them to study thought patterns and shape how we can rebalance the scales that Domino has attempted to disrupt. Some of the archives are also filled with rare books and pieces of antiquity deemed of special importance. We even have items from the Library at Alexandria. A historian's dream."

Sadie snorted. "That's putting it mildly. But how are they here?"

"You think this is the only Library?"

"There are more?"

"Quite a few, actually. This is by far the largest still around. The bulk of the Archives are moved every few hundred years to protect them, but the American-based Library has been their home for almost two centuries now."

Sadie looked out in amazement. She could spend a lifetime in this place and still never read every book it had to offer. She'd always found that history came to life through books, and this was a living monument to the past. She breathed it in, reveled in it.

"As I said, this is my favorite part," Valerie continued. "Watching someone experience this for the first time." She paused and looked over at Sadie. "I remember the first time your mother saw this, she had the same look you do right now."

"Wait… what? My mother, you knew my mother?" Sadie's hands began to shake; she grabbed the railing to steady herself.

"Yes, I was getting to that part. She was a Guardian here. Your father too. They were also my friends." Valerie stared down at her feet, then back out over the stacks of books, drones whizzing in every direction. She crossed her arms and took a deep breath before continuing. "I loved your mother. She was my best friend, and your father too. They were my family. And they gave everything for this place. They believed in the Library and the Guardian's mission, but they would never have done anything to hurt you, Sadie." Valerie smiled at her. "You're the spitting image of your mother. Of course your father is in there too, you have his eyes. It's strange. It's like having them back here, if only for a moment."

Valerie caught herself and returned her gaze to the Archives. "That's why when I saw you four years ago, that first day at the Smithsonian, I knew exactly who you were and I wanted to keep you as far away from this life as possible. But it seems fate has a mind of her own. Your parents loved you, Sadie, no matter what you may think about them, they loved you."

Sadie couldn't resist anymore, that familiar heat became too fierce for her to fight and she let a tear fall. Then another. And another. Until she was quietly crying, thinking about what she'd just learned. Her hands tightened around the metal railing in an attempt to steady the world that was cracking and shaking beneath her. Her whole life she believed that her parents didn't want her, that she wasn't good enough to be wanted. She'd fought hard to be the best she could so that no one would ever make her feel that way again. But none of it was true. She was loved, she was special. She wasn't alone.

One question still burned in her mind. The question that was always there in the background, like embers from a long-forgotten fire.

"Then why did they abandon me?"

"I… I don't know," Valerie responded as tenderly as she could. "We lost contact with them shortly after you were born. They were always on the run—Domino discovered their identities and your father, he was so cautious all the time. They didn't risk contacting us again. But I do know this: they never would've abandoned you. Not if they'd had any choice."

A choice, Sadie thought, *they didn't have a choice*. She hadn't been abandoned *by choice*.

"Have you heard anything from them since?" she asked, a glimmer of hope replacing the darkness inside of her.

"No, unfortunately… As I said earlier, you will always have a place here. I promise you that," Valerie continued with a tightness to her voice, "but you also have a family here. Your parents were my family and that relation extends to you, if you'll have us. Have me."

Sadie stared out at the buzz of activity before her. Walkways stretched out from her balcony along the sides of the room and all the way down, each level a catacomb of shelves with walkways reaching out across the expanse to join them together. She only now noticed the men and women walking along them, going about their regular routines while she quietly questioned her own existence. From her right, she heard a familiar voice.

"Hey, Bluebird." It was Killian, all patched up and walking on crutches. A doctor followed behind, telling him that he shouldn't be up and walking yet. Killian ignored those orders, of course, and continued toward Sadie and Valerie.

Sadie quickly wiped the tears away; she wouldn't let anyone else see her weakness.

"How are you feeling? Is your head okay?" Killian studied her with a worried expression, as if searching for signs of damage or distress.

"I'm fine, but I wasn't the one that got shot. How are *you*? Should you be walking on that leg?"

"Oh, it's fine. Just a scratch, that Soto has terrible aim." He winked, and the doctor huffed audibly behind him. "I brought this for you." He handed Sadie her bag. Immediately her headache returned, and she winced in pain as she placed the bag over her shoulder. "Are you sure you're okay?" Killian asked, noticing her reaction.

"Yeah, I just thought I'd shaken this headache finally."

"Here, let me see your bag, Sadie," said Valerie. She combed through it until she pulled out a small, black cylinder. "Do you know what this is?"

"I've never seen it before," Sadie replied, rubbing the space between her eyes to assuage the headache. Valerie snapped the cylinder in two and Sadie's headache dissipated. "*That's* what was causing my headaches all week? How did it get into my bag?"

"Best bet, a Domino operative slipped it in there at some point this week to test whether you really were a Nox Auris. I'm guessing if I were to take this to our techs, they'd say it was a low-level zeta emitter. Your headaches should stop from now on."

"Wait," Killian interjected, "could that be ramped up to cause a blackout?"

Sadie knew where he was going with this. *The lab… that piercing pain.*

"Theoretically, yes. We've never pushed it that far."

Killian turned to Sadie. "That's what happened to you! When we were trying to escape the lab."

"If that's true, then Domino is further along in their research than we previously thought." Valerie's expression returned to the cold, blank mask Sadie was accustomed to. "On that note, I should see to Mr. Soto. I'll leave you two be." She turned to leave. "And Sadie, think about what I said."

"I will," replied Sadie as she watched this newfound connection to her family walk away.

"So… how crazy is this place?" Killian chuckled.

"Pretty crazy, but don't you work here?"

"Not down here, this is all new to me. This is the Guardians' place. I had no idea this was even down here. Des definitely left a lot out..." The smile vanished from his face as he looked out over the room.

"I'm so sorry, Killian," Sadie said and placed her hand on his shoulder.

"I just don't understand. It's not like Desmond to do any of that." Killian's breathing deepened. Sadie could almost feel his inner turmoil erupting. She wanted to do something to fix it, to relieve his suffering somehow.

"I can't imagine how you're feeling right now, but I do know that your brother loved you. And he was truly sorry. He told me before... well, he thought it really."

"That's right! Nox Auris," Killian said, inhaling deeply, as if to suck in enough strength to push away the gravity of grief that pulled at him. "How does it feel to be one in a million?"

"A lot has definitely changed, not sure how much of it is related to that though." She shrugged. "Honestly, I don't even know what to do with these abilities."

"You'll figure it out," he said, looking at her with confidence and encouragement.

In his eyes, Sadie could see the truth, the genuine love and care that he had for her. She could feel his intensity. It was too much for her at the moment. She looked away.

"In the meantime, looks like we're both going to be sticking around this place for a while so might as well get to exploring," Killian continued as he hobbled down the path, beginning his expedition into the gigantic room.

Sadie took one last glance back toward the elevator, as if the entire course of her life had dwindled down to this choice. Take the elevator back upstairs to the Smithsonian, to her life as she had known it. Coasting through, as it were. Days spent reading reports, nights spent relaxing with a glass of wine in the company of Redy, weekends spent running around with Piper and her friends. Could she go back to that life, knowing what she knew now of the Guardians and Domino and their silent war that's been waging for millennia? ...Or stay down here? Learn. Fight. Live.

"Hey Bluebird, you coming?" Killian called out from the far balcony.

The elevator doors closed.

Epilogue

Elsewhere

Bruno Soto sat in the backseat of the blacked-out Lincoln, contemplating how he would get out of this one. Thus far in his life, he'd managed to stay relatively anonymous; the only Guardians to have ever seen his face were long dead and his name had been hidden under a false identity. Now, he was face-to-face with the entity his employers had long warred against.

He considered the ways he could escape the vehicle. He attempted to slide his left hand, being smaller since losing a second finger, out of the handcuffs behind his back.

"I wouldn't bother," said the driver of the vehicle. "Even if you do manage to get out of those, you can't get out of the car before we reach our destination." He had the smooth, husky voice of an older, but energetic man. Soto sat up to get a better view of his captor. It was too dark, but with every passing light on the highway he caught a glimpse of the man's salt and pepper hair.

"Oh, and where would the Library be? I've always been curious. You know, I think in another life, I could have been a Guardian too," Soto said with a slight twinge of fear rippling through his voice.

"We're not going to the Library."

"Where are we going then? I recall your boss asking you to take me to the Library."

"I don't work for the Guardians." The man paused. "In fact, you and I work for the same person. Councilman Ambrose."

"Is that right," Soto said. His pulse quickened; he pulled harder at the cuffs. Fear overtook him. The last time he saw Shawn Ambrose, the councilman had given him one last chance to prove himself. That had gone terribly wrong. "So we'll be going to see him then? I have the device I promised him. It's here, in my jacket pocket. Those dimwitted Guardians missed it back at the hangar. And I do have some interesting news for him. The girl, the girl I told him about, she is a Nox Auris. I *almost* had her tonight. I can get her again, I promise. Mr. Ambrose doesn't need to worry about that."

"Oh we already know about her," said the man. "It's being handled."

"Please," Soto yanked against his restraints once more in desperation, "I'll do anything the Council wants. Give me another chance."

The car came to a stop and the driver turned around to look at him. "We both know it's a little late for that. Ambrose sends his regards though," the man said as he screwed a silencer onto his 22mm Walther PPK.

∞

As he walked down the halls of the Archfall Sanctum, Shawn Ambrose's Lucchese boots clacked with the slow tempo of a man that no longer needed to rush anywhere after rising to the rank he had in his life. As the son of a Texan oil tycoon, he'd grown up in the lap of luxury. He had a knack for manipulating CEOs and didn't shy away from using this ability to further enhance his wealthy lifestyle. He soon became a fierce businessman, one only known by the upper echelon of society. Of course, his "talents" hadn't reached their full potential until he'd been recruited by Domino. Here, he was free to use his particular expertise to sway entire markets and nations on a whim.

Shawn turned into the central rotunda of the Domino Central Headquarters, a dimly lit room fashioned after the Pantheon in Rome. A giant skylight in the center of the ceiling illuminated a round table directly below; the only other light in the room came from the floor to ceiling aquarium taking up the north wall. It was filled with everything from blue tangs to hammerhead sharks. A sand shark skimmed the bottom of the tank as Shawn joined the four figures already sitting in shadow around the table, awaiting his arrival.

"I am happy to report that the Western Siberia ploy worked perfectly. We are already seeing results," said a man with a thick Portuguese accent from the far-left spot at the table. Shawn took the seat to the man's right and placed his white Stetson down. "And what updates do you bring us from the US, Senhor Ambrose?"

"The Escavez Affair worked out better than we could've even hoped; not only did our company, Lockwood Military Development, win the contract, but it seems that Dynamo Research has tanked under the pressure. Your call was spot on, Councilman Silva."

"And the issues you were having with Bruno Soto?" asked another figure. She was a beautiful, thin, blonde woman with a thick Australian accent.

"Soto has been taken care of, Councilwoman Taylor," said Shawn. "Don't worry your pretty little bonnet about that one, he won't be an annoyance to us any longer."

"Bonnet, really?" Councilwoman Taylor glared at him. "Grow up, Shawn, this isn't the wild west and I'm no damsel in distress."

"And you are positive he did not reveal anything to the Guardians?" a man wearing a black and white dashiki interjected, preventing any further escalation.

Shawn reluctantly released his icy gaze from Councilwoman Taylor. "Don't reckon he had the opportunity, Councilman Obi," he said, shaking his head. "My best man intercepted him just in time. Though he did give up one last interesting tidbit. Turns out his big surprise this time was a Nox Auris."

Gasps erupted from around the table. "Another one? So soon? Are you sure?" Councilman Silva asked from beside Shawn.

"That's the interesting bit. You see, we have reason to believe this girl is not only a Nox Auris, but the child of the last one—she's the daughter of John and Ally Scott, if our intel is correct."

"Councilman Ambrose, if that is true, I want her brought in." Up until this point, the final figure had remained silent. She was a small and unimposing woman, who often surprised people with her ability to speak with both the poise of royalty and the ferocity of a dictator that you wouldn't want to cross. She continued as she rose and walked over to the aquarium behind the table. "Where is she now?"

"I believe she's returned to the Library, but I have

a plan. She will presumably return to her regular life at some point, and when she does, I already have an operative in place at the Natural History Museum. I have no doubt that he'll be able to encourage her to think outside the Guardians."

"Good. I trust you to see this through then, Ambrose. We need her alive and on our side if we are going to have any hope of executing the next stage of our plan. I think it's time we move beyond our little skirmishes with the Guardians. I want them gone. I want to focus on a new era for Domino," said the woman as she began to pace before the aquarium wall. "Up to this point we've been content with parlor tricks. But I want more. I believe it's time we use our money and power to turn this world around. To shape it into one entirely of our making. *Onus Dominus.*"

The other members echoed, "*Onus Dominus.*"

Sadie's story continues in Book 2 of the Bluebird series.

Visit ElleHolmes.pub to sign up for our newsletter to get the
latest updates for the next installment due out in 2021.
If you enjoyed this story, please leave a review so other
readers can find the same joy you did.